See Bride Run!

by

Charlotte Hughes
New York Times Bestselling Author

Copyright © 2014 by Charlotte Hughes
Romantic Comedy
readcharlottehughes.com

All rights reserved, in whole or in part, in any format. The content should not be used commercially without prior written permission, except in the case of brief quotations embodied in critical articles and reviews. This book is provided for your personal enjoyment.

See Bride Run! was originally published as a Loveswept paperback in 1998, in a slightly altered form, by Bantam Press, a subsidiary of Bantam Doubleday Dell Publishing Group, Inc.

The content that follows is a work of fiction. Characters, incidents and dialogue are drawn from the author's imagination, and any resemblance to actual persons and events is coincidental.

Prologue

The wedding had the makings of a fairytale. The groom, Eldon Wentworth, was charismatic, movie-star handsome, and came from old money. Eldon had studied abroad, traveled the world, and was considered one of Atlanta's most eligible bachelors.

Annie Hartford was lovely with her fresh-scrubbed look, large, Kelly-green eyes, and blond hair that tumbled past her shoulders. Her gown—an haute couture Oleg Cassini—was a stunner: a strapless ball gown with a jeweled bodice that shimmered when she moved. From the waist, creamy satin spilled down multi-layered crinoline, creating a voluminous skirt.

A frothy veil was fixed in place by a small tiara with pink diamonds. It had shamed even the larger tiaras with their ornate multi-karat white diamonds, all pulled from a safe in Tiffany's and placed on a velvet tray for her perusal. Most people would not suspect how unique—not to mention costly—the pink stones were, but Annie had been raised in an environment where women recognized a precious stone at fifty paces, and most husbands purchased at least one ridiculously extravagant car.

That was Annie's world. At twenty-nine years old, Annie Hartford was sole heir to a billion dollar empire.

Now, on her wedding day, Annie paced about in one of the church's parlors—it was difficult to sit with all the crinolines—her thoughts swirling like confetti riding a wind gust.

Sitting on a velvet settee, the Hartford's long time employee, Vera Holmes, fretted. At sixty-something, she was still attractive. She had decided on her sixtieth birthday to stop coloring her hair, and the soft dove gray color only emphasized her nice skin. She was usually calm, but not today. She had picked off most of the light pink polish on her nails.

The wedding planner, Susan, had gushed over the bridal gown and tiara before quickly going over what they'd practiced at the rehearsal. "My assistant will tap on your door once the last of the attendants get near the altar, and you'll join your father in the narthex. Don't worry; my assistant will see that your gown and veil are arranged perfectly before you make your way down the aisle. Also, do not let the number of guests intimidate you," she added, "and remember to smile." She hurried from the room.

"Are you okay?" Vera asked.

"I'm perfectly fine," Annie said. She knew the guest list of six hundred was her father's way of showing off, as were the six hundred lobsters flown in from Portland, Maine during the night; and the small orchestra presently playing Mozart's *Eine Klein Nachmusik*, to early arrivals. Winston Hartford did *not* want an old lady with blue-tinted hair playing the organ at his daughter's wedding.

Annie glanced at the wall clock beside the door.

Forty-five minutes until show time . . .

Annie had not been looking for a husband when she ran into Eldon Wentworth at Hartford Iron and Steel, a 300,000 square foot facility of warehouse and processing center. The facility was massive by Atlanta's standards and had grown from the small company her great-great grandfather founded in 1930. She and her father were meeting for lunch to discuss an upcoming conference.

Eldon had been at the plant looking at ornamental iron for a property he had purchased. When he spotted Annie, he hurried over and introduced himself. "I attended Duke University with your brother," he'd said. "I spoke to you briefly at the funeral, but that was what . . . almost ten years ago? Hard to believe."

See Bride Run!

Annie looked him over. Dark blond hair, perfect teeth, medium build. Snazzy dresser; Ralph Lauren cashmere sweater, designer jeans, and Armani loafers. He was good looking enough that, under normal circumstances she might have noticed and remembered him; yet unlikely at her brother's funeral. She shook her head. "I'm sorry."

"I completely understand," he'd replied. "I just wanted you to know that I was proud to call Bradley a close friend."

"Thank you," Annie said.

Eldon had gone on to share funny tales of her brother's antics. Annie felt Bradley was nearby, laughing right along with them. "I was the quiet, well-behaved twin," she said, "and Bradley was the mischief-maker. Hard to believe we shared the same real estate for nine months." Eldon looked surprised. "Did you not realize Bradley had a twin sister?" Annie asked.

He was prevented from answering when they heard a noise in the doorway. Winston Hartford stood there, looking from one to the other. Annie froze. Despite the passing years, Bradley was seldom discussed in her father's presence. His death in an auto accident still held the man in a grip. Grief had changed the landscape of his face, scoring deep lines across his forehead and each side of his mouth. His heart seemed as brittle as the leaves on the azalea bushes after a freezing rain.

Annie had watched in disbelief as her father shook Eldon's hand and invited him to lunch, where they shared stories of Bradley's shenanigans. Annie could not help but wonder if Eldon was just a likeable sort or if her father was finally chipping away at the wall that contained his anger.

Thirty-five minutes . . .

Annie and Eldon dated only three months before becoming engaged, at which time Winston Hartford began grooming Eldon for a managerial role at the plant. Annie had to bite her tongue. That her father did not think a woman capable of running Hartford Iron and Steel was a constant irritant.

With the wedding only weeks away, Annie ran into Bradley's best friend from high school and college, nicknamed Jimbo. He had taken

Bradley's death especially hard.

"I heard you were engaged," he'd said. "Who is the lucky guy?"

"Eldon Wentworth," she'd said. "An old friend of Bradley's. You should hear some of the funny stories he tells." She noticed Jimbo's frown. "What's wrong?"

"Your fiancé is a liar, Annie. Bradley and Eldon were not friends," he'd said. "To my knowledge, they never even spoke."

Annie was stunned.

"Eldon wasn't at Duke very long. He was expelled during the second semester for cheating on an exam."

"Why would he lie?" she asked.

"It's no secret that you are the sole heir to a mega fortune. You need to dump the guy as quickly as you can and be done with him."

Thirty minutes . . .

Annie had called Eldon and immediately broke off the engagement. "You're a pathological liar. You and Bradley were never friends. You did not even know he *had* a twin when we met, which I find odd since he and I spoke by phone almost every day. I also know that you were kicked out of Duke for cheating on an exam."

"You're overreacting," Eldon had said. "Your dad loved hearing the stories and so did you. I gave you what you wanted."

Twenty-five minutes . . .

When Annie arrived home several hours later, she was summoned to her father's study. It reminded her of the time he had called Bradley and her in to announce their mother was leaving, and they would live with him. They'd been four years old at the time and did not quite grasp it until later.

"What do you think you're doing breaking off your engagement?" he demanded.

"Eldon lied," she said. "He never even met Bradley." She filled him in.

"I demand that you stop repeating rumors about Eldon. He comes from one of the oldest, most well-respected families in Atlanta?"

"Pass the business to me, Father," she'd said. "I know more about running Hartford Iron and Steel than most of your managers. I worked in the plant for five summers while growing up. I have ideas, *good ones*."

"Your place is by your husband's side, running the family estate, looking after the Hartford Foundation, and—"

Annie interrupted. "Giving dinner parties for your customers, sending hams to the employees at Christmas for ten years," she added. "I deserve a chance to prove myself within the company." She swallowed. "Or I quit."

He looked shocked. "Do *not* speak to me that way."

"I'm not going to marry a liar and a cheat just to make you happy," she had said emphatically. "I refuse to be bullied by you any longer."

Her father had slammed both fists on his desk. "You *will* marry Eldon," he'd shouted. "You *will* walk down the aisle wearing the dress and tiara that cost me a fortune. You will *not* embarrass me in front of six hundred people, not to mention the media. Do you know *how* I know?"

Annie remained silent.

"I just got off the phone with my banker. I have frozen all your accounts and canceled your credit cards. Your fancy sports car is not available to you at the moment. If you leave this house it will be by foot and with only the clothes on your back. You will be homeless."

Annie felt as though she'd been punched in the chest. She wondered if he had done the same thing to her mother or worse. That would explain why the woman had seemingly dropped off the face of the earth.

Ten minutes . . .

Vera and Annie gazed out the window of the church where her father's white stretch-limousine was parked. The plan was, once she and Eldon had taken their vows and the photographer his pictures, they were to be driven to the St. Regis where three adjoining ball rooms would accommodate the reception and luncheon. She and Eldon were to spend the night and board a plane for Venice the following day.

"What are you going to do, Annie?" Vera whispered, bringing her back to the present.

Annie looked at her. "I'm not going through with it. I'd rather be broke and homeless than marry a man I detest."

Vera smiled and said, "I knew that would be your answer. I slipped two thousand dollars inside your purse. I can drive you to a friend's house. She will be a good friend to you as well, Annie."

"Oh, Vera," Annie said, feeling the sting of tears. "I can never thank you enough for everything."

Vera was tearful as well. "Would you like for me to call your father in?" Annie dreaded it. Six hundred wedding guests. Her father's wrath would fly into her face like a horde of angry hornets.

And then it hit her: Winston Hartford was too smart to take a chance on something like this happening. He had changed her entire life within three hours of her breaking off the engagement; he'd had weeks to come up with a plan should Annie try to weasel out of the wedding. But what else could he do to her?

She feared the answer was standing right in front of her. He would go after the only person she had left that she really loved.

Annie frowned when the chauffeur suddenly jumped from the limo and hurried toward the back of the church. "What's wrong with Snedley?"

"He has prostate trouble, the poor man," Vera said. "Runs to the men's room every fifteen minutes." She sighed and headed for the door.

"Wait!" Annie said. "Where does that door lead?" she asked, motioning to a solid oak door on the opposite side of the room.

"To the back of the church," Vera said. "The Sunday school rooms and offices," she added, "plus a big kitchen and a couple of dining rooms. Why?"

"Does Snedley ever leave the keys in the limo? Is there a spare?"

"I don't know. Why are you asking?"

Eight minutes . . .

"I need for you to detain him when he comes out of the men's room so I can get away."

"Get away?" Vera frowned. "How?"

"I'm going to make a run for the limo."

"Oh, Lord!" Vera said. She looked like she might faint.

"I don't want you and Snedley to get into trouble. All you have to do is say you had no idea I was planning anything."

Vera nodded.

Someone knocked on the door.

Five minutes...

"That's the assistant," Vera said. "Just a minute," she called out softly. She looked at Annie. "Check the ashtray for keys. I seem to recall something about the ashtray. Now, listen carefully," she said. "Take the interstate south to Pinckney, Georgia. It is three hours away. Find Lillian Calhoun. I'll call you when I feel it's safe. Your father will be watching me."

Annie nodded.

Another knock, this one impatient...

Two minutes...

"I love you," Annie said and kissed her on the cheek. She threw open the door, gathered an armful of satin and crinoline and raced toward an Exit sign. The limo was parked some thirty feet away. Fortunately, the media had set up their cameras at the front of the church. There was nobody in sight.

It suddenly occurred to Annie that she had left her purse inside the parlor. "Dammit!" she said. She had no money, no driver's license or ID, no clothes, nothing! Just a stupid wedding gown.

She could not risk going back. It was now or never.

Chapter One

"Gin." Darla Mae Jenkins made a production of discarding her playing card and laying the others out so they resembled a fan. She gave her boss a smug look. "You owe me thirty-five cents," she said in a drawl thick as gravy.

Sam Ballard gave a grunt of displeasure as he looked over her cards. Darla had been known to cheat on more than one occasion, and he wasn't about to be taken in by the unscrupulous cardsharp. "You know what I think, Darla Mae? I think you've tucked a few aces in that fancy new garter belt you recently purchased."

"Why, Samuel Aaron Ballard, I cannot believe you're accusing me of cheating. You know darned good and well I'm as honest as a barn is broad." She suddenly stood, hands on hips, hazel eyes clouded with suspicion, and demanded, "How do you know about my new garter belt?"

"I should not have to remind you that word travels fast in small towns, and Pinckney is no different." He smiled. "Remember when this was *the place to* be for root beer floats, hanging out with friends, and catching up on the latest gossip."

"Yeah," she said. "Just walking in the door brings back a lot of fond memories."

Sam glanced about the Dixieland Café, which sat in the very heart of downtown Pinckney, Georgia. It had been built in 1913; the town had given birth to it after the courthouse was built and merchants began opening shops on the square and needed a place for lunch. Sam had a copy of the first menu which listed the Blue Plate Special—one meat, two side vegetables, and a biscuit for a quarter.

It had played a role in the Civil Rights Movement with lunch-counter sit-ins, and it had miraculously survived The Great Depression. Jimmy Carter had eaten at the Dixieland while campaigning in 1976 and again in 1980, both times giving short speeches and going on about what good food the restaurant served, especially the chicken fried steak which later earned the name, *The Jimmy Carter Special*.

Sam had purchased the café shortly after it had been scheduled for demolition. Everybody in town thought he was crazy, him being fresh out of law school with no practice to speak of and even less money; but he could not just sit back and watch the Dixieland get the wrecking ball. He'd used the same skills—carpentry and construction work—that had paid his way through college and law school, to get it cleaned up and operational. He had replaced the torn red vinyl that covered the stools sitting at the counter, as well as the seats in each booth. Volunteers, those who were equally opposed to the city tearing it down, helped Sam bring it back to its former glory, although it had taken almost a year to do so.

At least a dozen grainy, black and white pictures hung from the walls, photos of horse-drawn buggies, women in long dresses, children playing in the dirt street, back when time seemed less hurried. He'd had the pictures restored, enlarged, and reframed.

If someone had asked Sam if he needed the headache of running a restaurant, he would have said, "No way in hell!" but the Dixieland was more than a restaurant. Sam felt he had torn a page from a history book and brought it to life.

He checked his wristwatch. The breakfast and lunch crowd had come and gone, and the "early birds"—seniors who came in around five p.m. and ordered from a menu that offered a discount—would bring a new wave of business. In between shifts, employees from surrounding businesses often took their coffee breaks at the restaurant so they could enjoy a slice of pie as well.

Darla smoothed the wrinkles from her uniform and gave her light panty girdle a tug. Sam complained on a regular basis that her skirt was too tight and too short, but Darla claimed it helped her tips. Besides, Darla did what Darla wanted, and nobody could tell her otherwise. But the truth was, when Sam looked at it from a business standpoint he knew he had a goldmine in her. The customers loved Darla because she was fast on her feet, quick-thinking, had a fun sense of humor, and was, among all things, trustworthy, except when it came to cards. Sure, the truckers loved her long legs and shapely behind, but the woman offered so much more.

"You're right about the gossips in this town," she said. "If I had a nickel for every one of 'em, I wouldn't be waiting tables for a living. A girl can't so much as kiss a man goodnight on her front porch without everybody and their mamas knowing it."

"Perhaps you should try to be a little more discreet, Miss Jenkins."

"What are you talking about? I'm the queen of discretion."

"Which explains the eighteen-wheeler parked in front of your mobile home last weekend," Sam said.

She waved off the remark. "Oh, that was just an uncle visiting."

Sam nodded. "Ah, yes, another uncle."

"Don't get smart with me, Sam, or you'll be looking for a new waitress." Darla used that threat on a regular basis, but Sam knew she wasn't serious.

She glanced out the front window of the cafe as she spoke. "Great balls of fire! Would'ja get a load of that!"

Sam swiveled around on the red vinyl counter stool and gave a low whistle at the sight of the white stretch limo sitting in the middle of Main Street. "Well, now. I wasn't aware of any celebrities visiting Pinckney. Must be here for the Okra Festival," he added. He'd barely gotten the words out of his mouth before he noticed smoke seeping out from beneath the hood.

See Bride Run!

"Uh-oh, looks like trouble in Tinsel town. I'd better go see about it."

"Hey, wait for me," Darla said, following him out of the restaurant.

A number of people had already gathered on the sidewalk, including Mott Henry, the town drunk. From the looks of it, he hadn't shaved or bathed in days. He watched the excitement for a moment, then turned and moseyed down the sidewalk toward the liquor store, obviously more interested in buying his next bottle than the commotion in the street. The Petrie sisters, still spry in their eighties, stood at the edge of the crowd, each holding a brown sack from Odom's Grocery. They craned their necks to see over a group of teenage boys.

"Is anyone in there?" a man in the crowd called out. "You can't see diddly with them tinted windows."

"I can't figure it," Darla said. "Why would anybody put tinted windows in a danged limo? Shoot, if I was riding in one of those suckers, I'd want the whole world to see."

Sam was amused by the town's response to the limo. One would have thought a flying saucer had just landed on Main Street, and everybody was waiting for the hatch to open. It just proved the town needed more in the way of entertainment.

Mechanic, Bic Fenwick, owner of Fenwick's Towing and Garage, happened by at that moment in his tow truck. He parked on the side of the street, climbed from his truck, and hurried over. "What's the story here?" he asked Sam.

Sam shook his head. "I just got here. Darla and I saw smoke coming from beneath the hood. I figured I should investigate."

Bic knocked on the driver's window. "Hey there, did you know you got smoke comin' out from under your hood?"

Sam chuckled. "I'd say it was a given, Bic."

"Well, you never know what people can see with them tinted windows," Bic said. He pressed his face against the window and squinted. "You want me to take a gander at what's under your hood?" he shouted, as if the tinted windows might interfere with the person's hearing as well.

Sam figured whoever was in the limo was getting a good laugh.

The window whispered down some five or six inches. Sam found himself looking into a pair of incredibly pretty green eyes, so pretty, in fact that he tried to think of the exact color and decided they must be what people referred to as Kelly-green. Her face was equally pretty, framed by hair the color of ripened wheat. Some kind of net clung to the fat curls, and Sam thought he caught sight of a pink tiara.

He leaned forward. "Excuse me, miss, but you can't leave this thing sitting in the middle of the road. You're blocking traffic." As if to prove his point, a man in a pickup truck blew his horn. Sam waved him around.

Annie gave an enormous sigh. As if her day had not been bad enough. She had spent the last half hour trying to make it from the interstate to the town of Pinckney before the limo died because she could not bear the thought of walking eight to ten minutes in her wedding gown. Not only that, she was furious with Snedley. How could a paid chauffeur not know the limo was on the verge of having major problems? She supposed she should cut him some slack because his prostate problem had probably garnered much of his attention.

"Did you hear me, miss?" Sam asked. "You're going to have to move your vehicle. You're blocking traffic," he repeated.

Annie could not hide her annoyance. Did the man think her daft, for Pete's sake? She knew she was blocking traffic, but there wasn't a damn thing she could do about it. "Thanks for your input, Einstein," she said loudly, "but it won't budge so I don't have much choice in the matter."

Bic looked at Sam. "Einstein?" he repeated. "I don't think she appreciated what you said."

"Well, lucky for me I'm not trying to win a popularity contest," Sam told Bic, even though he was peeved that the woman had resorted to name calling. "I need for it to be gone before my early bird customers arrive," he added.

"How come you're worried about people parking at the curb?" Bic asked. "You've got that big parking lot on the side and back of the restaurant?"

"Because a couple of my early bird customers are in wheelchairs, and some of the others just have a hard time getting around. It's easier for their families to park in front of the restaurant and help them to the door."

"I'll see what I can do," Bic said. "Maybe I can figure out what's causing all that smoke." He addressed the woman inside of the car. "Miss, do you see a hood release in there?" he asked and told her where to look for it. He glanced at Sam and rolled his eyes. "'Least that's where you'd find a hood release in most cars. No telling where they put 'em in these big suckers."

"Probably next to the wet bar and Jacuzzi," Sam said quietly. The woman in the car might have the prettiest green eyes he'd ever seen, but damned if he was going to get involved in a verbal tussle with her. Sam heard a metallic click, and Bic opened the hood. Smoke billowed out like a mushroom cloud. "Jeez, Louise!" Bic said, backing away from the vehicle and snatching a cloth from his back pocket which he used to wipe his face.

"What's going on here?" a voice said.

Sam turned and found himself staring into Sheriff Harry Hester's face. He was so bald that most folks called him Howie—for Howie Mandel—behind his back.

Bic answered. "This here limo is putting out more smoke than a bonfire. I'm trying to figure out what's causing it."

Sam leaned close to the sheriff. "There is a lady inside. I may as well tell you, she's a bit mouthy."

"Oh, yeah?" Hester said. "We'll see about that."

Sixty-year-old Marge Dix elbowed her way through the crowd. Most considered her a sourpuss. "Would you just look at that?" she said, her voice bristling with indignation. "Here we have starving people in this world, and we got folks driving cars the size of mobile homes. I hope whoever it is doesn't plan on settling in Pinckney. I just can't abide such vulgarity. Makes me ill, that's what it does."

Darla, who had been quiet up to that moment, pretended to give

Marge a sympathetic look. "Then I wouldn't look if I were you, Marge, honey," Darla said. "If something made me that sick, I'd march right home, lock the doors, and pull the shades."

Marge regarded Darla. "The Bible says we should store our treasures in heaven."

"Some of us don't want to wait that long for nice things," the waitress replied.

Sheriff Hester stepped closer to the limo and tried to peer at the woman through the crack. "Miss, I need to see your driver's license," he said, "and I may as well tell you, a little kindness goes a long way in this town so you might want to be a bit more tolerant of our citizens."

"You go, Howie," Darla said.

Hester shot her a dark look. "Watch it, Darla Mae, or I'll write you a ticket for having an eighteen-wheeler parked in your front yard last weekend."

Annie gave another sigh. She should have taken a chance and gone back inside the church for her purse. She wished she could magically disappear; instead, it looked as though she was going to suffer her share of indignities.

"I'm sorry Sheriff, but I do not have my license with me." Annie waited, knowing he would derive a great deal of pleasure from that fact.

"Oh, really?" Sheriff Hester looked about the crowd. "Seems these rich folks don't have to follow the same rules as the rest of us," he said.

"That's precisely what I'm talking about," Marge Dix said to Darla. "Some people think they are better than us normal folks." Marge looked at the sheriff. "Driving without a license carries a stiff fine, doesn't it, Sheriff Hester?"

Sam frowned. He'd never cared for Marge Dix who was the town busybody.

"A fine?" Hester said. "Oh, yes. Not to mention possible jail time." A smile twitched the corners of his lips. He was obviously enjoying himself. "She'd better show me a registration for that thing, or there'll be a hanging in the courthouse square." Several in the crowd chuckled.

Darla threw up her hands. "I don't believe what I'm hearing." She looked at Sam. "Do something!"

Sam pulled Hester aside. "I would tone it down if I were you," he told Hester. "You don't want to get hit with a lawsuit. If someone can afford to drive a car like this they probably have enough money to keep a lawyer on retainer."

Annie was past being angry; she was furious. The man was no better than her father; out to make people feel small and stupid. "Then get your rope ready, Barney Fife," she yelled as loud as she could, "because I don't have the registration either."

Darla laughed out loud. "You go, girl!" Several of the onlookers cheered.

The sheriff colored fiercely. He stepped closer to the limo and leaned forward to get a better look at Annie. "Sam was right; you do have a mouth on you," he said, "but as an elected official, sworn to protect the citizens of this town, I do not appreciate you acting disrespectful to me."

"Let's get something straight, Sheriff," Annie said. "First of all, I'm no threat to *anyone*. I don't own a weapon and never have. You are free to search my vehicle.

"Secondly, I have the utmost respect for law officials, but I will not tolerate being publicly ridiculed just so you can look like a big shot. Further, I don't know that you aren't some kind of nutcase who would actually hang me in the courthouse square, shoot me, or lock me up for the rest of my life, so I consider that a threat. However, I do have rights so I'm allowed to call my attorney, and when he is finished with you, you'll regret ever laying eyes on me." Annie smiled. So what's it going to be, Sheriff?"

"She's good," Darla whispered to Sam.

Sam shrugged. "Not bad," he said.

In a flash, Sheriff Hester's demeanor changed. "How'm I supposed to know this automobile belongs to you?"

"You could give her sodium pentothal," Marge suggested.

Annie didn't hesitate. "This vehicle belongs to my father. I borrowed it."

"You borrowed it," Hester said flatly. "Who is your father?"

Annie glanced at the woman beside him, Marge something-or-other, who was clearly the town gossip. "I would rather not say at this time."

Hester seemed to understand. "Okay," he said to the crowd. I want everybody to back away from the vehicle. Not you, Bic," he added quickly. "You keep looking under the hood; see what you can find out." Bic nodded and went back to what he was doing.

"As for the rest of you, if you insist on hanging around you can stand on the sidewalk. You, too, Marge," he added. He looked at Sam and Darla. "I would appreciate it if you two would stay put."

"That's not fair!" Marge said.

"They're witnesses," Hester said, sounding irritated with her, "*not* that I should have to defend my decision. Now move to the sidewalk or go home," he added.

Marge gave him a dirty look but did as she was told.

Sheriff Hester turned back to Annie. "I hope when you speak to your attorney you'll tell him I did not drag you to the station for questioning, that I allowed you to sit in your daddy's comfy limo with the window rolled down only a few inches, and that I assured you every word would be handled in the strictest of confidence. This is not how I normally conduct my, um, interviews." He produced a small notebook and pen. "Now, then, where were we?"

"You asked me to give you my father's name," she said. "It is Winston Hartford. I am Katherine Anne Hartford, although I prefer to be called Annie since it is less formal."

"And where are you from, Miss Hartford?" Hester asked.

"Atlanta."

Sam let out a low whistle. Darla and Hester looked at him.

"What? Hester asked. "Am I missing something?"

"Depends," Sam said, not taking his eyes off Annie. "Your father wouldn't happen to be in the iron and steel business?"

"Yes," Annie said.

"Very impressive," Sam said.

"Do you know her father?" Darla asked before Hester had a chance.

"I know of him," Sam said. He looked at Hester. "Miss Hartford is heir to one of the biggest iron and steel companies in the southeast."

Annie blushed. She always felt uncomfortable when people discussed the family finances.

Harry hooked his thumbs inside his belt. He seemed to ponder Sam's words. "If that's true, then I'm very impressed, but without a driver's license or other form of ID, there's no way to prove it."

"You can't disprove it," Sam said.

"My father's picture, as well as his business and other ventures are all over the Internet," Annie said. "As is information about me." She looked at Hester. "I would hope that would serve as an I.D. for now."

"*For now*, what I'd really like is for you to step out of the car," Hester said.

Annie paled at the thought. A number of people were still watching from the sidewalk, including the nosy blabbermouth, Marge. Annie would be the laughingstock of the town once they saw her in all her wedding garb. "I would rather not," she said.

The sheriff looked surprised. "Is there a problem? Are you handicapped in some way? Do I need to send for a wheelchair?"

"No, nothing like that," she said quickly. "It's just—"

"I have been very patient with you, Miss," he said. "Now, please remove yourself from the vehicle."

Giving an enormous sigh, Annie hit the automatic door unlock and reached for the handle. The sheriff stepped back as she opened the door and tried to extricate herself from the front seat of the limousine. Her cheeks flamed a bright red as the crowd stared in disbelief. The woman in the waitress uniform hurried over and tried to help her. Once Annie was out and standing among them, everybody stared.

"Oh, my Lord," Darla said. "I've never seen anything like that."

Annie longed to crawl beneath a large rock and never come out.

Sam stared as well at what looked to be hundreds of yards of white satin and lace that made up the most elaborate bridal gown he'd ever laid eyes on. She still wore her veil although it hung askew, and her tiara looked as though it was barely hanging on. Seeing her face in the light was almost humbling. Her facial bones were delicate and very feminine, her skin flawless and glowing. Her mouth was full and sexy as hell. He could not help but stare openly.

"Jeez, Louise," Bic said, having come around from the front of the car.

He looked at Sam, and whispered, "Would you get a load of that crown on her head? She must come from royalty." He bowed low in respect and nudged Sam to do the same.

"That's not a crown," Darla said. "It's a tiara. A lot of brides wear them. I've never see a pink one."

"She looks like a bona fide princess to me," Bic whispered, still bowing. "How you reckon she managed to get that bride's dress in the car with her?"

Sam shook his head. Had he been a betting man, he would have wagered against that possibility. "Beats me." He looked at Bic. "Would you stop bowing for Pete's sake!"

"Well, now," Sheriff Hester said, clearing his throat loudly. "I don't think I've ever seen anything like this before. Are you supposed to be somewhere, miss, um—" He paused.

"No, Sheriff, I don't have anywhere I'm supposed to be," she said. "I fled the scene. That's how I ended up in this predicament."

"Honey, that dress is to die for," Darla said. "I know you didn't buy it off no rack. And I have to say," she went on, "Kim Kardashian's gown doesn't hold a light to you." Darla looked at Sam. "Am I right or am I right?"

He gave Darla a blank look. "I don't know anybody named Kim."

"Oh, good grief!" Darla said. "What's the use of having all those flat screens if you don't keep up with the hottest TV shows?"

"It's one of those Reality TV shows," Hester said. "My wife watches it."

Sam knew nothing about Reality TV, but he knew that Annie's bare shoulders reminded him of fresh cream. The gown was formfitting and jeweled from the waist up, revealing ample breasts and a trim waist. From there it flared like a bell. A very large bell, he thought.

The woman, Annie, caught him staring and looked amused. Or maybe Sam just *thought* she looked amused because he couldn't take his eyes off of her. She was a vision. Nevertheless, he felt foolish. "Yep, that is some dress," he said. "Only two things missing as far as I can tell," he added, "the groom and the church."

Darla glared at him. "Samuel Aaron Ballard, that was downright rude!"

Annie met his gaze. "Yes, it *was* rude."

"Don't listen to ol' Sam," Darla told her. "Last time he saw a bride, she was running fast as she could in the opposite direction."

Sam looked at Darla. "Thank you for airing my dirty laundry on Main Street," he said tersely.

"Would you two stop fussing long enough for me to do my job?" Sheriff Hester demanded. "Besides, I think it's time we gave Sam a rest about his fiancée running out on him. After all, that was years ago."

A sudden smile curved Annie's lips, and two dimples appeared. Sam felt as though a rug had just been pulled out from under him.

"Excuse me, Sheriff," Bic said. "May I speak to the lady one second?"

Hester looked greatly annoyed with the interruption. "Is it important, Bic?"

"Concerns her car."

"Is it bad?" Annie asked.

Bic gave another low bow. "I'm afraid you done blowed a head gasket, your um, highness," he said. "The part don't cost all that much, but

I'll have to take the head off the engine. I usually charge six bills for that, but for you—" He leaned closer. "I'll do it for half that price. I would like to have good relations with your country."

Annie did not know what to make of the man's behavior. "Excuse me, Mr.—"

"Bic," he said. "Just call me Bic."

"I'm Annie. And you need not bow." She saw that he was staring at her head. "Oh, the tiara?" she said. "It doesn't mean anything. It's just an adornment, of sorts." She paused, feeling embarrassed for the umpteenth time in one day. "As for the limo, I can't afford to have it repaired right now. I don't have any money with me."

Bic didn't look the least bit bothered by that fact. "That's okay. I can go ahead and tow it over to my garage, and we can discuss payment when you're ready. And under less stressful circumstances, I hope," he added and smiled. "I just want you to know that most folks in this town are real friendly."

Annie thanked him, then, turned to the sheriff. "So, what's it going to be?" she asked.

Sheriff Hester looked at Sam and shrugged.

"Okay," Sam said. "I think we can settle this easily enough." He regarded Annie. "Do you swear that this is your father's vehicle, and, if so, are you planning on returning it to him in a timely manner?"

"Yes, I swear it's his vehicle, and, yes, I plan to return it once I make repairs," she said. Annie was almost glad she didn't have the funds because she wanted to give her father time to cool off, although, realistically, that was not likely to happen. He would never forgive her. Ever. And it wasn't as if her father desperately needed the limo since he had a Rolls-Royce and a Bentley claiming two slots in their six car garage.

Sam turned to the sheriff. "See, Harry? The young lady is just borrowing the family car." Sam looked pleased with himself. "You can't arrest her for that." He leaned close to Hester. "Well, I suppose you could if you decided to play hardball with her," he whispered, "but you're going to end up looking like the bad guy."

Sam didn't know why he was going to bat for the woman; after all, she was a complete stranger, and she had not gone out of her way to be friendly. Besides, he knew Harry wouldn't lock her up. But he figured as long as he had an audience gawking from the sidewalk, he might as well do some fancy lawyer work and drum up a little future business.

He reached into his shirt pocket for his business card and passed it to Annie. "Give me a call if I can help. Also, I'm part owner of a used car lot in case you need, um, a reliable vehicle. Which seems to be the case," he added and pointed across the street where a construction trailer was surrounded by cars, trucks, SUVs, and even a couple of motorcycles.

She looked confused. "I thought you owned a restaurant."

"Yes," he said, "and we've got the best food in town."

"This card has you listed as an attorney."

"He's a multi-tasker," Darla said.

"You might want to hang on to my card in case Sheriff Hester has a change of heart and decides to haul you in."

"Harry better not arrest her," Darla said, cutting her eyes at the sheriff. "If she goes to jail, I go with her."

Agnes Moore, the town librarian, joined in. The crowd had circled the car again once Annie stepped out in her bridal gown. "I'll not only go to jail with you ladies, I'll notify the Friends of the Library and ask for their support."

The Petrie sisters, both elderly, stepped forth, almost shyly. "You can count us in," Edyth Petrie said. Sister Ethyl nodded vigorously.

Annie was touched. She had never met the women, but they were eager to help her if need be.

"Enough already!" Harry shouted. "I'm not going to arrest her, but I don't want to hear any bellyaching if she decides to take off in one of your pickup trucks."

Sam caught the sheriff's eye and shook his head. The man just kept digging holes and jumping into them.

"You know what your problem is, Sheriff?" Darla said.

"No, but I'm sure you're about to tell me."

"You've spent so many years looking at suspects and thinking the worst of people that you've forgotten how many good and kind people there are in this world. I'll take full responsibility for Miss Hartford," she said. "She can stay at my place as long as she likes. And she won't have to steal anyone's pickup truck because she can use my car."

"Not without a driver's license," Hester reminded her.

"And that brings me to your other problem," Darla said. "You can be a real jackass when you put your mind to it." Darla smiled at Annie. "Okay, it's all settled. You and I are going to be roommates." She paused. "But let me warn you, it's not going to be nearly as nice as what you're used to. I'm not rich, but I love my job and I have more friends than I know what to do with so I guess you could say I'm rich in a different sort of way." She fished a set of keys from her pocket, removed one from a silver key ring and handed it to Annie.

Darla looked at Sam. "I need a favor."

"Don't you always?" He suddenly smiled. "Your timing is perfect. You just told Annie you love your job."

"Don't let it go to your head, Sam," she replied. "Anyway, if you could please drive Annie to my place so she can change clothes that would be great. Lord knows she can't go traipsing around dressed like that." Darla paused and gave the dress a once over. "Although, as wedding gowns go, you struck pure gold with that one," Darla added.

Sam checked his wristwatch. He had already wasted more time than he should have, what with all the fuss, and he did not have time to listen to Darla sing the praises of Annie Hartford's wedding dress. "We need to get going," he said, his comment aimed at both women.

Darla gave Annie a closer look. "I think we're about the same size. Help yourself to anything in my closet. Once you've changed, Sam can drive you back, and we'll whip you up something to eat."

"You're very kind," Annie told Darla, feeling close to tears. She had lived with her father's bad moods, ill temper, and negativity for so many years she was amazed that Darla was willing to go out of her way to help a perfect stranger.

"I have no money at the moment so—"

"Did I *ask* you for money?" Darla said. "Honey, I don't expect anything in return. Not one thing. Even if you *tried* to pay me I wouldn't accept it, so there. Subject closed."

"All I have of value at this time is my dress," Annie said.

"Your dress?"

"I've no need for it." Annie knew that, even as beautiful as the gown was, she would never wear it again. Too many bad memories, she thought.

"You're *giving me* your wedding gown?" Darla asked, almost choking on the words.

"Yes. It's yours if you want it," Annie said.

"Oh. My. Lord." Darla's jaw dropped, her eyes rolled about in her head, and she swayed.

"Watch out!" Sheriff Hester said. "She's goin' down!"

He'd barely gotten the words out of his mouth before Darla went completely limp and sank toward the ground. Sam caught her just in the nick of time. He shook her lightly. "Darla? Are you okay? Darla, speak to me." She did not respond. Sam looked up. "She's out cold," he said.

Chapter Two

Thanks to the Petrie sisters, whose father had been a pharmacist and owned the local drug store for fifty years, they carried a veritable pharmacy in their oversized purses. No one was surprised when Edyth Petrie announced she had smelling salts and asked people to step aside so she could reach Darla.

Fortunately, Sheriff Hester immediately ordered everyone back to the sidewalk and threatened them with fines if they did not stay put. In a matter of seconds he produced a blanket from the trunk of his patrol car and Sam gently placed Darla on it and saw that her legs were covered. Even as worried as Annie was about Darla, she was touched by Sam's gesture.

Edyth knelt beside the unconscious woman, cracked an ampule of the salts, and waved it several inches from Darla's nose. Several people gasped when Darla bolted upright into a sitting position, wheezing, eyes blinking rapidly, and demanding to know why she was lying in the street.

"You fainted," Sam told her.

"No way!" she said. "I've never fainted in my life. Why should I start now?"

"It's my fault," Annie said. "I think I gave you quite a shock."

Darla looked from Annie to Sam and back to Annie. "Oh, I remember," she said to Annie. "You told me . . ."

"Easy does it, Darla," Sam said.

"You said I could have your wedding gown," Darla managed. "Do I still get it?"

Annie smiled. "If you promise not to faint again," Annie replied as she and Sam helped her to her feet. Annie looked at Ethyl Petrie. "Will Darla be okay?" she asked. "Does she need to be seen by a doctor?"

"She'll be fine," Ethyl said, "although she might experience a bit of irritation in her nasal passage. It will go away soon enough."

Darla did not seem to hear a word of the conversation as her gaze was fixed on Annie's gown, seemingly in reverence. "I never in a million years thought I would own such a dress," she told Annie. "I don't even want to know how much it costs because I might faint again, but it looks like it came right out of a fairytale. And that tiara! I know the stones aren't real—I'm pretty much a diamond expert thanks to a friend of mine—but they certainly *look* real."

Annie smiled.

"I feel like I need to pinch myself and see if I'm just dreaming."

"You are dreaming," an amused Sam said, "if you think any minister is going to let you walk down the aisle in a white wedding dress."

"Bite me, Sam," Darla said.

Annie noted the humorous light that passed between them and suspected they were only exchanging a little good-natured ribbing. They were obviously close friends, perhaps even lovers. Darla was certainly attractive enough, with her unusual dark red hair and great figure.

"Besides," Darla went on, "women wear white all the time these days, don't they Annie?" she asked, as though she considered Annie an expert on the subject.

"Absolutely," Annie said. "Even women who have already been married before," she added.

"Even those who've been around the block more times than most mail trucks?" Sam asked.

"Very funny, Sam," Darla said. "Perhaps we should inquire as to what color gown *your* next fiancée will be wearing."

"My guess would be gunmetal gray," Annie blurted, "to match her leg irons." Annie realized as soon as she said it she may have gone too far; she and Sam were strangers. But it felt good participating in their fun banter.

Darla burst into laughter. "So she can't escape," Darla managed to add as she doubled over with laughter.

Sam crossed his arms over his chest. "Having a good time, ladies?" His own smile was tight. "The only way I'm going to walk down the aisle is if some girl's daddy is holding a shotgun to my back. And since I'm, too, um, sophisticated to let something like that happen, I don't plan to spend the rest of my life shackled to *any* woman."

"You have a very romantic way of looking at love and commitment," Annie said, trying to pull herself together even though Darla had yet to stop laughing.

Sam arched one dark brow. "Excuse me, Miss Hartford; you must be confused. I'm not the one who stole my daddy's limo and high-tailed it out of town to escape wedded bliss."

Annie had a great reply on her tongue, but Sheriff Hester interrupted. "Okay, let's break it up," he said and waved his arms to get everybody's attention. "I've got work to do, and I don't have time to stand around yammerin' all day." He looked at Annie. "I'm not finished with you yet. I want to think on this some more. Don't go leaving town on me, y'hear?"

"Yes, sir." Annie nodded but wondered how he thought she was going to leave town without a vehicle or money to fix it. She couldn't even buy a bus ticket.

The crowd thinned. Darla gave Annie last minute instructions. "I'll see you in a little while," she said and hurried toward the restaurant.

Annie had no purse to store the key so she tucked it in her bodice. The sound of Sam's voice made her jump.

"My Jeep's parked behind the restaurant," he said. "Might be easier if I bring it here instead of you staggering about in that mammoth skirt," he added.

"Thank you," Annie said. "That would be helpful." Once he left her, though, she felt ridiculous standing on the sidewalk while strangers eyed her, probably wondering whether she was playing with a full deck. Bic Fenwick had backed his tow truck closer to the limo, and another man was in the process of hooking cables beneath the limo. Annie prayed they wouldn't scratch it.

Finally, Sam pulled up in a black Jeep Cherokee. He reached across the seat, lifted the door handle and pushed the door open for her. "Hop in," he said.

Annie took one look at the space on the passenger's side, and her heart sank. There was no way she would fit. She still could not believe she'd managed to fit inside the limo, even though she had pushed the seat as far back as possible and driven tiptoed. Funny thing about an adrenaline rush—one could sometimes accomplish the impossible. "This isn't going to work," she told Sam.

Bic, who overheard her comment, grinned. "Looks like we might have to strap you to the hood of his Jeep," he said. "I got plenty of rope if you need it."

Annie knew the man was teasing. "No thanks. I've already entertained this town enough for one day."

Sam climbed out of the driver's side wearing a scowl. He was clearly impatient to be done with the chore Darla had given him. "I don't know why you women go through all this fuss for a ceremony that only lasts twenty minutes."

Annie could hear the exasperation in his voice. "Yes, well, my father insisted that I make a grand appearance. It's what Eldon and his snooty family would expect."

"Who the hell is Eldon?"

"My fiancé."

"Oh, you mean the guy you left standing at the altar looking like a fool." He paused and glanced up at her. "Wouldn't it have been simpler to break off the engagement?"

"I tried. My father wouldn't hear of it."

"Have you always done everything your daddy told you to do?"

"Pretty much." She couldn't help but notice Sam's hair; thick and rich, the color of Brazil nuts. He had better than average looks, but instinct told her he probably knew it and used it to his advantage. "Are you almost finished interrogating me?"

Sam only became more annoyed. "I don't have to do this," he said. "I could leave you standing here in the middle of the street."

Annie gave him a tight smile. "But you won't because you're a gentleman."

He grunted. "Boy, have you got *me* all wrong."

"I think I'd do better if I sat in the backseat," she said, "but you'll have to help me get in."

"I never doubted it for a minute." Sam was glad the crowd had dispersed. Those few remaining were chatting among themselves, not paying any attention to the bride and her predicament. He opened the back door and stood aside for Annie to enter. She took a step up and tried to squeeze through the door.

Finally, Sam placed his hands firmly on her rump and pushed. Annie went through the door, falling face first onto the backseat. Sam dusted his hands. "There now," he said, making certain her feet, and the dress were inside before slamming the door. He climbed in on the driver's side.

Annie mouthed a couple of choice swear words as she tried to dig herself out of a mountain of satin and crinoline. "Why did you do that?" she sputtered.

Sam started the Jeep and pulled onto Main Street. "Because my patience has worn thin worrying about your dress problems," he said. "Now please sit back and be quiet till we get to Darla's."

Annie clamped her lips together tightly and ignored him as they made their way to the edge of town. Finally, Sam pulled off the main highway and drove down a dirt road, where an old mobile home sat beneath a stand of pines.

See Bride Run!

"This is where Darla lives?" Annie asked.

Sam pulled into a gravel drive and parked. "That's right. I know it doesn't look like much to a rich gal like you, but it's paid for and Darla loves it. Besides, you can't be too picky when she's giving you a place to stay for free."

Annie's feelings were hurt. "I don't know why you have to be so rude," she said. "I think Darla's place is just fine."

"Sure you do." He climbed out and opened the back door, then literally dragged her across the backseat and out of the car. Annie did not so much as glance at him; she gathered her mountain of skirts and made her way to the small deck that was attached to the front of the trailer.

Sam crossed his arms, leaned against the front of his jeep, and waited. He'd left his cell phone at the restaurant so there was no way to call Darla and check on things. He hoped The Bride did not dawdle. He wanted to get back to the restaurant before the dinner rush began.

Annie kicked off her Manolo Blahnik heels and carefully climbed each step leading up to the deck. Once she stood before the front door, she turned slightly so Sam would not see her reach inside her bra for the key. Not that he would bother looking. The man clearly disliked her, and it was just as clear why.

Annie stuck the key in the front door of the trailer, unlocked it, and pushed it open. She sighed. There was no way she was going to fit through the door. Even worse, the metal on either side of the doorjamb was rusty and jagged. The skirt would be ruined if she tried to force herself through.

"Dammit!" she cried, tearing off her veil and tossing it aside. "Dammit, dammit, dammit!" It had been a long day, and she felt close to tears. "This dress is cursed! *I'm* cursed!"

Now what? Sam thought, wondering what had set her off. She sounded like she was close to having a major meltdown, and he debated jumping in his jeep and taking off. He suddenly noticed her veil fluttering by in the breeze, taking the tiara with it. Like a kite, it flew to the top of a tree and became lodged in the branches.

29

He started for the deck. "Is there a problem?" he asked once he cleared the steps and stood behind her.

"Unzip me, please," Annie said, offering him her back.

Sam blinked several times. "Excuse me?"

"I can't fit through the doorway, and I can't force myself through without tearing this stupid skirt to smithereens." She paused and pointed to the damaged metal on the doorjamb. "I need for you to please unzip me," she repeated.

Sam was reluctant to involve himself further in the woman's problems, but once he saw the problem, he understood why Annie was so upset. He knew Darla would have his head on a platter if she found out he had refused to help Annie and it had resulted in damaging the gown.

It was not easy getting her out of the dress; Sam figured there must be a hundred yards of satin and crinoline. But from the moment he ran the long zipper down her back, almost to her tailbone, she had his undivided attention. Her skin was like alabaster dipped in rose petals. The sight of her bra and panties gave him pause. While the flesh-colored fabric offered a certain amount of decorum, Sam could not help but notice she was physically fit but curved in all the right places.

"What's wrong?" Annie asked. "Are you embarrassed that I'm in my underwear?" She might have been embarrassed as well had she not been tired, hungry, and irritable.

"Why should *I* be embarrassed?" he asked. "I'm fully clothed." He wasn't about to admit that he found her sexy as hell, and when Annie leaned forward to retrieve the dress and shoes, Sam thought he would have a coronary when her lush breasts threatened to spill from her bra.

"You, uh, don't seem to have a problem with modesty," he noted.

Annie just looked at him. "Would you rather I squeal and try to cover myself?" she asked. "Forget it. I've always been very athletic, and I try to take care of myself, so I'm not ashamed of my body. Nor do I embarrass easily when it comes to naked men."

Sam arched one brow. "Oh?"

"My brother did not always remember to lock the bathroom door so I was introduced to the male anatomy at a very young age."

Sam pondered her words. "So, you lied."

Annie glanced his way. "I beg your pardon?"

"When I was trying to prevent the sheriff from arresting you for stealing your father's limo, you made it sound like you were the only heir." Not that Sam actually believed Hester would throw her in jail.

"My twin brother died ten years ago in an auto accident," Annie said sharply, "so I was not lying."

"I'm sorry, first for your loss, and second for accusing you of lying. I've been hanging around Sheriff Hester too long. Losing your twin must've been—" Sam paused, trying to think of the right word. "Excruciating," he finally said.

"Yes," she said, "which is why I did not feel like announcing it in front of half the town."

Sam nodded. "That's understandable." He didn't blame her for keeping quiet about her brother's death during all the excitement, but he wondered if she had planned to set the record straight without him bringing it to her attention. If the sheriff checked her out and discovered she had lied about being an only heir, without checking the circumstances, which Hester was known to do, he would take great pleasure in making fun of Sam's "fancy street lawyering," as he called it. He would have accused him of being swayed by a pair of pretty green eyes or her daddy's money. That sort of ribbing bothered Sam in the beginning, but as time wore on he developed thick skin, and frankly, he didn't care what people thought of him.

Annie noticed Sam was trying to keep his eyes on her face, but his gaze wavered below her shoulders several times. "Is this the first time you've seen a woman in her underwear?" she asked.

Sweat beaded his brow despite the cool September evening. "Yeah," he said, "and I may as well tell you, I'm disappointed as hell."

She nodded, amused. "It shows." She looked at the mound of satin and crinoline at her feet and sighed. "Guess I need to do something with this," she said. "If I hadn't already promised it to Darla, I would just put a match to it."

It took a good half hour and was quite a task, but Annie managed to turn the dress inside-out, unhook several "extra" layers of crinoline, and, with Sam's help, fold each one as best they could.

"It doesn't have to be perfect," Annie said. "The dress will need to go to the dry cleaners. Darla will probably want to preserve it for future use. At least we can get it through the doorway now," she added, passing him the crinoline. "Have you, by chance, seen the veil?"

Sam pointed upward. "It's in the top of that tree."

"Oh, great," she said, her words riding on a sigh. "I don't have time to worry about it right now."

"But the tiara is barely hanging on. Aren't you concerned?"

"I'll look for it tomorrow," she said. She was suddenly eager to use the restroom after hours of trying to convince herself she did not need to go.

She carried the satin dress and jeweled bodice up the two metal steps that led to Darla's living room. She came to an abrupt halt. "Yikes!" she said.

Sam was right behind her, his eyes glued to her round bottom. He almost slammed into her. "What is it?" he asked, then glanced past her. "Oh, yeah, I forgot to tell you. Darla's grandmother was a big Elvis fan. When she passed away she left her Elvis memorabilia to her only granddaughter."

"Wow," Annie said. She stood in the small living room, holding her dress, gaping at souvenirs, collectables, decanters, and various keepsakes of the man who had amassed a fan club of many millions. "I've never seen anything like this," Annie said. Sam stepped inside the room holding her crinoline slips, and the room seemed to shrink in size. "It's like a museum," she added.

Sam nodded. "My thoughts exactly," he said, "but you'll never convince Darla that it's a bit much."

Neither of them said anything for a few minutes. Not only did Annie need to visit the powder room, she suddenly felt self-conscious standing there in her underwear. "I need to get dressed," Annie said. "After that I'm going to drink about a gallon of water."

"You must be thirsty," Sam said.

"Yes, very." Annie had no desire to explain why she was craving water. She had already shared too much by traipsing about in her underwear. "I suppose the bedrooms are that way," she said, nodding toward a door leading off the kitchen.

"There is only one bedroom," Sam said.

"Oh. Well, I hope the sofa is comfortable. I'll try to hurry." She went through a doorway and entered a short hall that led to the bedroom. It was neat, the bed made, everything seemed to be in its place, no Elvis memorabilia to crowd the room. She dropped the dress on the bed, and ducked inside the tiny bathroom. After seeing to her most pressing needs, she grabbed a glass on the sink and drank two glasses of water in a matter of seconds.

Annie felt much better. She returned to the bedroom where she'd left the gown in a big lump on Darla's bed. She knew how excited Darla was to receive it so she spread it out neatly and smoothed the wrinkles. She hoped Darla had better luck wearing it than she'd had. Finally, she opened Darla's closet and was greeted with a wardrobe that had been popular in the '80s. She searched for something that was less trendy at that time.

Sam dumped the mountain of crinoline on the sofa and sank into a chair, closing his eyes to block the Elvis clutter. He heard Annie moving about in Darla's bedroom and hoped she would soon be ready to leave. He could tell she did not like him—in fact, they both seemed to rub each other the wrong way—which was odd since most women liked him just fine. He wasn't bad to look at, and he was a successful attorney—well, as successful as one could be in a town the size of Pinckney, Georgia—and he was easy going and tried to get along with everybody. He liked to think he could be counted on. Of course, none of that was likely to impress a woman like Annie Hartford.

He had read all about her father in *Money Magazine,* which had listed his net worth and pictured his iron and steel facility. A blueprint, or diagram of sorts, had shown the sheer magnitude of the facility and state of the art equipment. The man looked like a pit bull; a bully, someone accustomed to have his way or else. The only kind word Sam had read was regarding the Foundation set up in the Hartford name and run by Annie.

What Sam had seen of Annie so far, excluding her hot looking body—was not impressive. She had breezed into town in a stretch limo that was worth only Lord knew what, in a dress that had obviously cost a fortune but meant so little to her that she had given it away. If she was anything like her father then she was bad news; a hifalutin' society queen whose only interest in a man was his breeding and the size of his bank account. And what of Eldon; her betrothed? How had he taken the news that his bride had sneaked away in her daddy's limo, just to get out of marrying him? Not to mention all the guests—probably hundreds—who had expected to see a wedding unlike anything they'd seen before. Who had made the announcement that there would be no wedding? All these things raced through Sam's thoughts like tickertape.

When Annie returned to the living room, she found Sam slumped in a chair, seemingly deep in thought. He took one look at her outfit, a navy shirt dress with large golden sunflowers, thick black socks, red tennis shoes that looked like clown shoe, and just shook his head.

"What?" Annie asked. "Too loud? Darla has a thing for sunflowers and her feet are at least a size bigger than my size seven."

"Forget the clown shoes. That dress is a little short, isn't it?" he said, trying not to ogle her long shapely legs.

"I tried on several," Annie said. "I'm taller than Darla so they're all short. I didn't want to spend any more time searching. I know you're in a hurry to get back to the restaurant before your dinner crowd shows up."

"Just be careful," he said. "This town has its share of rednecks and bikers. If one of them takes a liking to you he might decide to make you his woman." Sam was exaggerating again, but he knew if there was trouble, Annie was likely to be right in the middle of it.

Annie notice he had not taken his eyes off her legs since she had entered the room, and she could not help teasing him. "Why don't you come right out and say it, Sam. You like my short skirt because you like looking at my legs."

He sighed and shook his head. "See, I knew you would take it the wrong way. I should have kept my mouth shut and let you take your chances."

She could not hide her amusement. "So, you *don't* like my legs?"

"I did not say that. I think they're fine."

"You know what *I* think?" Annie said, unable to resist, even though it was a struggle to remain straight-faced. "I think *you* like my legs and want to make me *your* woman."

Sam almost gaped, then figured she was teasing. "No, thanks," he said, coming to his feet. "You're far too complicated and high maintenance for me." He headed for the door. "I don't need all that drama in my life."

Annie frowned at the somewhat stinging remark as she followed him out. Complicated? High maintenance? Sam Ballard obviously did not know her well, but then, how could he since she had only landed in Pinckney a couple of hours earlier. True, the circumstances of that meeting had been anything but normal so she could not blame him for thinking she had . . . issues.

"Well, now," she said, after locking the front door and pocketing the key, "I do believe I've been rejected by Pinckney's most eligible bachelor. I hope you won't mind driving me to the nearest bridge so I can jump."

Sam laughed as they walked toward the Jeep. "I must write Eldon and tell him what a lucky man he is to have escaped holy matrimony with you."

Annie got in on the passenger's side and strapped on her seatbelt. She waited until Sam joined her to speak. "Eldon is probably crying over a bottle of expensive scotch as we speak. He knows he lost the best thing he almost had, a woman with a filthy rich daddy who was grooming him to take over an iron and steel dynasty."

Sam glanced at her, and his look softened. "So that's the way it was, huh?"

"Yes, but I don't want to talk about me," Annie said. "I want to hear all about your life here in Pinckney. Do you have a girlfriend? Oh, what a silly question; I'll bet you have a dozen girlfriends," she said, before he could answer. "I'll bet you've got one *special* girl, though, don't you? Let me guess. She is uncomplicated and almost never requires anything of you, meaning she is very low maintenance. I'll bet her name is Lulu, and she's got boobs the size of cantaloupes. Am I right?"

Sam shook his head as he turned onto the main road leading into town. "You know, just when I think I could like you, you go and blow it for me."

They made the rest of the drive in silence. When Sam parked in front of the Dixieland Cafe, Annie politely thanked him for everything and climbed out. "Give Lulu my best," she said before closing the door.

Sam shook his head as he watched Annie walk into his restaurant. The woman was an enigma. She had just admitted that her fiancé had only wanted to marry her so he could get closer to her daddy's money and take over the man's company. If that was the case, why had Annie gone on the run? Why hadn't her father sent the fiancé packing instead? It sounded suspicious. Annie had already lied once, although he did not hold it against her considering the circumstances; but he couldn't help wonder what else she may have lied about. He had been fooled once by a woman; he was determined it would not happen again.

Darla whistled when she spied Annie in her sunflower dress and red tennis shoes. "Kinda short on you, kiddo," she said. "Too bad you're not waiting tables, we'd have to get a Brink's truck to haul your tips home. However, the shoes might be a turn-off. You want a cup of coffee? It's fresh."

"I would love a cup of coffee," Annie said. "Until I got to your place my poor stomach had not seen food or drink in about sixteen hours. I may have drunk your well dry."

"Why were you not eating or drinking?" Darla asked.

"That wedding gown is a real bear getting in and out of. Heaven forbid if you have to visit the little girls' room."

"What if I have to, you know, tinkle?"

"That's what I'm trying to tell you," Annie said. "It's next to impossible. I did not put anything in my stomach or drink water after ten p.m. the night before."

"But what if I can't hold it?"

"You have two choices," Annie said. "You grab a couple of your closest girlfriends and have them hold up the dress while you, well, you know."

"Are you kidding?" Darla said. "Two women can't fit in a bathroom stall with me and that dress." She lightly bopped her forehead with the ball of her hand. "What am I thinking? *I* won't be able to fit in a stall in that dress. What's the other choice?"

"You have someone call the Fire Department, tell the dispatcher a woman is trapped in fifty pounds of crinoline, and they need to bring The Jaws of Life."

Darla grinned as she filled a mug with the freshly brewed coffee and placed it in front of Annie, along with a glass of ice water.

Annie added cream and sugar and took a sip. "This is so good," she said.

"Sounds like we need to feed you before you starve," Darla replied. "Do you like fried chicken? Saturday is fried chicken night, and our cook, Miss Flo, makes the best in the world. Her daughter, Patricia, works in the kitchen also, and she specializes in biscuits, pies, and various other deserts."

"But I don't have any—"

Darla held her hand up. "Please don't talk to me about money," she said, "because I will reach across this counter and smack you."

"Fried chicken sounds perfect," Annie replied. "To tell you the truth, I'm so hungry I could eat soggy cardboard."

"Oh, bummer," Darla said, "We don't serve soggy cardboard on Saturday night. That's our Wednesday special."

"Remind me to make reservations."

Darla scribbled the order on her notepad. "I'll put a rush on it," she said.

As Annie sipped her coffee, she replayed in her head all that had taken place that day. She had decided to go ahead and marry Eldon after the harsh words she and her father had exchanged in his office the night she'd tried to call off the engagement. She knew married couples who still lived together long after their passion for each other had subsided. What some of them did instead was develop a passion for something else, usually some form of volunteer work. Since Annie already performed volunteer service, she had planned to increase her hours once she married Eldon. Her father would have to find someone else to throw his dinner parties and run his many errands because she would insist on moving, and if Eldon wanted a peaceful marriage, he would go along with it.

Annie thought she had settled it in her mind, but the morning of her wedding she was jolted awake by a suffocating panic attack and a sense of dread unlike anything she'd ever experienced. She realized she did not want to live a passionless marriage; she wanted to know what real and lasting love was like. She would always regret any embarrassment she'd caused her father by taking off like she had, but she would never regret leaving.

Except for Vera. Annie hoped she had not gotten Vera and Snedley in trouble by taking off like she had. She desperately wanted to call the woman, but her emotions were too near the surface to speak to her.

Darla set a plate of fried chicken in front of her. "Looks good, huh?" Darla said.

Annie forced a smile as Darla refilled her coffee. "It looks great."

Darla winked. "Eat up! I'll check on you in a few." She hurried off with her coffee pot.

Annie had to agree with Darla's assessment of the fried chicken when she tasted it. It was crisp on the outside and almost melt-in-her-mouth tender on the inside. It was served with a small side salad, real mashed potatoes and gravy, seasoned green beans, and a hot buttered biscuit. Despite feeling anxious about Vera, Annie was able to eat quite a bit.

"That was a wonderful meal," she said, when Darla picked up her plate. "Tell Flo and Patricia I want to be adopted into their family."

"You'll think twice about that if you ever witness Flo's temper," Darla said. "She threw a skillet at me once when I said her meatloaf was dry; and she got after Sam with a paring knife a couple of years back when he refused to give her a raise."

"You don't think she really meant to hurt either of you?" Annie asked.

"I think she probably acts tougher than she really is, but who knows? Just to play it safe, I've done nothing but praise her meatloaf ever since. Sam, on the other hand, refused to give her the raise."

"That makes him stubborn or brave," Annie said. "Which is it?"

"I would have to say both. He told Flo that nobody but *nobody* pulled a knife on him, and he threatened to have her arrested if she ever did it again. Anyway, he put her on thirty days probation. Well, Flo is just like the rest of us; we need a paycheck. So she changed her tune and became the nicest person you'd ever want to work with. She supposedly apologized to Sam after her thirty days, and a couple of weeks later, he gave her the raise."

"So the moral of the story is . . .?"

"Sam is a fair man. He pays better wages than the other restaurant owners in this town, and we always get a nice Christmas bonus and cost of living increase in January. Just don't push him."

"I think it's great he gives a cost of living increase," Annie said, "what with the economy being on shaky ground."

Darla laughed. "What do you know about the cost of living and the economy, Annie?" she teased. "That's something you'll never have to worry about."

"Being rich isn't always what it's cut out to be," Annie said.

"Spoken like a true rich person."

"Um, Darla, I need a small favor," she said, changing the subject.

"Name it."

"I would like to text someone who is probably very worried about me. I was wondering if I could borrow your cell phone."

"Sure, but you can call the person if you like. I've got unlimited minutes."

"I'm afraid I'll get emotional if I talk to her. Right now I just want her to know I'm okay."

"I'll grab my phone from my purse."

Annie had just finished texting Vera that she was safe and had a place to stay when half a dozen chattering women walked through the front door.

"Good evening, ladies," Darla called out. "I've already set up your regular table. I'll have your drinks ready in just a sec."

"No rush, Darla," one of them said.

"Who are those women?" Annie asked.

"They are members of the Pinckney Social Club and Support Group," Darla replied. "You must be widowed, divorced, or separated in order to join. I'm sure you fit in there somewhere. Come on over, I want you to meet them."

"I'd rather wait," Annie said, still feeling foolish after all that had occurred once she rode into Pinckney on a cloud of smoke. "I can meet them later."

"Listen to me, Annie," Darla said. "You're going through a difficult time right now, and that's what the support group is all about, helping each other through the good, the bad, and the ugly. Plus, you'll be able to make new friends. As I see it, you need all the friends you can get right now."

Chapter Three

"Hey, everybody," Darla said, all but dragging a reluctant Annie with her to the table of ladies. "I want y'all to meet Annie Hartford from Atlanta. She arrived in town this afternoon driving a smokin' limo and wearing a gorgeous designer wedding gown." Darla hugged Annie to her. "She actually *gave* me the dress, the big sweetheart."

"Heard you fainted, Darla," a woman named Ira said, grinning.

"You would have fainted too, Ira, if you'd been me," Darla said, "but I'd rather not talk about it right now because I'll start getting all emotional. I just wanted to introduce Annie—she's feeling a bit shy at the moment—I know y'all will give her a big Pinckney welcome."

The six women at the table smiled and nodded, a couple of them stood and shook Annie's hand, including a slender, middle-aged woman with a frosted pixie haircut, and wire framed glasses. "I'm Lillian Calhoun," she said. "Welcome to Pinckney, honey." She motioned for Annie to take the chair next to her.

Annie recognized the name. "My friend, Vera Holmes, told me to look you up," she said once she had sat down.

"I've not seen Vera in a long time," Lillian said, "but she is such a dear person." Lillian paused. "But *you*, young lady, are an amazing woman. We all heard how you ditched your fiancé, jumped in your father's limo, and hit the road. We think you were mighty brave to do what you did, don't we girls?"

"I don't understand why you didn't just call off the engagement," a dark-haired woman name Cheryl Camp said.

"I tried, and it did not work. You would have to know my father to understand. He does not play fair."

"Her father has a hellacious temper," Lillian said, "and he will go to all lengths to get his way. Trust me, Annie is better off without him."

Annie looked surprised. "How do you know about my father?"

Lillian blushed. "Me and my big mouth," she said. "I've just heard things about the man."

"From Vera?" Annie asked.

Lillian hesitated. "Yes. Please don't be angry with her for telling me. I think she just needed someone to talk to at the time. Like I said, we go way back."

Annie found it odd that Vera had shared personal information about her with someone Annie had never even heard of until that day. "I could never be angry with Vera," she said. "She raised my brother and me when our parents divorced."

"Yes, I know," Lillian said. "From the looks of it she did a fantastic job."

Annie lowered her voice. "I suppose Vera told you about my twin brother."

"She did. I'm so very sorry you had to go through that. Just don't beat yourself up for leaving like you did," Lillian said. "Some relationships are so unhealthy you have no choice but to walk away."

Annie suddenly grinned. "Actually, I ran like hell."

Darla caught the last comment as she arrived carrying a large oval tray with salads and beverages. She placed the tray on a metal tray stand. "I'll never know how Annie was able to run in that dress *or* how she managed to climb into the limo to begin with."

"Desperate times cause for desperate measures, right?" Lillian asked Annie and winked.

Annie nodded. "Absolutely."

"We also heard how Sheriff Hester showed his behind," she said. "If anybody needs to be hanged in the courthouse square he would be my first choice after the way he behaved. He will never get another vote out of me."

"I didn't vote for him last time," an Asian woman sitting on the other side of Annie said. Her thick, shiny black hair hung straight down her back, not a strand out of place, making Annie think she would be perfect for a shampoo commercial. She offered Annie her hand. "I'm Kazue. I'm a seamstress. Lillian and I do a few jobs together."

Annie looked at Lillian. "What is it you do?"

"Interior decorating," Lillian said. "Kazue specializes in window treatments and bedding. She makes me look good."

"Nonsense," Kazue said. She looked at Annie. "The woman is gifted, and we get a lot of word-of-mouth jobs," she added. "We get business from Savannah, Atlanta, Athens, Albany, Columbus, you name it. And not just locations in Georgia," she added.

"We finally had to hire extra personnel," Lillian said.

Darla finished serving the drinks and salads. "I take it everybody wants the fried chicken dinner."

"That's why we're here," one of the other members said.

"And I thought you ladies came to see me," a male voice said. Annie glanced around to find Sam Ballard standing behind her. He'd changed into dark brown dress slacks, a crisp white shirt, and a brown and beige stripe tie.

"Uh-oh, girls," Lillian said. "Sam has discovered our secret." She batted her eyelashes at him. "We only pretend we're here for the fried chicken," she said, "but the real reason we come is to get a gander at the best looking lawyer in town."

"Hey, I can't help being handsome," Sam said. "I was born this way."

Darla was writing the order on her ticket pad and looked up. "You're meeting a client?"

43

He nodded. "I shouldn't be long. I trust you'll hold down the fort." He glanced at Annie and his smile faded, even as his gaze lingered. "I'll leave you ladies to your dinner," he said. "I'm sure you have a lot of catching up to do since last week."

Nobody spoke until he walked away. Finally, Lillian nudged Annie. "What was that all about?"

Annie could not get over how nicely Sam had looked. Not that he hadn't looked good earlier in a pair of khakis and a casual shirt, she reminded herself, both starched and ironed. She noticed Lillian, and the others waiting for her reply; even Darla looked interested.

"I don't think Mr. Ballard likes me very much," she said. "You know, running out on my wedding the way I did. I think I remind him of the time he was, um—" She paused, trying to think of a polite way of saying it.

"I believe the word you're looking for is *jilted*," Lillian said.

"Oh, good grief," Kazue said. "That was how many years ago? Four? Five?"

"Five," Darla replied, "and I don't mind telling you, I'm sick of all the ribbing. It's not funny. We need a new scandal. Right now people are talking about my new garter belt. Is that desperate or what?"

"Why did you buy a new garter belt?" Ira said. "Have you not heard of panty hose?"

Everybody at the table got a good chuckle, including Annie. Kazue shook her head sadly. "Where have you been, Ira? The garter belt is for *after* hours. I'll bet Darla has a teddy to match."

"Damn right," Darla said, "both are black and red. And for those times when I really feel like getting kinky, I have a Tweety Bird outfit." She was prevented from saying any more when the bell rang, letting her know her food was up.

"She was teasing," Lillian said.

"Don't be so sure," Kazue replied. "This is Darla we're talking about."

The restaurant started filling up. "If Sam doesn't hire someone to help Darla soon I don't know what the poor girl is going to do?"

"Why is she the only waitress working on a busy night like this?" Annie asked.

"The last girl was kind of a smart aleck," Lillian said, "which did not go over well with Darla *or* the people in the kitchen. Needless to say, she did not last long. There are two girls working the morning shift; one of them has been coming in most evenings to help. I don't know why she isn't here tonight. Don't worry," Lillian added. "Sam knows Darla is working alone tonight. He'll cut his appointment short."

"I know this is none of my business," Annie said, "but what made him buy a restaurant when he has a law degree?"

Lillian looked at her. "Just like a lot of us, Sam couldn't bear the thought of the city tearing down this building, but I think most people were overwhelmed at the amount of work it would need to bring it back to what Sam refers to at its glory days. Thankfully, a lot of people showed up to help; several retired contractors, as well as plumbers, an electrician, painters, you name it. All free of charge.

"As for the used cars, he wasn't looking to start another business. An old friend of his showed up one day, asked if he could rent the empty lot next to Sam's law office since Sam owns both pieces of property. When his friend went to auctions to buy cars or traveled out of town to pick up one or two, Sam ended up waiting on customers, and wouldn't you know it, he is so well-liked in this town that he started selling them like lemonade on a hot day. His friend offered Sam a full partnership. The extra money suited Sam just fine because he was trying to build his practice. I'm sure all the expenses involved in renovating the restaurant took a huge bite out of his savings account."

"Sounds like he has multi-tasking down to an art," Annie said.

Lillian smiled. "I'm just guessing, but I think he'd like to get out of the used car business. Between the restaurant and his practice, he has his hands full." She paused. "I don't mean to change the subject, but where are you staying?"

"Darla has kindly invited me to crash on her sofa for the time being."

"Hope you like Elvis," Ira muttered under her breath.

"I heard that," Darla said, coming by to pour fresh coffee and tea.

"How long do you plan to be in Pinckney?" Ira asked.

Annie was too embarrassed to admit that she had *no idea* what she was going to do, that she had been in such a hurry to escape her wedding that she had forgotten her purse, meaning she was indeed flat broke at the moment, so broke she was having to borrow Darla's clothes.

"I don't have transportation to leave at the moment," she said. "My father's, um, limo is in the shop. I'm not sure *what* I'm going to do," she said. "I just want to stay as far away from Atlanta as I can."

"So stay in Pinckney for a while," one of the other women named Cheryl said. "You could rent an apartment for a few months, see if the town suits you. You should look at Hillcrest Apartments," she added. "They're really nice; all high-end appliances and granite countertops. They can even furnish them for you. I could drive you over tomorrow since you don't have transportation at the moment."

"I think I need to find a job first," Annie said, "before I look for a place to live. I don't have much cash on me since I left my purse at the church in my mad rush to escape."

"Where do you bank?" Cheryl asked. "I can take you there first."

Annie blushed. "I'm afraid that's not an option." All eyes were on her. Annie figured they would find out the truth before long so there was no sense keeping it a big secret. "I did not want to discuss my personal problems," Annie said, "but all my accounts are frozen, and my credit cards canceled."

"Why am I not surprised?" Lillian said. "Your father is a real bastard."

Annie was surprised by Lillian's harsh comment, but she suspected the woman knew more than she was saying.

"I can give you money until you get on your feet," Lillian said.

Annie shook her head. "No. This is my problem. I should have guessed what my father would do once I tried to call off the engagement. I think it's safe to say he has washed his hands of me."

"Okay, so you have a place to stay, at least temporarily," Cheryl said. "You'll need to find some kind of job. Problem is, this is a small town and jobs are scarce. But I have a good friend who runs an employment agency, so who knows? What kind of work have you done?"

Annie wished she had an impressive resume she could whip out, but that was not the case. "I've never really worked," she said. "I did not attend college. I had hoped to go to join my brother at Duke University, but that was not to me. After I graduated from high school, my father sent me to finishing school."

"Finishing school, huh?" Cheryl said. "Isn't that the same thing as charm school?"

"Not like the charm school of yesteryear," Annie said, "where the student's GPA was based on how well she married. The school I attended emphasized personal growth. I was taught etiquette and poise, of course, but we reread all the classics, stayed on top of current affairs, attended plays and operas, took cooking and nutritional classes, studied early childhood education, and—" She paused and look about. "What?"

"All that sounds great," Cheryl said, "but did you learn any job skills?"

Annie shook her head. "Unfortunately, no," she said.

"So what have you been doing since you graduated from this school?" Ira asked.

"I take care of the estate and plan dinner parties for my father," she said. "I run a lot of errands for him."

The women at the table stared at her but remained silent.

"I'm sure there's something you can do," Cheryl said. "You may have to start at the bottom and work your way up," she added.

"What would the bottom be?" Annie asked, hoping it wouldn't entail taking off her clothes.

"You can make beds, can't you?"

Annie smiled. "I'm sure I could if somebody showed me how."

Ira dropped her fork. Cheryl stared back at her, mouth agape.

"You've never made a bed?" Cheryl whispered.

Annie chuckled. "I'm teasing. Of course I know how to make a bed. I had to train housekeepers."

"What's wrong here?" Darla asked, arriving with their fried chicken dinners. "Everyone looks so serious."

"Oh, we were just discussing what kind of job Annie might be able to find in Pinckney," Cheryl said. "She doesn't have much experience."

"I've already thought about the job situation," Darla told them. "I'm going to get Sam to hire her."

Darla barely got the words out before Sam came through the swinging doors leading from the kitchen. He had dispensed with the tie and rolled up his shirt sleeves. He quickly looked around as though assessing the situation, grabbed an armful of menus and met a party of four who stood just inside the front door.

Annie was having trouble finding her voice. "You mean as a waitress?" she asked. When Darla nodded, she went on. "But I have no experience."

"Then you're very lucky that you're going to be trained by the best," Darla informed her.

"He doesn't even like me," she said.

"Maybe he *does* like you and that's the problem," Darla said, "but that's neither here nor there. Sam might balk in the beginning, but he'll eventually come around."

Annie shook her head. "I don't think—" Annie paused and sucked in air. "I've never carried a tray. I can barely carry a glass of water without spilling half of it." But Darla had already shot off like lightening to the next table.

Lillian covered Annie's hand with hers. "Listen to me, Annie," she said in a soft voice. "Don't ever tell yourself you can't do something. I was terrified when I opened my store. Terrified! Don't let it stop you. Just take a lot of deep breaths and move one foot in front of the other. You'll be okay. I promise you."

"No. Absolutely not. I can't believe you would even suggest it."

Darla kept silent as Sam counted the day's earnings from the cash register and made out a deposit slip. They were alone. Flo and Patricia had already clocked out and headed home. Lillian had driven Annie back to Darla's place.

"Sam, just tell me this. What do you have against Annie?"

"I don't even know the woman, how can I have anything against her?"

"Then what have you got against me?"

He looked up in surprise. "Now, that's a dumb question if ever there was one."

"You obviously don't care about my health. And if you don't care about my health, then—"

"What the hell are you talking about? What's wrong with your health?"

"I'm getting old."

"You're thirty-five, for Pete's sake. That's not old. Anybody who can dance all night at that redneck bar on the edge of town, then come in the next day and work a double shift is definitely not old. You're in your prime, Darla Mae Jenkins."

"I can't keep up like I used to. I have corns on my feet trying to run this place by myself. My corns have corns. Do you know how unattractive that is, Sam? Why do you think I had to go out and buy that expensive new garter belt? It's to keep men looking there and not at my feet."

"Maybe you should try going home at a decent hour once in a while. Here's a thought. Go to the library and pick up a few good books."

"Oh, now that sounds fun," she said. "Do you go to bed every night with a good book?"

"Most nights I do." When she gave a snort, he looked at her. "I'm thirty-five years old, too, honey. My hell-raising days are over."

"Don't you ever get lonely?"

"I'm too damn busy to get lonely," Sam said, "but that doesn't mean I don't enjoy female companionship. I'm human."

"The fact is, you promised to hire someone before the Okra Festival, and now it's less than a week away. You know what that's like. There is absolutely no way I can handle those crowds by myself."

"I've got an ad in the newspaper."

"Forget it. By the time someone responds, I can have Annie trained. The festival starts a week from yesterday."

"Then I'll find someone with experience."

Darla's lips were pressed into a grim line as she reached beneath the counter for her purse. "Good night, Sam."

He glanced up, surprised. "What, you're not even going to wait for me to finish closing out? At least let me walk you to your car. You know I don't like—"

"I don't need for you to walk me to the car," she said. She unlocked the front door and left without another word.

Annie was waiting for Darla when she arrived home. She had showered and dressed in a pair of Darla's cut-offs and tee-shirt. Unable to sit for long thanks to a bad case of nerves, she'd scrubbed Darla's kitchen and bathroom until they sparkled, and she'd washed a load of towels. Finally, she had dusted the living room, taking great care with the Elvis decanters.

"Place looks nice," Darla said as she came through the door, "but I don't expect you to clean."

"I was jittery. What did Sam say?"

Darla slumped into a chair and kicked off her white uniform shoes. "He's going to think about it."

"At least he didn't say no."

"I'm beat," Darla muttered.

"Can I get you something from the kitchen? A glass of iced tea?"

Darla gave her a weary smile. "No, thanks. As soon as I grab a hot shower I'll be good as new. Think I might drive over to Ernie's."

"Who's Ernie?"

"It's a place not a person. Just a little waterin' hole on the edge of town," she added. "I usually go have a cold beer and it relaxes me so I can come back and get some sleep. Hey, you might be interested in going. Meet some of my friends. It's only nine-thirty, and it's Saturday night. The place will be hoppin'."

"Sure, I'll go. I can change back into the dress I had on earlier."

"Most folks wear jeans. It's a country-western bar."

"Your jeans are probably too short on me."

"I've got a pair that needs hemming. They'll probably do. I also think I have an extra pair of boots that will fit you if you keep those thick socks on."

The two women were on their way a half hour later. Although Annie was exhausted and would have preferred climbing into a comfortable bed, or sofa, she figured it would be rude not to go with the woman who was offering her a place to stay. Besides, it was to her advantage to meet as many people as she could, since the subject of her employment wasn't yet settled. She was more than a little nervous at the thought of working at the Dixieland Cafe. What did she know about waitress work?

It was her own fault for not standing up to her father years ago when she was planning her education. She should never have let him send her to some dumb finishing school, where the staff was more interested in teaching her to set a lovely table or plan a party for one hundred guests than how to support herself.

Now here she was, almost thirty years old, and didn't have a clue what she was going to do with her life. Annie frowned when Darla pulled into the parking lot of a large one-story cinderblock building. The place was surrounded by motorcycles and pickup trucks, some of the trucks so high off the ground it would have taken a stepladder for her to reach the door. "Is this it?" she asked, although a massive neon sign flashing beside the road clearly spelled out Ernie's Place.

"This is it," Darla said, parking beside a truck with a full gun rack in the back. "Do I look okay?"

Annie wasn't sure how to respond to someone wearing a leather miniskirt, tank-top blouse, and a blue-jean jacket. "Let's just put it this way, Darla. You will definitely stand out in a crowd in that outfit."

The woman smiled. "Thanks, darlin'. That's just the kind of thing a girl likes to hear. Come on. Let's play."

Annie climbed out of the car and followed Darla toward the building with mounting trepidation. If the music blaring outside the building was any indication of how loud it was inside, she knew she was in for a long night. But her poor eardrums were not prepared for the moment when Darla opened the door, or the loud squeal Darla gave the moment they stepped inside.

At first Annie thought her friend had hurt herself somehow, but a second later Darla threw her arms around a man's neck. Annie decided the woman must be very happy to see him. And he to see her, from the way he picked her up and swung her around as if she were weightless. The two carried on for a good five minutes while Annie entertained thoughts of climbing into the backseat of Darla's car for a long nap.

"Hank, it's so good to see you," Darla said, giving him another hug. She glanced at Annie as though realizing for the first time she was standing there. "Oh, I want you to meet my new roommate, honey. This here's Annie. Annie, meet Hank, my old boyfriend. We go way back."

Annie smiled and offered her hand, but Hank obviously decided a bear hug more appropriate. By the time he set her down, Annie was certain all the bones in her body had been crushed.

"C'mon and let me buy you pretty gals a cold one," he said, dragging them toward a bar that ran the entire length of the room. Darla paused a number of times to speak to someone she knew. By the time they reached the bar, Annie's head was splitting from the music.

"What'll it be, miss?" the bartender asked her. He wore overalls and looked as though he'd been plowing a field all day.

"Just give me a diet soft drink," she said, and received a good deal of ribbing from Darla and Hank, both of whom ordered a draft beer. Annie had barely managed to take a sip before a tall red-haired man named Jesse tapped her on the shoulder and asked her to dance. She turned him down, only to have Darla insist she dance with him because he was a friend of hers. Annie soon found herself trying to keep time to a tune with fiddle music and before long she had more dance partners than she knew what to do with.

Sam was surprised to find Darla's lights off and the car gone when he pulled into the driveway of her mobile home. She'd rushed from the restaurant in such a hurry that she'd forgotten her wallet. She had pulled it out when she'd cashed her tips out at the end of the night, swapping change and small bills so Sam wouldn't have to worry about going to the bank to replenish them. He knew she was ticked off at him, and it wasn't the first time, but she would eventually get over it. The bottom line, he was still owner of the Dixieland Café, and Darla would just have to accept the fact that she was his employee.

It didn't take Sam long to figure out where the two women had gone. With it being Saturday night, he knew his star waitress would be sitting in Ernie's. 'Course tomorrow she'd be as hung over as a Shriner at an annual convention, and the church crowd would have her hopping like a barefoot young'un on a hot sidewalk. She'd be in a sour mood and probably get into a verbal battle with Flo or Patricia.

Sam had no desire to go to Ernie's, but he knew he had to get Darla's wallet to her, despite her frequent bragging about never paying for a drink. Sam backed out of the drive, and as he headed in the direction of the redneck hangout, he tried to imagine Annie in such a place. He couldn't.

Pleading exhaustion to her current dance partner, Annie returned to the bar, only to find Darla and Hank missing. The bartender in overalls returned wearing a grin. "Some of your dance partners have taken a shine to you," he said. "They want to buy you a drink. Several, in fact. What'll you have?"

"I don't want anything right now," Annie replied as politely as she could, considering her head felt as though it was ready to split open. "Would you happen to know where my friend went?"

"She left with that other feller. Said to tell you'd she'd be back in a jiffy."

"When you see her, would you please tell her I'm waiting for her in the car?"

"What do I look like, Western Union?"

"I'm sorry to impose—"

"I'm just havin' fun with you," he said, his chubby face breaking into a grin. "I'll tell her."

Annie made her way out the door, leaving a good portion of the noise inside. She passed a couple of men sitting on the tailgate of a truck but pretended not to see them.

"Hey, baby, you lookin' for some comp'ny?"

"No thanks," she said, and kept on walking.

"Hey, that ain't no way to be," one of them said as he caught up with her. "What'd I ever do to you?"

"Please—" She stopped and turned. He was a beefy fellow but she wasn't sure if she should be scared or amused. He spit a wad of chewing tobacco on the ground, and she shuddered. "I have a splitting headache, and I just want to be alone," she said. She resumed walking. Where the hell had Darla parked?

"I got a headache powder in the truck."

Sure he did, Annie thought. And she had a hundred dollar bill in her pocket.

It finally hit her that Darla's car was missing, and the thought of being stranded at a place like Ernie's almost made her weep. Why would Darla have left her? Especially knowing she didn't have a dime to her name? She didn't even have enough money to call anyone. Besides, who would she call?

"You can drink it down with a cold beer, and that headache'll be history."

Annie saw a car turn off the highway into the parking lot, and she prayed it was Darla's. She almost went weak with relief when it turned out to be a Jeep driven by Sam Ballard. He pulled up beside her.

"Out slumming tonight, Annie?"

"I beg your pardon?"

"If you're looking for trouble, this is the place to find it." Sam slammed the Jeep into park and climbed out. Annie noticed the stranger's friend had come up and both of them towered over Sam.

"I asked you what the hell you're doing and who these men are?" he almost shouted.

Annie's jaw dropped. "I don't have to take this—"

The man next to Annie nudged her. "Do you know this guy?"

"Yes, I—"

"I happen to be her husband," Sam said, his words clipped and precise. "She has a new baby at home waiting to be nursed. She told me she was running to the store for disposable diapers."

"Oh, well—" The man looked from Sam to Annie and back to Sam. "Hey, man, we don't want to cause no trouble between married folks. Me and my brother was just passing through town." He regarded Annie. "You should be home with your kid, lady." He looked at the other man. "C'mon, let's get outta here."

Annie was glad it was dark and nobody could see the crimson color on her face. "That was despicable," she told Sam.

"Would you rather see me get beat up by the rhino brothers?" He didn't give her time to answer. "Where's Darla, and what the hell are you doing in a dark parking lot with some men you don't know?"

"I don't know where Darla is, and I don't have to answer your questions."

"Great. Then I'll just leave you here to fend for yourself." He turned and climbed back inside the Jeep.

"Wait!" Annie hurried over. "Darla's car is gone. She took off with some guy named Hank."

"So you decided to wait for her in a parking lot filled with drunk rednecks and bikers. Great idea, Annie," he said, sarcasm ringing loud in his voice. "Now I see why your father had to make your decisions." He regretted his choice of words the minute they left his mouth, the very second he saw Annie's face fall. But, dammit, she could have gotten in bad trouble there.

Sudden tears stung her eyes. "You can just go straight to hell for all I care." She started walking.

He pulled up beside her. "I'm sorry, Annie. That was a lousy thing for me to say. Get in the car, and I'll take you back to Darla's."

"I'd rather walk."

"You can't walk. It's dangerous this time of night."

"I can take care of myself. Contrary to what you might think," she added angrily.

They had reached the highway. "I'll bet you don't even know how to get to Darla's trailer."

Annie wasn't listening. It had been such a miserable day, not to mention humiliating as hell, and her head felt as though it would explode. She had spent the better part of the evening wondering what she was going to do with her life and cursing the fact that she hadn't taken charge long ago. The last thing she needed was for Sam Ballard to show up and rub her nose in it.

"Annie, I'm warning you, either get in the Jeep, or I'll personally put you in."

She kept walking.

Sam gunned his engine and parked a good distance ahead of her. He climbed out, then slammed the door so hard, his Jeep rocked on its wheels. Teeth gritted, he closed the distance between him and Annie, then, without warning, hefted her up and threw her over his shoulder. She kicked and squealed like a stuck pig.

"Shut up, dammit!" he ordered. "Folks'll think I'm kidnapping you." She screamed louder, and he gave her a sound whack on the behind.

Annie saw red. She kicked her legs and flailed her arms and finally grabbed a handful of his hair. Sam let a few obscenities fly before he realized someone had pulled up behind them. He turned but was blinded by headlights. He blinked several times before he realized it was the highway patrol.

"Dammit to hell, Annie, look what you've done now." He heard the door open and close, was barely able to make out the silhouette of a patrolman.

"What's going on here?" the uniformed man said.

Annie continued to pummel Sam in the back but glanced around at the sound of another's voice. "Oh, Officer, thank God you're here. I'm being abducted."

"Abducted, huh?" The patrolman spit what looked like a wad of chewing tobacco on the ground, and Annie wondered if everybody in Pinckney chewed it. "Well, we don't put up with the likes of that in Pinckney, Georgia ma'am." He reached for his gun. "I reckon I don't have any choice but to shoot him."

Chapter Four

In disbelief, Annie watched the patrolman pull his gun out of the holster and aim it at Sam. She screamed. "No, wait!"

"Put her down, pal," the armed man said. "I'm warning you, I got this sucker aimed right for your goozle."

Sam sighed heavily and dropped Annie to the ground. She landed in a heap.

"Now move away, lady, so I can finish him off."

"Officer, please let me explain," Annie cried, crawling along the gravel as fast as she could. She pulled herself up by the man's pants leg. "He, uh, Mr. Ballard here, was only offering me a ride. I was lying about being abducted."

"He probably told you to say that, didn't he?" The patrolman pushed her aside. "You need to turn your head, miss. I've done this sort of thing before, and it ain't a pretty sight."

"Oh, my God, no!" Annie threw herself in front of Sam, acting as a shield.

Sam stood there with his arms crossed over his chest, the lines in his face tense, as if holding himself in check while Annie sobbed and carried on like a character in a bad soap opera. "Okay, Buster, you've had your fun. I'd like to go home now."

The other man chuckled and stuck his revolver back in its holster.

"Listen, Sambo, you're going to have to learn to start charming the ladies a little better. You can't just throw a woman over your shoulder like a sack of taters and haul her off. You have to buy them flowers and candy and—" He paused and looked around as though wanting to make sure they weren't overheard. "You might have to write a few lines of poetry. It don't matter if it don't rhyme."

Annie's head swiveled from side to side. "Excuse me, but do you two know each other?"

Sam looked at her. "This is Johnny Ballard, my cousin. Folks call him Buster. He's a real prankster."

"So all this was just a big joke at my expense," she said. She glared at Sam. "You let me grovel and beg for your life like some idiot nutcase. How dare you!"

A car screeched to a halt, and Darla jumped out and came running. She looked panicked. "What's wrong? Is somebody hurt?"

"Well, now, ain't you a sight for sore eyes," Buster said. "Why don't you and me go for a spin in my patrol car. I'll even let you play with my siren."

"Annie, what's going on?" Darla asked.

Annie tried to explain everything that had happened since she'd last seen her friend. It was all she could do to get the words out, what with her stammering and sputtering. Her heart was still racing.

"Didn't the bartender give you my message?" Darla asked. "Hank needed cigarettes. I told the bartender to tell you I was going to the convenience store not far from here, and that I'd be right back. Only, I didn't know Hank was going to hang around and look at dirty magazines."

"Would you please take me home?" Annie asked, realizing that she was trembling. "You're welcome to go back to Ernie's and stay as long as you like, but I'm exhausted."

"Sure, honey. We can go."

"I'll walk back," Hank said, having come up in the meantime. He kissed Darla on the cheek. "I'll call you, babe."

Buster put his hand on Annie's shoulder. "I hope I didn't scare you, young lady. Sam and I are always cutting up."

"Actually, I think the whole scene was disgraceful," she said. "I hope you have your little notebook handy because you need to file assault and battery charges."

Buster looked startled as he reached into his pocket. "Is this for real?"

"I'll let you decide," Annie told him. She balled her hand into a tight fist, swung around with all her might, and slammed it into Sam Ballard's face. Sam, caught off guard, reeled back, lost his footing and sank to the ground.

Darla gave a squeal of surprise. "Oh, no!" She looked at Annie. "Why did you do that?"

Annie hitched her chin high. "He had it coming."

Buster hurried over to the fallen man. "Hey, Sambo, are you okay?"

Sam shook his head as if to clear it. "Holy hell, Buster, she knocked me off my feet." He glared at Annie, who looked quite pleased with herself.

"She sure did," Buster said. "That's assault and battery if I ever saw it. You want to press charges? 'Course, you know folks are gonna tease you something fierce about being beat up by a girl."

"Buster—" Sam tried to interrupt.

"The good news is they'll probably forget about that nasty business when your bride-to-be skipped town. Hey, buddy, I'm with you no matter what you decide."

"Please get her out of my sight," Sam told him.

"Don't bother," Annie said. "I'm out of here." She spun around on her heels and stalked toward Darla's car, with Darla right behind, asking for an explanation.

"He isn't going to be as eager to hire you now," Darla said.

Annie told her what had occurred as Darla drove them back to her mobile home. "Why didn't you say something sooner," Darla demanded. "I would gladly have waited my turn to slug him."

Annie was still fuming the next morning as she replayed in her mind the good-old-boy routine she'd witnessed the night before between Sam and his cousin. And to think, she had tried to shield Sam's body with her own to keep Buster from shooting him! They were probably still laughing over the whole thing. She had done nothing but make a gigantic fool of herself since she'd rolled into town in a smoking limo, wearing enough satin to make sheets for everyone in Pinckney.

She would never be able to hold her head up in front of the townspeople. They'd probably insist she wear the words "town idiot" embroidered on her blouse.

Annie heard the floor creak and turned as Darla staggered down the hall looking like something the cat would refuse to drag in. "What's wrong?" she asked.

"I'm sick," Darla said. "I think it's the flu."

"Oh no. Can I get you something?"

"You can go get my shotgun out of the closet in my bedroom and put me out of my misery."

"Sit down, and I'll pour you a cup of coffee," Annie said, getting up from her chair. Darla made it to the sofa and collapsed. "Do you have any cold medicine on hand?" Annie asked.

"No. I never get sick." She coughed and moaned. "I haven't been sick since—" She paused. "I don't remember when."

Annie poured the coffee and carried it to her friend. "You take it black, right?"

Darla mumbled something to the affirmative. "What time is it?" she asked as she raised the cup to her lips.

"Ten o'clock."

"I'm supposed to be at work by ten forty-five to set up for the lunch crowd. There's no way I can make it feeling like this. You'll have to go in for me, Annie."

"Me!" Annie almost shrieked the word. "But I don't know the first thing about waitress work."

"You said yourself how you used to plan big parties for your father's friends and clients," Darla pointed out. "All you have to do is smile at everybody and try to get along with Flo and Patricia. If you make them mad, you're screwed."

"Shouldn't I call Sam first and tell him you're sick? Let him make the decision?"

"He's probably home nursing his shiner, but there's an older woman and a kid who graduated from high school some months ago who work the breakfast crowd," she said. "You have to do this for me, Annie. I could lose my job, and somebody has to be there to serve those customers."

Annie was truly torn. After losing her temper and punching Sam in the face, he might just wring her neck when he saw her again. "What am I supposed to wear?"

"I have a couple of clean uniforms in my closet."

Annie checked her wristwatch. There wasn't much time to argue, considering she had to take a shower and put on a little makeup. She took a deep breath. "Okay, I'll do it. He may toss me out of the place the minute he sees me, but I'll give it my best shot." She was already headed in the direction of the bathroom.

Annie showered and dressed in record time, then applied her makeup quickly and sparingly. The uniform was too short—no surprise—but there wasn't much she could do about it at the moment. She started for the front door, promising to call and check on Darla later, then, it hit her. "Oh, no. How am I supposed to get to work?"

"My car keys are on the kitchen table."

"But I don't have my license and Sheriff Hester—"

"Forget about him. Just park the car in the back of the restaurant. You can tell him I drove you. He's not likely to take you in and interrogate you."

Shaking her head and wondering how her life had become so confused, Annie grabbed the keys and hurried out to Darla's car. It was in

See Bride Run!

sad shape. The seats had been taped and stitched so many times, it resembled a patchwork quilt. Annie thought of the custom pearl colored Jaguar with its powder blue interior presently sitting in the garage at home, and she realized she had always taken those things for granted.

Never again. She didn't have to be rich, and she didn't have to drive a fancy foreign car, but she wanted the security of knowing she could make it on her own. Just like Darla, Lillian Calhoun, Kazue, and the others, who had proved to everyone, as well as to themselves, that they had what it took to survive in this world.

Annie was still deep in thought when she pulled into the driveway in back of the Dixieland Cafe. She was a few minutes early, but it would give her time to get everything set up just right. She pushed through the back door and found herself in the kitchen with Flo and Patricia, neither of whom looked particularly pleased to see her. Her former resolve started to slip.

"Who the hell are you?" Flo asked, pausing in her work to scrutinize her. "And why . . . ?"

"My name is Annie Hartford, and I desperately need your help."

Patricia put a fist on her hip and cocked her head to the side. "Oh, yeah?"

"Darla's sick, and there's nobody to take over but me. But I don't know the first thing about waiting tables. I was hoping the two of you could show me the ropes, so to speak."

The two women exchanged looks. Flo cocked her head to the side. "Does Sam know about this?"

"No. He will probably toss me out of this kitchen the minute he sees me, but you know how it is when a friend needs help. I couldn't say no."

"He ain't gonna toss you out of *my* kitchen," Flo said. "If he so much as tries the last thing he'll see is my fat behind going out the back door."

"Then you'll help me?" Annie asked, a pleading note in her voice.

Flo sighed heavily. Patricia pressed her lips together in a grim line. "I'll help you as much as I can," Flo said, "but I got my own job to do.

You need to go out and talk to Gladys, the head breakfast waitress. She can show you what to do."

Annie thanked them profusely, pushed through the swinging doors, and came face-to-face with a squatty, thick-waisted woman with gray hair and thick-framed glasses. Her pale yellow uniform was as crisp as a brand-new linen tablecloth, but her shoes made annoying squashing and sucking noises when she walked.

"Who are you?" she asked.

"Annie Hartford. I'm covering for Darla today. She's got the flu."

"Most likely it's a hangover."

"No, I saw her myself. She's really sick."

Gladys sighed as though the world had just settled on her shoulders. "Okay, let me show you around. I reckon I can help you set up for lunch since my assistant waitress is dumber than cow dung. I might as well warn you, it gets awfully busy once the church crowd hits, but I'll show you some shortcuts that'll help. It's all about being prepared."

By the time the church crowd arrived, Annie had received a crash course in waitressing from Gladys and the girls in the kitchen. Although she felt breathless and jittery, she kept telling herself to smile, write her order legibly, and smile some more. She politely ignored the table of teenage boys who kept dropping their forks so she would have to stoop down in her short skirt to retrieve them.

She felt she was doing an okay job until Sam Ballard walked through the door. One sight of him and the shiner on his right eye and Annie lost control of the small tray she was carrying. Four iced-tea glasses crashed to the floor, causing everyone in the restaurant to jump and search for the source of the commotion. Annie immediately stooped to retrieve it.

"Don't touch that!" Sam said, his voice ringing loud with command. "You'll cut yourself."

Too late. Annie winced as a shard of glass jabbed her right index finger. She had been in such a rush to clean up that she'd been careless. Sam knelt beside her, his look thunderous. "What the hell are you doing here?" he demanded.

A wave of apprehension coursed through her. Why had Darla just assumed she could saunter into the place ready for work without talking to Sam first? "Darla's sick. She asked me to cover for her."

His eyes darkened as he held her gaze. "Oh, she did, did she?" he asked, mockery invading his tone. "Well, she can look for another job after today."

"But—"

He wasn't listening. "Go in the kitchen and ask Flo to take care of your finger. I'll clean this up. Then I want you out of here."

"Who's going to wait on these tables?"

Annoyance hovered in his eyes. "That's not your problem now, is it?"

She tried to disguise her own annoyance in front of the customers. "You're mean and hateful, Sam Ballard, you know that? Is it a sin for one of your employees to get sick?"

He stiffened, as though she'd just punched him in the eye again. His look seemed to drill right through her. "Darla's not sick. This is all just a ruse for her to get her way. Besides, it's none of your business how I treat my employees."

She was unnerved by his hostility and wished now that she'd slugged him in both eyes. Deciding it would be best to hold her tongue and walk away from the situation Annie stood and hurried toward the kitchen.

Flo took one look at her and grabbed a first-aid kit. "That glass went pretty deep," she said, once she'd cleaned the wound. "Wouldn't hurt to have a stitch or two in it."

"I don't have time to go to the hospital," Annie said. "Just do the best you can." Her voice cracked.

Patricia came over. "What's wrong with you? You gonna cry over a little cut like that?"

"That's not it," Annie said, then blurted the whole story. "Sam told me to get out, and he said he was going to fire Darla."

"Fire her?" Flo said angrily. "Over my dead body." She finished wrapping the finger and checked her work.

"Why do you care?" Patricia asked. "You don't even like the woman."

"I ain't got nary a thing against Darla Jenkins 'cept for that smart-aleck mouth of hers. But Sam ain't got no right to fire an employee just because she's sick. What's going to happen if one of us gets sick? We gonna get canned too?"

Sam came into the kitchen with the tray of broken glass just as Flo and Patricia clocked out and started for the back door. "Where do you two think you're going?" he said, dumping the glass into a trash can.

"We quit," Patricia said.

"Wait just a damn minute!" he ordered, stopping both women in their tracks. "What's this all about?"

They did a double take at the sight of his bruised eye. "We just heard you plan to fire Darla for being sick. And that you're sending this poor child home after she came in and did her level best to take over when there was no one else."

Sam shot an accusing look at Annie. "You just have to cause trouble for me, don't you?" he said.

She crossed her arms and pointedly stared. "If you think I'm going to keep quiet when you threaten my friend's job, you're wrong," she said matter-of-factly. "I was only trying to help out because there was no one to work in Darla's place."

"And she was doing a fine job of it till you came in and stirred things up," Patricia said.

"Am I supposed to ignore what you did to my eye?" he asked Annie.

Flo's own eyes widened. "You popped him in the eye?"

Annie nodded. "He played a very cruel joke on me."

"Then he obviously had it coming. I ought to take my frying pan to you, Sam Ballard," Flo said. "What's gotten into you?"

Just then a tall bearded fellow pushed open the swinging door. "What do you have to do to get served in this place?" he demanded.

Sam pasted a smile on his face. "Sorry, sir, we had a little emergency.

I'll be right out." He appealed to Flo and Patricia. "You can't leave now. The dining room is filling up fast."

"Then you'd better make a decision about Darla and Annie," Flo said.

Sam scowled. "I am *not* going to base my decisions on what you and your daughter think should or should not happen. I still own the Dixieland Cafe, and I'll run it as I see fit."

"Okay, see ya," Flo said. She started for the door once more, with Patricia on her heels.

"Hey, fellow, I don't have all day," the customer said. "Either somebody waits on me now or I'm leaving."

"Okay, hold it!" Sam said. He turned to Annie. "Go wait on the man. Give him anything he wants on the house." When Annie didn't so much as budge, he raked his hands through his hair. "What *now*?"

"In the future, when you tell me to do something, I would appreciate it if you said please."

"Please," Sam said between gritted teeth, wishing Buster had gone ahead and shot him the night before.

Annie left the kitchen with a fresh bandage on her finger and a smile on her face.

Relieved to have that problem out of the way, Sam turned to his kitchen employees. "Okay, Darla keeps her job, but this is absolutely the last time we settle matters this way. If you don't like one of my decisions, we talk it over, but the final decision is mine. I will not tolerate a mutiny. Understand?"

"You're the boss," Flo said, taking her time card and clocking in once more.

"That's right," Patricia agreed, doing the same. "We just work here, what do we know?"

Sam shook his head and started for the door, but Flo stopped him. "You really need to do something about that shiner, Sam. And please—" She paused and chuckled. "Puh-leese don't let anybody find out that skinny gal gave it to you."

"Might not be a bad thing," Patricia said. "At least they'd forget about him being jilted."

Sam closed his eyes and shook his head. It just never ended.

It took Annie a good fifteen minutes to get the dining room under control again, but once she explained injuring herself, the customers were more than understanding and left good tips to boot. The teenagers dropped their forks twice more, forcing her to do her stoop-but-don't-let-them-see-up-my-skirt routine, before Sam sauntered over with clean ones.

"I see you boys are having difficulty holding on to your flatware," he said. "My waitress is busy with other tables and doesn't have time to keep fetching it like a golden retriever. Why don't you just motion for me next time your fork slips from the table."

"Are you asking us or telling us?" a lanky youngster with curly hair asked.

"I'm trying to come to a gentleman's agreement," Sam said smoothly. "My waitress has spent more time at this table than the others. I hope you'll remember that when it comes time to tip her."

"What happened to your eye, man?" another youth asked.

Sam placed his hands on the table and leaned forward. "One of my customers ticked me off. If you think I look bad, you should see him."

"Hey, we're cool," the curly-haired boy said, and the others nodded in agreement. "We're almost ready to leave anyway."

Sam smiled. "I'm glad we could have this little chat." He walked away.

Annie was taking an order at a booth nearby and couldn't help the small smile that lifted one corner of her mouth. Sam had taken up for her! Once the teenagers paid and left and she cleared the table, she saw six dollars in the center of the table.

By the time the last customer straggled out, Annie had cleared the tables and wiped down the counter and stools. She offered Sam a cup of coffee, but he declined.

"We need to talk," he said in a cool tone.

Something tightened in the pit of her stomach at the sound of his voice. He indicated a booth. "Have a seat." When she hesitated, he added, "Please."

Sam sat directly across from her. He measured her with a cool, appraising look. "Don't ever do that again," he said.

Annie studied him as well. She had already noted how good he looked in his navy sweater and khakis even with the shiner; up close she could see how the sweater set off his blue eyes. However, the two lines that ran across his brow told her he wasn't too pleased with her at the moment. "Don't ever do what?" she asked.

"Complain to my other employees about something I've done."

She took a deep breath. "I'm sorry, but I was bleeding, and I was upset. Flo wanted to know what was wrong."

"I make the rules here, Annie. I operate my businesses as I see fit. If you want to work here, you'll respect that."

She hitched her chin up. "You had no right to threaten Darla's job just because she's sick."

The lines deepened. "Darla is not sick. She's pouting so she can have her way. This is not the first time she's pulled something like this. But I shouldn't have to explain my reasons to you, now, should I?"

"I'm not trying to be difficult to get along with," she said, "but I've spent my entire life following someone else's rules whether I thought they were fair or not. I'm not going to make that mistake again."

Sam noted the stubborn tilt of her chin, and despite being annoyed with her, he had to admire her for the way she was taking charge of her life. He clasped his hands together and leaned closer. "Okay, here's the deal," he said. "You have a problem, you come to me. I'll be glad to discuss it, and I promise to be fair-minded. Agreed?"

She nodded. "That certainly sounds reasonable." Her eyes suddenly widened. "You mean I've got the job?"

"For the time being. I can't help but appreciate the fact that you came in at the last minute and all, and you didn't do nearly as bad as I thought you would."

"Gee, Sam, was that supposed to be a compliment?"

He ignored the comment. "I'll need your Social Security number."

Annie scribbled it on a napkin and handed it to him. "How's your eye?"

"It hurts like hell. Why do you ask?"

"I've never punched anybody like that. You and your cousin scared me half to death."

"I didn't do anything. Buster acted alone."

"You could have said something. Instead, you let me make a complete fool out of myself."

Amusement flickered in his eyes. "I'm genuinely touched that you were willing to use your body as a shield to protect mine."

Annie's spine went ramrod stiff when she realized he was making fun of her again. Her mouth took an unpleasant twist. "Perhaps I acted rashly," she said in a grudging voice. "I probably should have grabbed Buster's pistol and shot you myself."

He almost laughed, but he feared she'd throw the napkin holder at him. Instead, he stood and walked to the door. "I have to check my messages across the street," he said. "Just in case somebody is looking for a good used car." He glanced over his shoulder. "I'll be back in time for the dinner rush. You'd better grab yourself something to eat while it's quiet. And stay away from sharp objects," he added, motioning toward her finger.

With growing frustration, Annie watched him cross the street to his car lot. He even looked good from the back. He paused here and there to check on a car or wipe a smudge of dirt off a fender with the hem of his sweater; then, he unlocked the construction trailer that served as his office. She shook her head, wondering if they would ever be able to spend time together without locking horns.

Annie went into the kitchen, where she found Flo reading the Pinckney Gazette and Patricia glancing through a catalog. She ordered a grilled-cheese sandwich, and they were quick to instruct her how to make it herself since they were taking a well-deserved break. She did so while peeking out front from time to time to make sure a customer hadn't appeared.

"You'll know if someone comes in," Flo said. "That bell over the door is loud enough so we can hear it in the kitchen."

Annie made her sandwich and pulled a stool up to the long metal table, where they sat. Flo shared her newspaper with her. They sat in companionable silence until Annie finished her lunch and returned to the front. Several people came in for coffee and pie. Annie used her spare time to straighten up beneath the counter and restock the condiments. She came across a fall schedule for the community college and leafed through it. Classes had already started, but late registration was permitted for an extra fee.

Something stirred inside of her as she studied the courses offered in accounting, one thing she did happen to know something about. The classes began at eight a.m., she would have time to take a couple before she had to be at work, if she could get along with Sam Ballard well enough to keep her job.

If only she had a car.

Or even a bicycle, for that matter.

The bell on the door jangled and Lillian Calhoun walked through the door. She gave Annie a big smile. "You got yourself a job! Good for you."

Annie smiled. "Yes, and I've done very well in tips for my first day."

Lillian offered her a high five. "I just stopped by to place a to-go order," she said. "What do you recommend?"

"The special tonight is meatloaf, squash casserole, and green peas with pearl onions, and, of course, Patricia's famous biscuit."

"Hmm. The last time I had Flo's meatloaf it was a bit dry." Lillian had barely gotten the words out of her mouth when something metal slammed against one of the walls in the kitchen, startling both of them. "On second thought, I believe I *will* have the meatloaf," Lillian said.

Annie smiled. "Excellent choice," she said, writing the order on a ticket and hanging it in the window.

"Would you like a cup of coffee on the house while you wait?"

"I'd love it." Lillian reached for the community college catalog. "What have we here?"

"Oh, I was just checking through the fall schedule and wishing I could sign up for a few of the courses."

"Why can't you? You could take morning classes."

"That's not the problem. The problem is, Darla lives way out in the boonies, and I don't have transportation. I could buy a bike, but it's quite a distance."

Lillian looked thoughtful. "Let's see. Kazue has an extra bike I bet she'd lend you, and my place is only a few blocks from the college and less than a mile from here." When Annie just stared at her, she went on. "I have a garage apartment. It's not bad, and the furniture's okay. Just needs sprucing up. You could rent it by the week if it would be easier on you, and I'd be willing to give you the first week free, if you'll clean it."

"You would?" Annie asked.

Lillian laughed. "Why wouldn't I? You would do the same for me if you could."

"Yes, of course." Annie realized she would indeed, and that made her feel pretty good about herself.

Lillian patted her hand. "That's what it's all about, honey."

Flo slid a Styrofoam container into the window between the kitchen and dining room and Annie put it in a sack. But when Lillian pulled out her wallet to pay, Annie stopped her. "This one's on me," she said. "It's not much, but it's what I can do at the moment."

Lillian studied her as she tucked her wallet back into her purse. "You're going to be okay, Annie Hartford. In fact, you're going to do better than okay. Here's my card. It has my home address on it. Come by tomorrow and see the apartment. I think you'll like it."

Annie was still pondering those words long after Lillian left.

Somebody believed in her! Somebody actually believed she was capable of doing anything she set her mind to.

There was only one problem. Money. She needed to sign up for the courses as soon as possible if she had any hopes of starting this semester, and there was no way she could hope to make enough in tips that quickly. She needed a temporary loan, and there was only one person she knew to go to.

She would ask Sam Ballard for the money.

Chapter Five

The lunch and dinner rush did not go so well. Sam was on hand during both, busing tables, seating customers, and when there were more tables than Annie could handle, he took orders and served the food as well. He was relieved that Gladys had taught Annie how to use the cash register, and other duties, meaning he would not have to take time to do so right in the middle of a mad rush.

Annie raced through the dining room, trying her best to keep up, but she was so nervous having Sam there that she spilled or dropped almost everything she touched. A glass of iced tea slipped from her fingers and doused a truck driver sitting at the counter. He'd been flirting with Annie from the moment he walked in the door, but his smile faded abruptly as the cold beverage soaked the back of his shirt. Sam hurried over with a towel, and the three stood there looking at one another for a moment.

Annie batted her lashes at the customer. "Was that as good for you as it was me?"

Sam looked at her as though she'd lost her mind, but the trucker howled with laughter and ended up leaving her a big tip.

"What's wrong with you?" Sam asked, once he had a moment to speak to her. "I feel like asking people if they have health insurance before you wait on them. All my profits are being eaten up by broken plates and glasses."

Annie was too embarrassed to admit that part of the problem was him. He watched her constantly, her every move, and she was equally aware of his. She didn't know if he expected her to run off with the money in the cash register or what. "I've never done this kind of work before, and this is my first day," she said. "Besides, one waitress can't take care of this crowd. I'm doing the best I can."

"Of course I know one waitress can't handle it," he said. "That's why I'm here. I put an ad in the newspaper. Unfortunately, I've only had two responses, and neither had experience."

"Sort of like me, huh?"

Sam didn't respond. He knew she was trying, that she was also nervous, and it probably did not help that every time she looked up she found him staring at her, which would make anyone nervous. One reason he watched her was to make certain he was there for her if she needed him; the other reason . . . well, hell, he would have to be made of stone not to notice those legs and that tempting behind.

"Let's just try to get through the night without seriously injuring anyone, okay?" he said.

Annie bit back the sarcastic reply on her tongue; after all, she needed the job if she was going to get her life in order. And she needed a loan. Instead of mouthing off at him as she was tempted, she offered him a smile. "I appreciate your being patient with me, Mr. Ballard. I know I can do this job; I just need more practice. And I promise to pay for every single glass and plate I break."

Sam looked perplexed. *Mr. Ballard?* Nobody called him that. As Annie walked away he watched her warily. She was up to something.

By nine thirty, the customers were gone. Sam had cleaned off most of the tables and the counter. Annie didn't know if he was doing it to be helpful or if he feared she'd break more dishes, but she went behind him wiping everything down and performing the tasks Gladys had listed. Flo and Patricia had already cleaned and mopped the kitchen and clocked out for the night.

Sam was getting ready to clear the cash register. "I'll buy your change if you like," he told Annie. "That way I don't have to go inside the bank and get it."

"Oh, okay." Annie reached into her apron pocket, pulled out her tip money, and spread it on the counter. "I'm afraid I don't have much change," she said.

Sam was disappointed for her. She'd worked both the lunch and dinner shift, and all she had to show for it was a few lousy bucks. He glanced over his shoulder, an apology on his lips, then froze when he saw the mountain of bills in front of her. "Looks like you did okay."

"I think I did," Annie said. "I've got about one hundred dollars here. Oops, I've got more in my other pocket. Looks like thirty dollars and change. Is that good?"

Sam was stunned. Darla did pretty well in the tip department, even when she shared the floor with another waitress, but she had been at it for years. That Annie had garnered that much in tips on her first day, especially in a family restaurant that closed at nine, was pretty impressive.

"That's damn good," he said.

"Especially when I told folks they didn't have to tip me to begin with," Annie said.

"You told your customers they didn't have to tip you?"

"I was honest. I told them I was brand new at waitressing, that I would appreciate any pointers they could give me, but under no circumstances did I expect a tip. They insisted."

Sam wasn't quite sure what to think since Annie had experienced a number of mishaps and even one or two calamities that would have sent many customers running for the door. Obviously the people she had waited on had been forgiving. "I'm glad you did well," he said at last. "Hopefully things will get easier as time goes on."

Annie cleared her throat. "While we're on the subject of money, I'd like to discuss the possibility of a small, short-term loan."

Sam arched one eyebrow. "You just made one hundred and thirty-something bucks in tips and you want a loan?"

"Yes, I need to borrow four hundred dollars." She reached into her pocket for a slip of paper. "I've got it all figured out. I'm willing to pay one point higher than the bank pays in interest, and I've scheduled my payments so that I'll have the debt paid off in three weeks. I'll probably be able to pay you back sooner, but I added the extra week just in case."

Sam reached for the paper. Surprisingly enough, she did have it all figured out, including the interest rate, late payments, and penalties. He shrugged. "Hell, Annie, I can just give you the money for as long as you need it. You don't have to go through all this. May I ask what you plan to do with it?"

"I want to take a couple of courses at the community college. I can fit them in before I have to be here for my lunch shift. My goal, at least for now, is to earn an associate degree in accounting."

Sam did not know what to make of it. Winston Hartford could have sent his daughter to any school she chose and in any country. Why hadn't he done so, and why was Annie only now looking to start her education at a less expensive technical college? None of it made sense, but the last thing Sam wanted to do was get personally involved in Annie's problems.

"Do you know anything about accounting?" he asked.

"Enough to know that I would be good at it." Annie did not want to go into details so she kept it simple. "I often volunteered to help out in the business office of a small girl's school I attended in Boston. Math had always come easy for me so I decided to pay attention in case it was a skill I could learn later on."

"Of course, the semester has already begun in the two courses I want to take, Accounting 101 and Intro to Business Concepts. I may have to wait until the next semester, but I'd like to try and get in if possible. I thought maybe if I did well enough, I might one day become a CPA."

Sam was thoughtful as he took in her determined look and stubborn chin. She was a hard worker, even if she was the queen of accidents. There was more there than fluff, he told himself. "Annie, I have a sneaking suspicion that you can do anything you set your mind to."

Annie felt her jaw drop. His words almost brought tears to her eyes. Other than Vera and Bradley, and, of course her grandfather when he was alive, nobody had ever really expressed a belief in her until she came to Pinckney. Now everybody seemed to think she was more than capable. "Thank you, Sam. I appreciate that. I sort of feel that way too."

He reached into his back pocket and pulled out his wallet, then fished out four one hundred-dollar bills. He slid them across the counter. "I don't charge interest to my employees and friends, and I don't need a repayment plan. You just pay me back when it's convenient. That's how we do business in a small town like Pinckney."

She was genuinely touched and almost sorry she'd given him that black eye. "Thank you," she said. For a moment they just gazed at each other in silence. Finally, she folded the bills and put them in her pocket.

"Well, I need to let you finish what you're doing, and I should go check on Darla. I called a couple of times today, but I didn't get an answer. Probably took the phone off the hook so she could sleep."

"Uh-huh." Sam looked doubtful as he came around the counter. "I need to walk you to your car."

"That's not necessary."

"Yes, it is." He led the way to the front door, unlocked it, and they stepped outside.

"Darla really did look and sound terrible this morning, Sam," Annie said as she made her way to Darla's car.

"She'll be fully recovered when you get back. By the way, Darla can get real competitive when it comes to tips. You might want to avoid telling her how well you did on your first night."

"Thank you for telling me," Annie said. "I certainly don't want to say or do anything that might harm our new friendship." A new and unexpected warmth surged through her, and she almost wished she didn't have to leave. But she had been worried about Darla all day, and she wanted to make sure the woman was okay. "Well, good night, Sam."

See Bride Run!

"Good night, Annie."

She climbed into the car and started the engine. Sam was still watching as she pulled from the parking lot and drove in the direction of Darla's mobile home. Her concern for Darla suddenly shifted, replaced by thoughts of Sam Ballard.

When Annie pulled into the driveway of Darla's mobile home, she was surprised to find the lights off, including the front one. She figured Darla must be sleeping. Luckily, she had the key. She groped for the door; fortunately, the key slipped easily into the lock. She stepped inside the trailer and felt for the light switch.

"Hold it right there or I'll blow your head off," a male voice said, frightening Annie so badly, she thought her knees would collapse. The light came on, and she found herself facing the biggest man she'd ever seen. He had to be at least six-foot-six, with a barrel of a chest and thighs that made her think of tree trunks. His hair was jet-black, his jaw dark with stubble. He held a shotgun, and it was aimed at her.

"I'm not armed," she said, holding her hands over her head. "I have a little money. It's yours if you want it. Just leave and don't hurt us."

"*Me* leave?" he asked in disbelief. "Who the hell do you think you are telling me to get out of my own house?"

"Bo, who are you talking to?" a sleepy Darla asked, coming down the hall in her bathrobe. "Oh, hi, Annie, how'd your first day go?"

"You know this lady?" Bo asked.

"Bo, put that shotgun down before you scare poor Annie."

"Who?"

"Don't you ever listen to anything I say?" Darla asked.

"Annie's staying here till she can get on her feet. I got her a job at the Dixieland Cafe. Don't you recognize the uniform, numbskull?"

Annie watched him lower the shotgun and thought her bladder would give.

"Oh, yeah," he said. A wide grin spread across his face as he grabbed her hand and pumped it furiously. "Nice to meet you, Annie. I'm Darla's husband, Boswell Jenkins. Bo, for short," he added.

Annie looked at Darla. "I didn't know you were married."

"Actually, Bo's my ex-husband," Darla said. "They sent him to prison for writing bad checks and a few other nonessentials. I was so mad, I divorced him." She smiled. "But he's out for good, and he's promised to change his ways, so I've decided to take him back." She punched him in the chest playfully. "Big ole goofball didn't even tell me they'd decided to let him out early."

Bo pulled Darla tight against him and kissed her hard. "That's because I wanted to surprise you, Baby. And make sure nobody was warming my side of the bed while I was away."

Darla put her arm around Annie. "How'd it go today?" she asked. "Make any good tips?"

Annie had to pry her tongue loose from the roof of her mouth in order to speak. "I did okay, I guess."

"I'm sure you did fine," Darla said. "And your tips will increase once you get the hang of things. Was Sam mad that I didn't show up?"

Annie was having a terrible time keeping up her end of the conversation. "He was at first, but he got over it."

"How 'bout a cold beer, Annie?" Bo asked.

She was glad he'd put his weapon away. "No, I'd better not. Listen, Darla, you won't believe who offered to rent me her garage apartment today. Lillian Calhoun."

"No kidding?"

"She said I could move in tonight, as a matter of fact. It all happened so fast." She told Darla about wanting to sign up for classes at the college and how close Lillian's place would be to work and school. "I was hoping you wouldn't mind running me over to her place since I sort of promised I'd be there after work." It was a lie, and Annie hoped Lillian wouldn't mind her barging in at that hour, but she had no desire to spend the night at Darla's with Bo and a shotgun on the premises.

"Are you sure that's what you want to do, honey?" Darla asked. "You know you're welcome here."

"I know, and you're very sweet to offer it to me, but I'd really like my own place. After living with my father most of my life, it'll be a special treat." She looked at Bo. "And I'm sure the two of you have a lot of catching up to do."

Darla and Bo exchanged a tender look. Finally, Darla turned to Annie. "I don't need to drive you to Lillian's. Bo's pickup truck is parked in back—we decided it best to hide it so the town gossips wouldn't have a heyday—anyway, he can take me to work tomorrow."

Annie couldn't mask her relief. "Is it okay if I hang on to this uniform for a couple of days? Until I get one of my own?" she added.

"Go ahead and keep it," Darla said.

"Oh, no, I—"

"I have three more just like it," Darla said. "Remind me tomorrow to tell you where to buy an extra. They aren't expensive. Now, do you know how to get to Lillian's place?" Annie was given brief directions before she was whisked out the door by an anxious Bo.

"I promise I won't try to shoot you next time you visit," he said, grinning.

She smiled. "Thank you." Annie hurried out to the car. She couldn't wait to get out of there, even if it meant sleeping in the backseat of Darla's car.

Annie was on her way in minutes. One thing Darla had not taken into consideration when she'd given directions to Lillian's place was the fact that Annie knew absolutely nothing about Pinckney, or the landmarks that were supposed to help her find her way. It was after eleven o'clock by the time she found Lillian Calhoun's house. The place was dark.

Annie pulled away from the curb and drove for a few minutes, wondering what she was going to do. She was dog-tired, and her eyelids were beginning to sag. She'd passed a motel, but it hadn't looked very appealing, and she was wondering if she crawled under the sheets whether she wouldn't find herself sharing space with some unwanted critters, when suddenly she found herself in front of the Dixieland Cafe. The lights were still on, and Sam was sitting at the counter doing book work. Thinking maybe he could give her the name and address of a decent hotel, Annie pulled into a parking space out front. Sam was obviously deep in thought, because he didn't look up until she knocked on the door. He glanced over his shoulder, then did a double take at the sight of her. He hurried to let her in.

"What's wrong?" he said quickly.

"May I come in?"

"Yeah, sure. Why aren't you at Darla's?"

Annie told him about Bo and her reasons for not wanting to stay. "I was hoping you might know of a nice motel."

"So, Bo Jenkins is out of the slammer, huh?"

She nodded. "Just got out today. Darla had no idea. I went by Lillian's house. She has offered to rent me her garage apartment. But there wasn't a light on anywhere, and I didn't want to wake her."

"You don't have to stay in a motel," Sam said. "You can stay at my place."

"I beg your pardon?"

"Don't give me that look. I have a mean housekeeper. She'll protect you from me."

Annie sighed her relief. "Well, in that case. Are you sure you don't mind?"

"I wouldn't have invited you otherwise." He checked the clock over the cash register. "Damn, I didn't know it was so late. Do you want to follow me?"

Annie hesitated. "Sam, are you sure? I feel like I'm imposing. All I've done is rely on other people since I got here. I really wanted to be independent, you know?"

"Being independent doesn't mean you can't accept help when you're in a jam."

Annie regarded him. He appeared to be so strong and confident, she was certain he'd never had to ask for help. "Well, I appreciate it," she said.

"Don't mention it."

"Why are you still here?" she asked curiously as he began closing his ledger and stacking everything.

"I was trying to get caught up with my book work. As usual I'm late filing my quarterly taxes."

"Why don't you hire someone to do it?"

"I fired my CPA because he screwed up everything. Which is why I'm in such a mess," he added. He carried the books to the door, then, balanced them on one hip while he unlocked it. "Maybe I'll hire you once you get your license," he added as he motioned for her to go through first.

She waited for him to lock up. "How many CPAs are there in Pinckney?" she asked.

"Two or three, I guess." He opened his Jeep and tossed the ledgers onto the front seat. "We can always use another one."

Annie followed Sam through town, in the opposite direction of where Darla lived. All the buildings and houses faded away until there was only blackness on both sides of the car.

Finally, Sam turned off the main road and drove down a long winding drive until he reached a white two-story farmhouse. Annie parked behind him in a circular drive where rosebushes grew along a white fence.

The porch light was on, giving Annie a clear look at the concrete porch that stretched across the front of the house, so unlike the wooden porches in new construction. Oversized rocking chairs shared space with glazed pots containing red geraniums, and a green metal glider sat at one end with a distressed coffee table of sorts that Annie suspected held trays of lemonade and sweet tea in the summer months.

"I love old houses," Annie said. "How old is this one?"

"About sixty years old. It has been renovated a couple of times." Sam unlocked the front door and stepped back so Annie could enter first. A large piece of furniture held a lamp that lit the hall leading from the front of the house to the very back, as well as a flight of stairs climbing to the second floor. Wide-planked floors, shiny with varnish squeaked beneath Annie's feet.

A door toward the back of the hall opened, and a plump woman with a dumpling face stepped out. She wore a pink bathrobe and matching sponge curlers in her hair. She gave a sniff of annoyance at the sight of Annie.

"Well, Mr. Sam, what have we here?" she asked, her voice ringing with disapproval.

"Martha Fender, meet Annie Hartford from Atlanta. She'll be staying the night. I assume we have a guest room available."

The woman's tone changed immediately. "Yes, of course. She can stay in the blue room. It has a nice view of the lake."

"You're on the water?" Annie asked. When Sam nodded, she went on. "Do you fish?"

"I don't have a lot of time for fishing, but Martha brings her friends and family out from time to time."

"I love fishing," Martha said. "It's so relaxing."

"Do you catch many fish?" Annie asked.

"Oh, yes. That lake is full of wide-mouth bass. We always have a big fish fry afterward."

"I've never fished before," Annie confessed. "Perhaps I can join you sometime, but only if you invite me to the fish fry afterward because I love fried fish with lots of tartar sauce," she added. "I can practically eat my weight in fish and hushpuppies." She paused. "In the meantime, please accept my apologies for disturbing you. I unexpectedly found myself with no place to stay tonight, and Mr. Ballard was kind enough to invite me to spend the night beneath his roof. Not that I'm surprised. Everyone has been so kind since I arrived."

Martha seemed to warm toward Annie. "That's the way we do things in Pinckney," she said. "We don't turn people out. Are y'all hungry?"

Annie hated to admit that she was starving. Bad enough that she was presently homeless.

"I'll make a couple of sandwiches," Sam told Martha. "Go back to bed. I'll make sure Annie gets settled in."

"You'll find plenty of towels and toiletry items in the bathroom cabinet," Martha said. "Let me know if you need anything." She took a second look at Annie's uniform. "Do you have luggage?"

Annie was further embarrassed to admit that she had the clothes on her back and nothing else. Sam seemed to pick up on it.

"It's a long story, Martha," he said. "I'll lend her one of my pajama shirts."

"Very well," she said and started down the hall. "Goodnight. Sleep well, Annie."

"She's nice," Annie said once she heard the bedroom door close.

"She can be grouchy if the mood strikes her," Sam replied. "Are you hungry? I forgot to eat dinner tonight, and I didn't see you eat anything."

"I had a biscuit."

"That's hardly enough to keep you going. Come with me." He led her toward the back of the house and into the kitchen. He motioned to an island in the center of the room. Although it contained drawers and cabinets for storage, one side was devoted to seating. "Sit down and rest your feet," Sam said.

"Gladly." Annie was thankful to do just that after being on them all day.

As Sam pulled out packs of meat and cheese, she studied the kitchen. It was enormous, with white cabinets, wide plank floors, and stainless steel appliances. "How long have you lived here?" she asked.

Sam pulled out a jar of dill pickles and set them on the island. "Almost five years."

"Do you have family nearby?"

"No. My parents moved to a retirement community in Hilton Head several years back so my dad could play golf every day, but they visit every few months. I have a younger sister," he added. "She's married with two boys, ages three and four. She and her husband live in Connecticut. He's a stockbroker in New York. And a damn good one, I might add because he has doubled my investments."

"Do the two of you keep in touch?" Annie asked, recalling how often she and Bradley called each other once he left for college.

"We talk once a week. Everybody comes here for Christmas. Which is cool," he added, "because this place has five bedrooms. One belongs to Martha, but there is always plenty of room. We also go on vacation together."

"So, what do you want? Ham, salami, roast beef, sliced chicken?"

Annie stood. "I'll have whatever you're having," she said, "but I really don't expect you to wait on me. If you'll tell me where the glasses are, I'll get us something to drink. I'd like to have milk."

Sam pointed to a cabinet. "I'll have the same," he said. "How about ham and Swiss cheese on rye?"

"Perfect," she said. Annie grabbed the milk carton from the refrigerator and filled two glasses. Once she ate a sandwich, she helped Sam put things away.

"Take a look around," Sam said. "Make yourself at home."

Annie peeked into several rooms. A formal living room ran the length of the front of the house. The furniture was clearly of good quality with a couple of antiques thrown in as accent pieces.

The den was large, yet cozy, with its stone fireplace and overstuffed furniture in navy and khaki stripes. An entertainment center took up one wall, boasting an enormous flat-screen TV that Annie guessed was at least sixty inches wide. She chuckled. "I'm thinking you should buy a larger flat screen."

"Hey, I need a big one. This is where the guys come during football season."

"I like your place," she said, returning to the kitchen. "But you're missing something."

He looked at her. "Like what?"

"A family," she said. "And a big dog lying in front of the fireplace," she added.

"I wouldn't mind having a golden Lab," he said, "but I'm not too keen on the idea of having a family."

"You're going to let one bad experience affect the rest of your life?"

"I like things just the way they are," he said matter-of-factly and in a tone that did not invite conversation.

"I should probably mind my own business," she said. "Besides, I'm not exactly an expert on relationships or I would not have skipped out on my wedding, nor would I be practically broke and in hiding. If it weren't for the kindness of others, I'd probably be sleeping in a homeless shelter tonight."

"You're not exactly destitute, Annie. I know who your father is, and I know he's worth mega millions."

"How do you know that?"

"Hartford Iron and Steel is only three hours from here," he said. "Most people have heard of it. I also read a lengthy article about your father and his company some months back. Plus, Hester hired someone to check you out."

"So much for trying to keep a low profile," she said.

"Want to know what Harry said when he found out you were the only heir to a vast fortune?"

"I can't wait," she muttered.

Sam chuckled. "He said you must be crazy to walk away from all that money."

"What did *you* say?"

"Well, I have an advantage over Hester since I also checked your old man out on the Internet. Some of the remarks about your father were unflattering. I told Hester you were probably tired of being bullied."

Annie looked surprised. "You actually said that?" When he nodded, she went on. "That's *exactly* why I left. It wasn't *all* about him trying to push me into marriage; that was just one of many ways he tried to control me, and I suspect he did the same thing to my mother."

"What's the story on her?"

"My father told so many lies it's hard to know what really happened. When Bradley and I were four years old, he told us she was leaving and we would never see her again."

"Do you remember her?"

Annie shook her head. "No. The only thing I remember is being so sad that I tried not to think of her. I suppose I blocked a lot. Our housekeeper, Vera, became our nanny, and she raised us. Bradley and I adored her. I still do."

"Have you ever tried to find your mother?"

"No. Bradley and I were led to believe—again, this was what our father told us—that she was leaving and that she did not even want us."

"That must've hurt like hell."

"Thankfully, Vera was able to convince us otherwise most of the time; but she had to be careful what she said because we were little and might repeat it, and she would be fired. She could easily have found another job, but she refused to leave us."

"He must have really hated your mother," Sam said.

"I think he hates all women. He has no respect for them. When I was older and realized how mean he could be at times, I thought of looking for her, but I had no idea how to go about it. And even though I knew my father had probably told us nothing but lies, I worried that she might have a new family, and, even if Bradley and I did find her, she might not want to see us."

Annie shook her head sadly. "And then we lost Bradley, and for a long time nothing really mattered. It was hard enough to just get out of the bed in the morning and put one foot in front of the other. I thought she would at least attend his funeral, if she was still alive."

"How do you know she didn't?"

"I think she would have made herself known to me. After all, I was an adult by then. Afterward, I realized she would not have had a chance because I did not leave my father's side. He was inconsolable. I thought it might change him for the better, but he was consumed by anger. I should have left. I could have moved into a place of my own and started a new life. I could have gone to college. But I was afraid to leave him. Even though he was still angry and bitter, I thought he needed me. So I stayed. I kept myself busy so I wouldn't have time to think. I did not realize I would still be with him almost ten years later. Then Eldon showed up. My father pushed us into getting engaged. I discovered in the meantime that every word that came out of Eldon's mouth were lies; no wonder he and my father hit it off so quickly. I just wanted out."

They were quiet for a moment. "I know what it's like to discover you aren't really in love with the person you're supposed to pledge your life to," Sam said. "It's like your oxygen supply is cut off; you're constantly trying to find a way to get out of it."

"I thought you were jilted."

Sam shook his head. "The only reason I'm telling you this is because I understand what you're going through."

"But why did you let everybody think *she* walked out on *you*?"

"Guilt."

"Have you ever regretted your decision?"

"Not even once. You'd probably enjoy a hot shower about now," he said.

"That sounds like a great idea," she said. "I'm beat."

"I can give you a t-shirt and bathrobe," he offered. "I can't help you with the rest of, well, you know."

"No problem," Annie said. "I do my laundry in the bathroom sink before I go to bed. And pray that it's dry when I have to put it on the next morning."

Sam laughed. "I'll show you to your room."

Annie followed him up a flight of stairs and down a spacious hallway. He pointed to a closed door. "That's my room, in case you need something during the night." Two doors down, he led her inside a pale blue bedroom with a mahogany sleigh bed. On each side, night tables held magazines and books. A fat comforter and oversized pillows in white looked inviting, and a floral settee and matching chair sat in front of the fireplace. An ornate mirror hung over the mantle.

"It's lovely," Annie said.

He nodded. "Lillian Calhoun decorated it," he said. "I might let her do my room next. There is a private bathroom through that doorway," Sam said. "Hold on, I'll be right back."

Annie spent a few minutes looking around. She would have enjoyed sprucing up the home she shared with her father, if only to soften the rooms a bit with new rugs and draperies. Her father did not like change, but that did not stop her from redecorating her bedroom, and turning what was called the "sewing room" into her office.

Sam returned with a couple of t-shirts, and a navy bathrobe. "This should get you through the night," he said. "Maybe you can take some of that tip money and buy a few things." He paused. "Well, good night."

"Sam?"

"Yeah?"

"Thank you. And thanks for listening. I didn't mean to talk your ear off."

"You're going to be okay, Annie." He exited the bedroom without another word.

Chapter Six

"... so you see, I couldn't very well go through with it now, could I? I mean marriage is hard enough without marrying someone you wish would fall into a pit of quicksand and sink to the bottom. Am I right?" Annie took a sip of her coffee.

"You did the right thing, dear." Martha Fender sat across from Annie at the kitchen table, a pair of wire-framed glasses perched at the end of her nose as she let the hem out in Annie's uniform. Martha had tossed it in the washer while Annie took another hot shower, which explained why she was still wearing Sam's bathrobe which was so large she had to hold it up so it wouldn't drag on the floor. She was reminded of her wedding dress.

"My father wanted me to marry a banker's son," Martha said, as Annie drank her coffee and nibbled on a slice of toast, "but my heart belonged to a mechanic. We ended up eloping."

"How romantic," Annie said.

"We never had much when it came to material things, and I had to work all my life cleaning other folks' houses, but I wouldn't have changed a thing. We had three beautiful children and almost forty years of happiness." She paused and looked up. "My Albert died of a sudden heart attack two years ago."

"I'm so sorry. I'll bet you miss him terribly."

"Oh, yes. Not a day goes by that I don't think of him. And I thank the Lord that He gave me a good man. Not every woman is blessed to have a good helpmate by her side."

"You're absolutely right," Annie said, "which is why I'm not sure I'll ever marry."

"Oh, but dear, you're still young. You have your whole life before you. Don't you want children?"

"Yes, I've always wanted a big family. But after living with a domineering father, I fear I might unconsciously choose someone with his traits. That happens, you know."

"Would you like to know a secret, Annie?"

"Sure."

"Okay, get ready because it might be life-altering." Martha smiled.

Annie leaned closer. "Do tell."

"We *teach* people how to treat us."

Annie straightened in her chair and regarded the woman. "I never once considered that," she said, "but, again, you're right. I did not stand up for myself because it was all I knew. I'll bet if I had carried a big board with me and knocked him over the head every time he opened his mouth he would have learned to shut up. You think?"

She and Martha looked at each other, and the next thing Annie knew they were howling with laughter.

In the next room, Sam tried to ignore the conversation and concentrate on the news program he was watching. But there was no ignoring Annie. He discovered right away that when she was around, his eyes and ears were fixed solely on her. He wasn't sure what that meant. Perhaps it was merely a physical attraction. No surprise there, since she was both bright and pretty. But there were parts of her personality that warmed him. Annie Hartford never met a stranger, it seemed. She'd already won over his moody housekeeper, simply by being herself.

"A horse whip would have accomplished the same thing," Annie said, "and would not be as burdensome to carry around, nor would I risk getting splinters in my hand."

Martha wiped tears from her eyes. "Are you always like this?" the woman asked.

"Yes," Sam called back. "She never shuts up. And when she's not talking she's breaking dishes."

Annie leaned close to Martha. "I could probably use a horsewhip about now."

"I heard that," Sam said.

"I'd better hush," Annie whispered. "If he fires me I won't be able to buy underwear."

Martha shook her head, but she was still chuckling. "There now," she said, biting the thread and holding the uniform up for inspection. "You've got a good two inches added to the length."

"Thank you, Martha," Annie said. "You don't know how relieved I am. Of course, my tips are likely to suffer. Darla says the shorter the dress the bigger the tips." She winked. "I don't know how Darla avoids frostbite in the winter."

"I'm glad you'll be moving into Lillian Calhoun's garage apartment," the woman said. "Darla Jenkins is a sweet girl, mind you," she added, "but she's a little wild for my tastes."

"You know what I think?" Annie said. "I think Darla *wanted* people to think she was going out all the time and having fun so they wouldn't feel sorry for her. When I was looking through her closet to find something to wear, there were so many books stacked up on the floor that she could have started her own library. I noticed a book on her night stand as well."

"Well, bless her heart," Martha said. "All this time she has been pretending to be somebody she's not."

In the next room, Sam was frowning as he recalled his conversation with Darla about going to bed with a good book once in a while. He would never have guessed she was trying to save face after Bo was hauled off to jail. If Darla partied as hard as she led people to believe, she would never be able to work as hard or stay as sharp as she did. He felt bad that he had not thought of it, but it gave him a new respect for her.

Martha smiled. "You know what I think, Annie. I think you are very wise for someone who hasn't turned thirty yet. You're going to do well for yourself. By the way, I'll be glad to come over and help you clean your new place."

"That's very sweet, Martha, but I'll let you in on a little secret. I'll bet that apartment doesn't have a speck of dust in it. That's just Lillian's way of trying to help without hurting my pride. I can't wait until I can do something nice for her."

Sam shook his head and took another sip of his coffee. What was it about Annie that automatically drew people to her? He had to admit she was the most open person he'd ever met, and she genuinely cared about others. Unlike her father, he thought.

Still . . . Sam wondered if Annie might return home if she got over her mad spell. She was used to the good life. She did not carry trays and clean tables; people did it for her. How long would she be content to live in a garage apartment when she could easily return home to a mansion and a life of luxury?

He was going to have to steer clear of Annie before he did something stupid like fall in love with her.

"Oh, Lillian, it's absolutely adorable!"

"You really like it?"

"I love it."

The two women were standing in the living room of Lillian's garage apartment. Lillian had pulled the dustcovers from the furniture, and Annie was amazed that everything looked brand-new. A massive coffee table sat in the center of the room, piled high with books and magazines. "It's so cozy," she said. "I can imagine sitting in that antique rocker reading a good book."

"I decorated it for my friend, Mildred, when she came to live here several years ago after her husband died," Lillian said. "She absolutely refused to live in my house—said two women under one roof was one too many." Lillian suddenly looked sad. "Then, last year, all of a sudden she was gone. I miss her."

"I'm sorry for your loss," Annie said. "Was it a peaceful passing?"

Lillian gave Annie an odd look before she burst into laughter. "Oh, she isn't dead. She met a retired stockbroker at the bingo parlor, and it was love at first sight. She crammed everything she could into one small suitcase, and they took off in his RV to see the country. I get postcards now and then. I expect to receive a wedding announcement one of these days."

"That's wonderful. You must have a very youthful friend."

Lillian nodded. "I'm happy as long as she's happy." She motioned to the large bay window at the front of the apartment. "Kazue made all the window treatments and bedspreads. There's one bedroom and a bath and a half. You should have plenty of room," she added.

"It's perfect," Annie said, "and I promise to take very good care of it."

"Oh, honey, I don't doubt that for a minute."

"I'm prepared to pay you the first week's rent."

"No way," Lillian said. "Our agreement was you'd get the first week free in exchange for cleaning it."

"But it's not dirty."

"Oh, it needs dusting and sweeping and mopping. I noticed some cobwebs in the bedroom."

"Cobwebs? Oh, my, that'll take me all of thirty seconds."

"And you'll want to scrub the bathrooms since they haven't been used in a while. You should find cleansers beneath the sink, as well as various supplies Mildred left behind, most of them unopened. And there's a stackable washer and dryer in the storage closet just off the kitchen."

"Not that I'll need that right away," Annie said, laughing. "This is the only outfit I have to my name at the moment. I was wondering if there's a Salvation Army store or Goodwill in town. I need to pick up a few things."

"Honey, we can do better than that." Lillian checked her watch.

95

"What time do you have to be at work?"

"Eleven-thirty."

"That gives us two hours. Let's go."

"Where are we going?"

"It's a surprise."

Annie followed Lillian out of the apartment and down the stairs. "Go ahead and get into my car," Lillian said. "I'm just going to grab my purse and lock up."

They were on their way in minutes. Annie was delighted to get a closer look at the small town. She smiled when they passed the community college. "I plan to enroll first thing in the morning," she told Lillian.

"Good for you. Kazue says you can use one of her bicycles for as long as you need it. Shoot, she'd give it to you if you wanted it."

"Uh-oh, I just thought of something," Annie said. "I hope I don't run into problems registering because I have no identification," she said, wishing she had grabbed her purse before she left the church. "I probably already have one strike against me for enrolling late."

"Let me know if they give you a hard time in admissions," Lillian said. She chuckled. "I know everybody who works there, and I dare them to give my new friend any grief."

Annie felt a surge of joy that Lillian already considered her a friend. They arrived at the Second-Time-Around Shop a few minutes later. Lillian parked her car. "Believe it or not, we have a few well-to-do ladies in Pinckney who wouldn't think of wearing the same outfit twice. They donate their clothes here because all the proceeds go to the women's shelter. I've heard you can buy an entire wardrobe for less than fifty dollars. I've never shopped here personally, you understand. I mean, the last thing I want is to run into one of those snooty old biddies from the ladies' club, wearing her linen suit. Know what I mean?" She laughed. "I'd have to go out of town to wear them." She paused before going inside. "Now, let me do all the talking because I know how things are done in this town."

"Oh, good," Annie said. "I get to see a real pro at work."

They stepped inside and a well-dressed woman with white hair smiled at them. "Elaine, meet my new friend, Annie," Lillian said. "I insist that you give her the best possible deal or I'm going to spread awful rumors about you around town." Lillian winked at Annie.

"Nice to meet you, dear," Elaine said, shaking Annie's hand. She turned to Lillian. "I'm so glad you're back. You know that teal suit you were admiring on Marion Jones at the Christmas bazaar." She glanced around as if to make sure there was no one else in the shop. "She brought it in last week. Just five minutes after you left," she added. "And it's in A-one condition."

Lillian gave Annie a sheepish smile. "Well, I may have come in once or twice," she muttered out of the side of her mouth. "But we'll let that be our little secret."

Annie grinned, found her size, and began flipping through the racks. She was surprised but delighted to find the clothes in such good condition. An hour later, she followed Lillian out of the shop carrying three plastic bags and a good start on her new wardrobe: two pairs of jeans, several cotton shirts, and a lightweight jacket. She'd also picked up a couple of nightgowns, and a pair of sneakers that looked as though they'd come right off the rack. Lillian carried a sack as well; it contained the almost new teal suit.

They climbed into Lillian's car. "I'll have my seamstress jazz the suit up a bit," Lillian whispered as though she feared someone had bugged her car and would find out what she had done. "Add teal satin to the collar and lapels, change the buttons, add a kick-pleat in the back, and Marion Jones will never suspect it was her suit."

Annie had already decided she would do her shopping at the second hand store from that point on. "I need to make one quick stop if you don't mind," she told her shopping partner. "I have to pick up socks and lingerie. And maybe a little makeup so I don't scare people."

"That's not likely to happen with your complexion, dear." Two minutes later they pulled in front of a Kmart. Annie hurried in to get what she needed while Lillian stepped into the book store next door. When they arrived home, Annie was touched to find Kazue had already dropped off a bicycle and left a nice note.

"Check out the giant front basket," Annie said. "It looks to be about two feet wide. A person could easily fit a thirty pound dog in it. Not that I'm planning to get a dog," she added quickly since Lillian was now her landlady.

"That is an industrial sized basket," Lillian said, "the kind paperboys used at one time. It'll be perfect for lugging books and groceries."

"If you see Kazue before I do, please tell her I said thank you."

Lillian smiled and nodded. "I only see one problem. How do you plan to ride a bike in your uniform?"

Annie chuckled. "I've already thought of that," she said. "I'll wear my regular clothes and change once I get to the Dixieland Café. Speaking of which, I'd better get ready for work. I'll put the bicycle in the trunk of Darla's car so I can ride home afterward."

"You know how to get to the café from here, right?" Lillian asked. When Annie nodded, she went on. "All the streets are lit up at night, and the sheriff and his deputies patrol the area. It's very safe," she added.

"I'm not worried," Annie said. Then she thought to herself, unless Sheriff Hester decides to arrest *me*.

"And try not to be nervous on your second day on the job," Lillian told her. "It takes time to learn. Just be yourself, and your customers will love you."

Annie smiled, took several steps forward, and hugged the woman. Lillian looked surprised. "What was that for?"

"For being so good to me, that's what."

Annie arrived at work wearing jeans and a cotton shirt. Her uniform and panty hose were tucked in a bag. Sam, who was sitting at the counter reading the newspaper, frowned. Here, he'd made all these promises about how he wouldn't gawk at the woman the way he had the day before, and she had to come in wearing a pair of behind-grabbing jeans that would have sent a preacher's blood boiling. "I hope you're not planning to wear—"

Annie disappeared into the rest room without a word. Five minutes later she came out ready for work. Darla almost bumped into her coming through the kitchen door.

"Well, hey there, missy. Who let the hem out of that uniform?" She winked. "How d'ya expect to make any tips in this joint?"

Annie looked thoughtful. "I suppose I'll have to rely on my excellent waitress skills. What do you think?"

"No comment," Sam said, and earned a dark look from the two of them. He stood. "I'm out of here."

"And not a moment too soon," Darla muttered.

"I heard that, Darla, and I'll remember it when it's time for your next raise."

"Raise? Did I hear someone say raise?" Darla glanced around as though trying to find the source. "I don't think that's a word we use very often in this place."

"I'd love to stay and chat," Sam replied, "but I've got a man coming in who wants to divorce his wife. Says all the woman does is nag. Imagine that."

Darla frowned at him. "I'm no lawyer, Sam Ballard, but that is not grounds for a divorce. Women were born to bitch and moan, and the only way to put an end to it is take them to the mall."

"I'll remember to advise my client of that," he said.

Annie, who was filling saltshakers, chuckled. "And what exactly were men put on this earth to do?" she asked.

Sam turned to look at her, a thoughtful expression on his face. "We were put here to hunt for food, discover uncharted territories, and protect the weaker sex."

Darla threw a paper-towel roll, and he caught it. "Weaker sex, my foot!" she said loudly.

"I believe that's my cue to leave," he said, dropping the roll onto a nearby table and hurrying out the glass door. He managed to close it behind him before another roll hit the door.

Annie was still watching in amusement as Sam crossed the street to get to his office. She didn't hear Darla come up beside her.

"Well, well, we can't seem to take our pretty green eyes off of the man, can we?"

Annie blushed. "Nothing wrong with looking."

Darla nudged her. "You didn't spend the night with Lillian. I called first thing this morning, and she said you hadn't arrived yet."

The blush deepened. "It's a long story, and this place is going to fill up with customers any moment now."

"I'm not budging from this spot till I know, girlfriend."

"I stayed at Sam's."

"Aha!"

"His housekeeper was there. It was perfectly innocent."

"If you say so."

"The man doesn't even like me, for Pete's sake."

"Which explains why he can't take his eyes off of you."

"He watches me because he's afraid I'm going to break every plate in the house," Annie protested. She was thankful when three men walked through the door. Darla didn't make a move to go to them. "Are you going to wait on them or am I supposed to?" Annie asked.

"Why don't we take stations? I'll work the counter and booths, and you grab the tables. Then, tomorrow, we'll switch."

Annie grabbed three menus and hurried to the table. The restaurant filled up in no time, and although Annie stayed busy, it wasn't as hectic as the day before when she'd been the only waitress. Of course, Sam had helped, but it was much better having another waitress on the floor, even if it meant giving up a substantial amount of tips.

Once the rush ended, Darla and Annie ordered a sandwich and ate in the kitchen, taking care to listen for the bell over the front door.

"Did you tell Darla that Patricia and I saved her job yesterday?" Flo asked Annie.

Annie shook her head. She didn't particularly want to get involved in any more disputes. Unfortunately, Patricia didn't have that problem. She gave Darla a blow-by-blow account of what had occurred in her absence.

Darla looked genuinely touched. "Gee, I appreciate you guys sticking up for me like that. Sam can be such a pain sometimes. I don't think he'd really fire me, although he has threatened to a number of times."

"That's never going to happen," Annie said. "He's too smart for that."

"You should'a seen the way he was following prissy britches yesterday," Flo said, motioning to Annie. "Not only that, he couldn't take his eyes off her. Guess he liked that short uniform she had on."

"He was *afraid* to take his eyes off of me," Annie said, "for fear I would break every dish he had. I think I may have come close."

"Had nothing to do with broken dishes," Flo insisted. "It was that short skirt."

"You never should've let the hem out of it," Darla told Annie. "Sam Ballard is considered the most eligible bachelor in Pinckney, Georgia."

"I don't think Sam has marriage on his mind," Annie said.

"You're probably right," Darla said. "The only thing he's interested in from a woman is a little action."

They all laughed. Flo choked on a biscuit, and Patricia came close to performing the Heimlich on her. They managed to pull themselves together for about thirty seconds, then, fell into another fit of laughter.

"Excuse me, ladies," a male voice said. Sam Ballard was standing at the pickup window wearing a frown. The women had been laughing so hard, they hadn't heard the bell over the door announcing an arrival. "There's a customer out front who would like pie and coffee."

"Oh, Lord!" Darla said, getting up right away. She hurried through the swinging door leading from the kitchen to the dining room.

"That man takes life too seriously," Patricia said as Annie cleaned the remnants of hers and Darla's lunch. "He needs to lighten up."

When Annie returned to the dining area, she found Sam sitting at the counter discussing business with the customer who'd wanted the pie and coffee. He was going to town on a slice of pecan, even as his gaze flitted to Darla every few seconds.

Darla smiled at Annie in such a way that Annie knew something was up, she just didn't know what. She wet a cloth and began wiping off the stools at the counter. Sam and the man finished their business and shook hands. Sam looked at Darla. "How 'bout giving Tom a coffee refill," he said.

Darla smiled. "My pleasure." She reached for the pot.

"That was the best pecan pie I've had in a long time," Tom told Darla. "Tastes just like what my mother used to bake."

"Why, thank you, Tom," Darla replied in a syrupy voice. "I baked it myself."

"No kidding?"

Darla fluttered her lashes. "I bake all the pies here."

Annie turned her head so the customer would not see her smile.

"Wow," Tom said. He looked at Sam. "You've got yourself a helluva waitress here."

Sam nodded. "Yes. They threw away the mold when they made Darla."

"I'll bet you bake those biscuits too," Tom said, leaning his elbows on the counter.

"As a matter of fact, I do."

Sam nudged Annie. "This is when Darla does her best work," he whispered. "You might want to take notes."

The corners of Annie's mouth twitched. Even as she watched Darla, she could not help noticing how nice Sam smelled. His aftershave had a light musky scent that made her want to get closer.

"Note the body language," he said. "She's leaning slightly forward, chest thrown out, one hip thrust to the side. If I tried that, I'd end up in traction."

Annie giggled in spite of herself. Darla's eyes drifted toward them. She gave one wink and went back to her business.

"Note her tongue sliding in and out," Sam went on, "flitting across her full bottom lip. Keeping it moist," he added. "You know what the poor guy is thinking."

"She's quite good," Annie said.

"Also, she touches his hand from time to time as if to emphasize something she is telling him. The poor guy doesn't stand a chance."

"But what about Bo?" Annie asked.

"This is business," Sam says. "It has nothing to do with Bo."

"Aha, he's reaching into his shirt pocket for his business card. Asking Darla to call him sometime," Sam added. "And now the grand finale. He's going for his wallet . . . he's taking out a bill. I'll bet you fifty cents it's a ten spot."

"I don't know," Annie said. "That's a pretty big tip for pie and coffee. I'm thinking more like five."

Darla took the money, gave Tom a huge smile, and tucked it in her apron pocket. The man almost tripped over his own feet as he made his way out the door.

Sam and Annie waited for Darla to say something, but she did not look their way. She cleared Tom's dishes and wiped the counter, all the while humming a tune. Flo and Patricia watched from the ticket window.

"Okay, Darla," Sam said, "what'd he leave you?"

Darla looked offended. "A waitress never discusses her tips."

"Annie and I have money riding on it."

"So do me and Patricia," Flo said. "And neither of us appreciates you telling him you make the biscuits around here. You don't even know how to make canned biscuits."

Darla gave them a coy smile. "I'll give you a hint. We would not have the light bulb if it weren't for this man."

Sam sighed heavily. "Thomas Edison invented the light bulb, Darla. He's not pictured on any currency."

Darla shrugged. "That's correct, Sam, but Thomas Edison would never have been able to invent the light bulb had this particular gentleman not discovered electricity with his kite-flying experiment."

Sam and Annie looked at each other, stunned. "Benjamin Franklin!" Sam whispered. "That's a hundred bucks!"

"I want to take waitress lessons from Darla," Annie said. She walked away, swinging her hips from side-to-side as she'd seen Darla do; only she gave an exaggerated effort.

Flo and Patricia whistled and clapped, Darla offered her a high-five. Sam swallowed hard. It was going to be a long shift.

Chapter Seven

It was shortly before eight o'clock when Darla told Annie she could leave early. Business had been so slow that Annie had already cleaned her station, wiped down the booths and tables, filled the condiments, as well as the salt and pepper shakers, and cleaned the laminated menus with vinegar and water.

"There's no need for both of us to stay," Darla said. "Weren't you planning to pick up a few things at the grocery store?"

"Yes," Annie said, "but I'm in no rush. Besides, I'm sure Bo would love it if you came home early."

"He's having dinner at his mama's tonight," Darla said. "He'll be by for dessert later so I won't be alone since I told Sam I would close tonight. Go on and take care of your errands while it's still early."

"That's sweet of you," Annie said, "but you have to promise to let me stay one night so you can leave early."

"Okay, deal."

Annie clocked out, changed into her jeans, and was on her way a few minutes later after pulling her bike from the trunk of Darla's car.

As Lillian had told her, most of the streets were lit up with old-fashioned lampposts, which made it easy for Annie to find her way, and the fact that Lillian's house was only ten minutes from the restaurant was an added convenience. But instead of pulling into the driveway at Lillian's,

Annie passed it and headed in the direction of the grocery store. She was thankful Kazue's bicycle had a basket on the front; it would certainly make grocery runs easier.

Sam quickly closed his office and climbed into his Jeep as soon as he saw Annie leave the restaurant on a bicycle. He knew he had no business following her home. For one thing, she was an adult, perfectly capable of finding her way. Secondly, she was taking a safe route. She would not be traveling down back roads or dark alleys, and only a complete imbecile would accost her right on Main Street, one of the most heavily patrolled areas in town.

So why the hell was he following her?

Not that he wasn't enjoying the view. Each time she rose slightly off her seat to pedal harder, he caught sight of her perfect behind. He was tempted to get closer but didn't for fear of being discovered. Finally, disgusted with himself for what he was doing, he slowed and turned on his blinker. He needed to go home and stop thinking about Annie Hartford. But just before he was to turn, he saw her pass Lillian Calhoun's house. He frowned. Where was she going? Had she accidentally missed her turn? He could not imagine anyone getting lost in Pinckney, but Annie's mind was probably running in a dozen different directions. He turned off his blinker and drove on.

Annie pulled into the parking lot of the Piggly Wiggly supermarket some minutes later and attached the bike to a metal bicycle stand using a rubber-coated cable and combination lock that Kazue had provided. She went inside the store, grabbed a shopping cart, and immediately forgot about the limited space in the bike's basket. Upon checking out, she discovered she had purchased more than she'd planned.

Of course, the basket was larger than most and would hold a lot. She would just have to stack 'em high and ride back to the garage apartment slowly.

From across the parking lot, Sam watched Annie come out of the store with a loaded cart. He frowned. Now, how the hell did she expect to get all those bags into the basket on that bike? He sighed. Women did the damnedest things sometimes.

Annie positioned her cart beside the bike, opened the lock, then straddled the bike and began loading the sacks into the basket. By the time she put the fourth bag in, she was having serious doubts as to whether she'd be able to get home with them. What had she been thinking?

Annie mentally crossed her fingers for good luck and began to pedal. She could feel every heavy item she'd purchased—the half gallon of milk, a box of laundry detergent, two whole frying chickens because they'd been on sale, not to mention the large pack of hamburger meat that she planned to divide and wrap for the freezer.

And a whole lot more.

She struggled to keep the bike upright, but it wasn't easy considering she was on a hill. No wonder the trip to the store had been so easy. She vaguely remembered coasting down the incline. The front of the bike had a tendency to pull left. She decided she must've put most of the heavier items on that side.

She didn't hear the pickup truck come up behind her, but when her bike drifted toward the center of the road, the driver laid on his horn, scaring her half to death. The front wheel veered far left, and Annie tried to right it, but she overcorrected and lost control. The bicycle went down; she and her groceries along with it. She winced as her right knee and elbow scraped asphalt, then, she skidded down the hill some twenty feet before coming to a stop. Her right ankle yowled. Annie did not know if she had twisted it or broken the darn thing; pain was pain. When she glanced up, she found a mess; cans rolling down the hill, eggs broken with the yellow oozing from the carton. A can of soda pop spewed in her face.

Suddenly a car screeched to a halt on the road above her, and she prayed it wasn't a cold-blooded killer because there was no way she could run. The next thing she knew, Sam Ballard was standing over her, holding a flashlight.

He shook his head sadly. "I'll be generous and give you an eight-point-five on that fall."

Annie blinked back tears of frustration and embarrassment. "Very funny, Sam," she said. He got down on his haunches, and even though she was hurting, Annie had to admit he had very nice haunches.

"Hey, are you okay?" he asked, his voice genuinely concerned.

"What are you doing here?" she asked.

Sam tried to avoid an outright lie. "I saw you come out of the Piggly Wiggly with enough groceries for a family of four. I was afraid you were going to have trouble getting back to your apartment."

"You were spying on me," she said.

"I prefer to use the word *observing*. Are you hurt?" he asked. "Do I need to take you to the ER?"

"I think I sprained my ankle, but I don't need to go to the hospital," she said. "I've got a couple of scrapes, nothing life-threatening."

"I'll help you to my car, then, I'll try to chase down your groceries."

"All of my plastic bags are torn."

"I've got bags in my backseat that I've been meaning to return to the Piggly Wiggly's recycling can. "Okay, let's get you vertical." Using great care, he pulled her to a standing position, but the minute Annie put weight on her right foot, she gave a yelp, threw her arms around him and shifted her weight onto her left foot.

"Perhaps we should rethink the ER," Sam said, even though he liked the way Annie's body felt against his.

"I know it's just a sprain," she said, "because I once sprained my ankle playing tennis, and it feels exactly the same. If we go to the ER we'll be there half the night. They'll take an x-ray, tell me it's not broken, then, wrap it and send me home."

"Yes, but they will probably give you really good drugs for the pain."

"I'm more concerned as to how I'm going to get up a twenty foot hill," she said.

"I'll carry you."

"I don't know, Sam. It's pretty steep."

"Good thing you're just a little runt. Put your arms around my neck." Annie did as she was told, and Sam swept her up. "Okay, hang on," he said and started up the incline. It did not take long; he put her in the front seat of his Jeep. "I'll try to hurry so we can get you home and take care of your injuries," he said, and grabbed a number of bags from the back seat.

A car filled with teenagers sped by, and he yelled for them to slow it down before he noticed something in the road. He put it in one of the bags and carried it to the car. "I'm afraid those kids ran over your chicken."

"No!" Annie looked like she might cry. "That is so sad."

"It was already a goner, Annie. I promise it didn't feel any pain."

"I know, but it's like the poor thing had to die twice."

It took some time, but Sam finally managed to gather up the food items. Once he'd loaded the bags into his Jeep, he put the bicycle in back and drove toward Annie's apartment. He parked out front, climbed out of the car, and hurried around to her side. "You got your house key handy?" he asked.

She handed it to him. He dropped it in his shirt pocket, then, without warning, scooped her in his arms once again. Annie protested. "You need to stay off that ankle," he said.

"How am I going to work tomorrow?"

"Obviously, you're not going to be able to, but let's try to solve one problem at a time." Once he reached the top of the stairs, he paused to unlock the door. He carried her inside, glanced around, and set her down on a chair, propping her leg on a matching ottoman. Her jeans were torn at the knee. He ripped them farther.

"Hey, these are my good jeans!" she cried.

"Hush. I need to get a closer look. Man, this is serious!"

Annie leaned forward. "How serious?"

"I might have to amputate."

She pushed his hand away and took a look for herself. "It's not that bad. I can slap on two or three Band-Aids and nobody will notice."

"I wouldn't be too sure about," Sam said. "I've seen the way men look at your legs."

She shrugged and tried to get a good look at her elbow. "What do you think?" she asked him.

"It could have been a lot worse. Let's take a look at your ankle." He untied her sneaker and, very gently tried to pull it off.

"Ouch!" Annie jerked her foot away as pain shot through her ankle and radiated up her calf.

"I have to look at it, Annie," he told her. "Now try to be brave. Remember, you'll probably bear children one day. You might as well get used to dealing with pain."

"What do you know about giving birth?" she said derisively.

"Are you kidding? You wouldn't believe the stories I've heard from friends of mine who were in the delivery room with their wives. Now, try taking a few deep breaths to keep your mind off it."

"I don't believe this. I've got a sprained ankle, and you're teaching me Lamaze techniques." Nevertheless, she groaned and carried on as he gently pulled her sock free.

"Hmm," Sam said.

"Does he have all his toes and fingers?" Annie asked, noting that, despite the pain, Sam's hands felt very nice on her.

"Yes, but she's definitely on the plump side."

"It's sprained, isn't it?" Annie asked, afraid to look.

"Hard to say. Is it normally black-and-blue and puffed up like a blowfish?"

Annie leaned forward once more, trying to take stock of her injury. Her anklebone was now hidden beneath a bulge. "Oh, no! What am I going to do?"

"First we have to treat your wounds," he said. "Do you have a first-aid kit?"

"There is one in the hall closet," Annie said. "Lillian's friend left a lot of stuff behind."

Sam returned carrying an oversized first-aid kit plus a box of various other medical supplies. "You lucked out, Annie Fay," he said. "Lillian's friend must have worked for the Red Cross."

"My name is not Annie Fay," she said.

An easygoing smile played at the corners of his mouth. "Yeah, but it fits, don't you think?"

"Absolutely not! I'm not Annie Fay or Annie Mae or Annie Jo. I'm just plain Annie."

"Nothing plain about you, Miss Annie," he said, kneeling before her.

"Oh really?" she said, trying to remain casual and indifferent to his comment. Had he just flirted with her or was she imagining it? She struggled with the uncertainty that he'd aroused in her, and when he glanced, she felt impaled by his gaze. They both froze, stunned by conflicting emotions.

A shadow of annoyance passed across Sam's face, and he looked away. He had no business flirting with Annie because, as the old cliché went, she could be here today and gone tomorrow. Her father might not be the easiest man to get along with, and he had certainly kept his daughter on a short leash, but this was the first time Annie had stood up to him, and she had done so in a big way before disappearing. For all Sam knew, the man could be frantically searching for her. He could have had a change of heart.

The question that kept running through Sam's mind was whether she would go or stay.

"What's wrong, Sam?" Annie asked, noting the hard look on his face.

"Huh?" He shoved his thoughts aside. "We're going to have to get you out of those jeans," he said.

"Is that just a ruse to get me naked?"

"I don't have to resort to chicanery to convince a woman to take off her clothes. I've discovered most are only too happy to oblige."

"Oh, brother!" Annie laughed. "You have one inflated ego. If you don't mind, would you please go into the bathroom and grab the bathrobe hanging on the back of the door?"

"What happened to the girl who strutted about in her bikini underwear at Darla's?" he asked.

Annie waved off the remark. "That was before I knew you," she said.

Sam just looked at her. "I'm going to need time to wrap my head around that." He headed toward the bathroom. When he returned he was carrying a chenille bathrobe that had clearly seen better days.

"Please tell me this doesn't belong to you," he said.

"I found it in the bedroom closet."

"Boy, that's a relief. I felt ice water racing through my loins just looking at it." He stood there for a moment. "We have to get you out of those jeans," he said.

"Nice try, Sam."

"I'm serious. Otherwise, I can't treat your wound," he said. "You're going to have to stand up."

"Easy for you to say."

"I'll help you," he said. "Put your hands on my shoulders, and try to put all your weight on your left foot."

"Easy for you to say," she repeated but managed to do as he said. He reached for the fastening on her jeans. "Excuse me," Annie said, swatting his hand. "What do you think you're doing?"

"I'm helping you out of your jeans."

"No, thank you."

"Do you have a better idea?"

"Turn around, please."

Sam sighed, but did as he was told.

Annie moaned and groaned as she struggled to get the jeans past her hips; no easy task when she could only stand on one foot.

"Are you okay?" Sam asked and glanced over his shoulder. He wished he hadn't when he noticed her tiny satin boxer shorts. Her thighs were well-toned, creamy smooth, and sexy as hell.

"You're looking," Annie said.

"Sorry." Sam turned his head so that he was facing the opposite direction.

"I'm almost done," Annie said. She had finally managed to shove the jeans to her feet and slip into the bathrobe. "Okay, you can turn around now," she said. "I need to sit."

Sam gently lowered her into the chair and, taking great care, pulled the jeans free.

"I need to clean the scrapes on your knee and elbow," he said, reaching for the bottle of peroxide he'd found, as well as a bag of cotton balls. He cleaned her injuries as gently as he could. "I'm not sure what this is," he said, holding up a brown bottle, "but it says it heals and protects." He applied it to her knee, and Annie gave a light squeal.

"It burns!" she said. "Quick, blow on it," she said.

Sam did as he was told, but it wasn't easy while laughing at her antics. "Stop acting like a big baby," he said, trying to sound stern.

"Why don't you put it on yourself?" she said.

"I don't have any wounds."

"I can do something about that. Get me a knife."

He pretended to look hurt. "Is that any way to talk to me after all I've done to help you?" he said. He looked through the box. "Aha! An ice bag," he said. "It will help get the swelling down." He stood and made his way to the kitchen.

Annie was beginning to fret on a major scale. Of all times to sprain her ankle, she thought, feeling pretty miserable. It wasn't just about money; she felt she was letting Darla down, and she had no idea how she was supposed to ride a bike to her classes. She offered Sam a smile when he returned with the full ice pack. He had been so helpful; the last thing she wanted to do was whine.

Sam propped Annie's foot on a throw pillow from the sofa and placed the ice bag on her ankle.

"That's cold," she said.

He nodded. "That's why they call it an ice bag," he said, "as opposed to a heating pad."

"You're such a comedian."

""You need to try and stay off your foot," he said, then made a production of dusting his hands. "I'm afraid that's the best I can do until I receive my medical degree."

"Thank you, Dr. Sam."

"Don't mention it. Just do me a favor. Next time you need groceries, call me; and I'll either drive you to the store or lend you my Jeep." He gathered the medical supplies, including the used cotton balls, and carried them down the short hall to her bathroom. When he came back, he found Annie smiling. "What's so funny?"

"I was going to invite you to have ice cream with me."

"Sure. You want me—" He stopped abruptly. "Oh, damn, the container is sitting on the backseat in my Jeep, isn't it?" He hurried out the door to his car and grabbed the bags. He knew which one held the ice cream because it had leaked through the paper sack onto his seat. "Damn," he muttered, and hurried up the steps. He tossed the ice cream, bag and all, into her freezer, grabbed a wet cloth, and went back down to his Jeep. He cleaned it as best he could and headed upstairs again.

He found Annie hopping toward the kitchen on her left foot. "What do you think you're doing?" he said, his eyes fastened to her behind.

"Getting our ice cream."

He followed her into the cozy kitchen and pointed her in the direction of the table and chairs that shared space with the living room. "Sit," he ordered and went into the living room for the pillow and ice bag. Once he had both in place, he held up one hand. "Stay."

"What do you think I am," Annie asked, "an old hound dog?"

"No. A hound dog would have stayed put. I'll get our ice cream as soon as I put away your refrigerated items. Are you in pain?"

"Yes. I saw a bottle of Motrin in the medicine cabinet," she replied. "That might help."

Sam headed to the bathroom. He returned with the Motrin, filled a glass with ice and water and handed both to Annie. "Thank you, Sam," she said. "I really appreciate your help."

"You're welcome." He put her milk and orange juice in the refrigerator and reached in another bag. "Hmm, I suppose you want these sanitary napkins and feminine deodorant spray in the bathroom." He shot her a disarming smile that she chose to ignore. "Ah, yes, and here we have pink disposable razors, whitening toothpaste, and mint-flavored mouthwash. Oh, look, acne cream?" He looked at her. "You don't have acne."

Her look was deadpan. "That must mean it is working. Why don't you just stick all my toiletry items in one bag, and I'll put them away later."

"You bought a Mickey Mouse toothbrush?" he said in disbelief.

"It was half price. I'm trying to live frugally."

"That explains this day-old bread. Is it worth eating stale bread just to save a few cents?"

"I've eaten day-old bread plenty of times while volunteering at the soup kitchen in downtown Atlanta. I can't tell the difference."

"When did you have time to perform volunteer work?" he asked. "From what you've told me, your father kept you pretty busy."

"He made sacrifices because he figured it would make him, as well as the company, look good. I was glad to do it, not only because I enjoy helping people, but because it got me out from under his thumb."

"You're a nice person, Annie," he said and reached for the last bag. "Uh-h, this is not good," he said, pulling out a large bag of potato chips and a bag of mini-candy bars. Do you know how much fat is in this stuff?"

Annie was more than a little peeved. "Do I look like I need to be on a diet?"

He shrugged. "Okay, forget I said anything. You probably have this incredible metabolism that the rest of us lack."

"I run five miles a day and I only allow myself a certain amount of junk food."

"Wow, do you have any idea how many calories are in a single serving of potato chips?"

Annie sighed. "Sam, would you just put my refrigerated items away and leave the rest?" she said. "I don't need a running commentary on everything I bought from the grocery store."

"Okay, suit yourself," he said, doing as she asked.

"Now, may I have some ice cream?"

He reached into the freezer and pulled the bag out that held her butter-pecan ice cream. He opened the container. "Uh-oh, we'll have to drink it. It's not exactly in solid form." He grabbed two plastic glasses from the cabinet and filled them with the thick liquid. He carried them to the table, along with spoons and napkins.

Annie looked more than a little surprised. "I don't believe it," she said. "Bradley and I had an action figure cup just like these. They came from MacDonald's. I remember getting them like it was yesterday, but I was only three years old. Funny some of the things we remember." Annie shrugged and began working on her ice cream right away, fishing out chunks of pecans. Sam watched with amusement. He'd barely gotten half of his down by the time Annie finished.

She dropped her spoon into her glass and held her head with both hands. "Oh no, brain freeze!"

"That's what you get for drinking it so fast, you little piglet." He shoved his glass aside.

"Aren't you going to finish that?"

"I'm not big on sweets. My weakness is Patricia's biscuits."

"Mind if I have it?"

He set his glass in front of her. "Go for it. Slowly this time, so you don't give yourself an ice-cream hangover."

Annie took her time. When she finished she gave a huge sigh.

"What's wrong?" Sam asked.

"I had planned to begin the fall semester tomorrow."

"I can drive you."

She perked. "Would you?"

"I may even have a pair of crutches in my attic from when I hurt my knee a few years back."

"Was it a serious injury?" Annie asked.

"Damn right it was. I couldn't chase women for two whole weeks."

Annie responded with an eye roll. "Poor baby."

"I'll have to adjust the crutches since you're such a runt."

"I really appreciate it, Sam. And I won't forget. In fact, as soon as I can get around a little better, I'm going to cook dinner for you."

"You know how to cook?"

"I took cooking lessons in finishing school."

"I'm impressed."

"Don't be," she said. "I wasn't exactly at the top of my class."

"So where were you, exactly?"

"Well, what is the opposite of top?"

"You were at the bottom of the class? Is that supposed to entice me to come to dinner?"

"I just don't want you to have high expectations."

"How is the ankle?"

"It is still throbbing. Hopefully, the Motrin will kick in soon."

"There weren't instructions with the ice bag, but I think you're supposed to leave it on for twenty minutes, then, take it off for twenty minutes. I'll add more ice to it; you should really try to ice it on and off as long as you can."

"Yes, Dr. Ballard. It will give me something to look forward to."

"Why don't I help you and Mickey Mouse to the bathroom so you can brush your teeth before bed," he suggested, "and I'll take care of the ice bag."

"That would be great." Annie didn't put up a fuss as he scooped her up once more, stopping by the counter so she could grab her toothbrush. He set her down before the bathroom sink and hurried into the kitchen to fill the ice bag.

Sam was waiting outside the door when Annie opened it. He picked her up once more and carried her into the bedroom. The room smelled nice. "Is that your perfume I smell?"

"No, it's lavender. There are sachets in the drawers and the closet. I grew up with that smell. Vera used to buy them for me. She said lavender was calming."

He liked that the room held her scent. He placed her in a sitting position so he could pull down the covers. Once Annie was settled, he put a bed pillow beneath her foot, and, just as he was about to put the ice bag in place, he noticed the swelling had gone down some. Annie was happy to hear it.

"What time do you need to be at the college tomorrow?" he asked.

"My class starts at eight o'clock," she said. "Lillian registered me online so I won't have to spend time waiting in the office to do so."

"That's good news."

"People are so nice here, Sam," she said.

He smiled. "Or maybe they've just taken a shine to you," he said. He turned serious. "Now, listen to Dr. Sam . . . try to stay off your foot as much as possible, okay?"

"Yes, sir."

He grinned and tweaked her nose. "I like the satin boxers, Annie."

She gave him a smug smile. "I know. You haven't taken your eyes off them all night."

Annie was almost asleep when the phone on the nightstand rang, startling her. It was Darla.

"Oh, no, I woke you," she said.

"I hadn't fallen asleep yet," Annie said. "What's up?"

"Sam called and told me about your ankle. I wanted to check on you. Are you in pain?"

"Not unless I do something stupid like try to walk on it. I'm just sorry that I can't come in tomorrow. I hate leaving you in a lurch."

"Hey, I can handle it. Just as long as you can walk by the time the Okra Festival starts next week."

"I should be okay by then," Annie told her.

"I have another reason for calling," Darla said. "Bo and I've talked about it, and we've decided to remarry."

"Oh, Darla, that's wonderful!" Annie said, wanting to sound happy for her friend even though she had no idea if it was good news or not.

"We want to tie the knot at the Okra Festival. Bo already contacted the people in charge, and they said we could do it Sunday afternoon in the gazebo on the courthouse lawn. They think it'll be great publicity; they're even going to have the band play the "Wedding March" for us."

"How romantic!"

"And guess what, Annie? I'm going to wear your wedding gown."

"Correction; it's your wedding gown."

"Then you won't mind if I have it slightly altered?"

"You may do with it as you wish."

"Bo asked Sam to be his best man not more than ten minutes ago. I don't know if you're aware of this, but Sam was the only person who visited Bo when he was behind bars. It's because of Sam that Bo got out as soon as he did. Anyway, I was sort of hoping you'd be my maid of honor."

Annie was surprised at the request. She and Darla had only known each other a few days. "Oh, Darla, I'm touched," Annie said. "But surely you have a best friend—"

"She got married and moved to Ohio a year ago," Darla said. "Now she's expecting a baby in two weeks and can't travel. What d'you say? Will you stand up with me?"

"I'd be honored." Annie was already wondering where she would find a dress.

As if reading her mind, Darla brought it up. "You can go through my closet and choose anything you want to wear," she said.

Annie had a sudden mental imagine of her standing next to Darla wearing a dress with large sunflowers. "Um, that's okay," she said. "I want to buy something special for the occasion."

"Whatever you say, honey. Well, I'd better go. Bo is calling me from the other room."

Annie hung up the telephone and lay there for a moment, wondering where she was going to find a dress for Darla's wedding. Perhaps she'd call the secondhand store and ask the owner to check and see if she had something suitable in her size for an afternoon wedding.

It amazed her that she'd been in town only a short while and she already had a network of friends, each one unique in his or her own way. Winston Hartford would never approve of Darla and Bo, and he would find the ladies of the Pinckney Social Club quite laughable. He would make fun of Sam's law office and used car business, as well as the Dixieland Café. He would view Sam as a shiftless fortune hunter trying to gain Annie's affections and her inheritance because, *heaven forbid* that a man find her attractive and sexy.

Of course, there was a good chance that Annie had lost whatever she had stood to inherit, she reminded herself. Oddly enough, she did not care, and she would tell her father as much when she saw him, because she knew, sooner or later, he'd show up on her doorstep. Nobody, his daughter included, was going to get away with making him look foolish, not only in front of his employees and customers but in the media as well. She was going to pay and pay big. But she was going to draw a line in the sand when it came to her new friends. They had done nothing to Winston Hartford, and Annie would protect them at all costs.

Chapter Eight

Annie was ready and waiting for Sam when he rang the doorbell at seven-thirty the next morning.

"How's the ankle?" he asked. "I see you wrapped it. Good idea."

"It doesn't hurt like it did last night," she said. "I've used ice on it twice this morning. The bandage actually helps. I'm hoping by tomorrow I'll be able to work."

"I'd rather you stay off of it for a few days, Annie," he said. "Right now I can help Darla when she gets busy, but we're going to need all hands on deck for the Okra Festival."

Annie was too embarrassed to mention that she needed to make a living in the meantime.

"Does that go?" Sam asked, pointing to a purple, oversized tote containing two spiral notebooks.

"Yes. I found it in the hall closet. It should be large enough to hold my books as well. I'm hoping Lillian won't mind if I borrow it under the circumstances." She smiled. "It was either that or use a pillow case."

Sam grabbed the tote, opened the door, and held his hand out for the house key. Annie passed it to him, and, with the help of her crutches, managed to get through the opening. She waited on the outside landing while Sam locked up. He returned the key.

"We could shave off a lot of minutes if you'd let me carry you down the steps," he said.

Annie nodded. "I know, but I really need to get the hang of these crutches."

"Let me go ahead of you, then," he said, "just in case I need to break your fall."

"Gee, thanks for your vote of confidence."

He and Annie were so focused on getting her down the flight of stairs that they did not hear Lillian come up. "Oh, dear, what happened to your foot?" she asked Annie.

Annie paused and looked up. "I fell off Kazue's bicycle last night," she said.

"Oh, my goodness!" Lillian came closer. "Is it broken?"

"No, it's just sprained. I skinned my knee and elbow too. Real attractive stuff, if I may say so."

"Why didn't you call me?" Lillian demanded.

"Sam saw the accident and brought me home," Annie replied. "Luckily, your friend left a First Aid Kit and other medical supplies behind, including this Ace bandage."

"Do you think you should have a doctor look at it?" Lillian asked. She looked from Annie to Sam and back at Annie.

Annie shook her head firmly. "No, it's much better this morning. Sam is giving me a lift to school. By the way, thanks for taking care of the registration process."

"I'm so excited for you!" Lillian said. "Now, go out there and break a leg." Her eyes suddenly grew wide, and she slapped a hand over her mouth.

"It's okay, Lillian," Annie said with a chuckle, "and highly appropriate given the circumstances."

"You've got my number," Lillian told Annie. "Call if you need me."

They said good-bye, and Sam helped Annie into the passenger seat of his Jeep. It took only a few minutes to reach the college. Sam parked as close to the main entrance as he could get, then helped Annie out. "Go on in," he said, holding the door open so she could pass through. "I'm going to park the car."

Annie entered the building and immediately saw a set of double doors marked admissions. Her crutches slowed her down, but she was determined to do what she had to do.

A tall, angular woman wearing an old-fashioned beehive hairdo greeted her when Annie hobbled in. "Hi, I'm Annie Hartford, and—"

"Good morning, Annie," the woman said, giving her a warm smile. "I'm Betty, and I've been expecting you. Lillian did not mention you were on crutches."

"I'm nursing a sprained ankle," Annie said. "Nothing serious," she added.

"I have everything right here," Betty said, "including the books for each class. Your Accounting 101 class starts in fifteen minutes. You'll have a ten minute break before your Introduction to Business Concepts begins, but it's just down the hall. If you think you'll need assistance getting back and forth to your classes, I can assign a student, but I have a feeling, as pretty as you are, you'll get an offer or two without my help."

Annie smiled. "Thank you, Betty," she said. "You just became my BFF."

"Hey, we girls have to stick together."

Sam came through the door as Annie was paying for her classes. Betty took a long hard look. "Hello, there, Mr. Ballard," she said. "Are you considering taking a class?"

He pointed to Annie. "I'm with her."

"I see." Betty gave Annie a receipt. "You're all set," she said. "Looks like you have everything you need."

Annie could see she was trying not to smile. Sam grabbed her tote; the added books weighed it down. They stepped into the hallway, and Annie checked her schedule for the room number of her first class. "I don't have far to walk, it's just a few doors down. My second class is across the hall."

"What time should I pick you up?" he asked.

"The classes are back-to-back. I'll be out by twelve-thirty."

"Well, at least let me carry your books to your first class, Miss Hartford."

"Why, thank you, Mr. Ballard." She chuckled.

"What?"

"I feel like a kid again. I can't believe I'm actually going back to school to learn something I can use in the real world."

Once they reached the door to her classroom, Sam gave her a pep talk. "Now, don't be nervous," he said. "I know it feels scary, what with it being the first day—"

"I'll probably be the oldest one in the room." Annie had barely gotten the words out of her mouth when a white-haired man approached the door. He glanced at them curiously before going inside. "Maybe not," Sam said.

"Well—" Annie raised her eyes to his, and their gazes locked. "I suppose I'd better go in." But she realized she had no desire to leave Sam at the moment.

"Okay, listen," he said quickly. "I'll pick you up outside your second class. How 'bout we grab lunch afterward?"

Annie's smile was sincere. "Thank you, Sam." Without stopping to think about it, she leaned forward and kissed him on the cheek. He smiled and handed her the tote.

Annie realized Sam was watching her. She squared her shoulders, but the walk from the door to the teacher's desk was a long one, not because of the crutches but because she could feel everyone's eyes on her; hear her father's voice telling her she had no business getting an education; her job was to marry well and be an asset to her husband for the good of Hartford Iron and Steel.

The white-haired man happened to be the instructor, Mr. Barnwell, who accepted Annie's admissions slip and told her to sit where she would be most comfortable. "You're behind by two chapters, Miss Hartford," he said, "but you shouldn't have any trouble catching up as the first chapter is a pretty basic introduction to accounting. If you have questions, you can discuss them with me after class."

Annie smiled and thanked him, then looked for a place to sit. She resisted the impulse to hide out in the last row; instead, she took a seat at the very front. To some it might not seem like much, but to Annie it was one more instance of her taking charge of her life.

Class began. At some point she realized she was so engrossed in the lesson that she was no longer nervous.

Sam was waiting outside Annie's second class when she came out. A good-looking young man was carrying her tote. He paused at the sight of Sam and shot Annie a questioning look.

"Thank you for helping me, Nelson," Annie said sweetly. "You can just give the tote to my uncle."

The boy did as he was told, nodding at Sam quickly before returning his attention to Annie. "Take care of that ankle," he said, and headed down the hall.

Sam did not look happy. "Uncle?" he said.

Annie grinned. "I was joking."

"You actually thought it was funny?"

Her smile faded. "Obviously I was mistaken."

Sam started down the hall ahead of her. He wasn't sure why he was so annoyed, only that he was. Annie tried her best to catch up with him so she could explain.

"Hey, you don't owe me an explanation," he said. "I certainly wouldn't want to cramp your style, what with you surrounded by all those young studs."

"Sam, you are overreacting. I was just having a little fun with you, that's all. If it was in bad taste, I apologize. I would never intentionally try to insult you, what with all you've done for me."

"Oh, so you're being nice to me because you feel indebted?"

Annie felt like they were speaking different languages. "Perhaps I was feeling a bit giddy because I was finally able to do what I've wanted for years. I learned a lot today," she added.

Sam did not respond.

"Okay, listen up, Ballard," she said. "I've apologized. If you choose to stay angry with me that's your choice, but you're not going to ruin this day for me."

They had reached the main door leading out. Sam held one open so she could exit. Annie was glad to see his car parked beside the curb. Without a word, he opened it for her.

They rode in silence. When Sam passed her apartment, Annie didn't bother to inquire where they were going, since he'd invited her to lunch earlier. In all honesty, she would have preferred going home and propping her foot. A few minutes later Sam parked in front of the Dixieland Cafe. "We're having lunch *here*?" Annie asked, thinking it odd since Sam had lunch there almost every day.

"You have a problem with that?"

"Of course not," she said.

Sam climbed out of the car and helped her manage her crutches so she could exit the passenger's side. He walked beside her to the front door and opened it.

She came to a sudden halt at the sight of Darla holding a cake with the word, "Congratulations," scrawled across it. Lillian, Kazue, Ira, Cheryl, and even Flo and Patricia stood near Darla and yelled, "Surprise!"

"What's all this?" Annie said.

"We're celebrating your first day of class," Darla said.

"And we have presents for you," Lillian told her. "Look, crayons and glittery stickers, and paste, and—"

"We shouldn't have to tell you this," Ira said, "but you are *not* allowed to eat the paste."

Annie could not believe all the gifts on the table, just little things that hadn't cost much but were priceless as far as she was concerned.

Flo and Patricia gave a proud smile as they handed Annie their gift, a

Barbie lunchbox.

Annie was so genuinely touched it brought tears to her eyes. She turned to ask Sam if he knew about the party, but he had slipped out the front door. She watched him climb into his Jeep and pull away from the curb.

"What's his problem?" Darla asked.

Lillian shrugged. "Who knows? Poor guy," she added. "He's probably sick of being around all this estrogen."

Sam knew he had been rude by walking out on Annie's little party, but he had not been in the mood for socializing. Even so, he kept looking up from his desk, hoping to catch a glimpse of Annie. Okay, so he *had* overreacted when she had referred to him as her uncle in front of the college guy who couldn't seem to take his eyes off her.

Sam hoped Betty from the front office did not tell Annie that he had been sitting outside her second class for half an hour waiting for her to come out. He felt she had punched him in the gut by calling him her uncle, mainly because he feared that's how she felt. Perhaps she wasn't attracted to him. If that was the case, he needed to back off.

Correction: He should never have gone there in the first place.

The door to the Dixieland Cafe opened, and Lillian stepped out, holding it open so Annie could exit with her crutches. Kazue and Ira followed behind carrying a bag with her gifts. They helped her into Lillian's car.

That meant he didn't have to run her home. Good. He had better things to do with his time. A pickup truck pulled onto his car lot, and a couple got out. Sam watched them, trying to decide if they were looking for a lawyer or a good used car. Finally, they made their way to a newer-model truck sitting on the front row. Sam shrugged out of his jacket, rolled up his shirtsleeves, and went to work.

Annie sat in the overstuffed chair in her apartment, her foot propped on a cushion on the matching ottoman, the ice pack pressed against her ankle. Not only was her ankle sore from being on her feet all morning at school, she was tired from struggling with crutches.

Even worse, she was still down in the dumps after her spat with Sam. The fact that he had become so upset over her silly joke made her wonder what was really going on between them. Had she mistaken his kindness for friendship when there was more to it?

A knock at the door made her jump. She pushed herself up, and hobbled to the door. She checked the peephole and saw Sam. She unlocked the door and opened it. He held up her tote.

"You left this in my Jeep," he said. "I figured you might need it." He handed it to her.

"Thank you," she said. "I was so tired when I got back from the restaurant that I completely forgot. May I offer you something? A cup of coffee?" she asked. "Iced tea?"

He did not respond. Instead, he stepped inside and pulled her into his arms. Annie was too stunned to do much about it, the next thing she knew he was kissing her. She dropped the tote as his kiss deepened. She sensed an urgency as he pulled her against him. When he finally released her and backed away, Annie had to grab the chair to keep from falling.

"Would your uncle kiss you like that?" he demanded. Without waiting for an answer, he swung around and exited the apartment.

Annie awoke early the next morning to a chilly apartment. She grabbed a blanket from the closet and wrapped it around her, then, headed for the kitchen to make coffee. She was surprised how much better her ankle felt, there was almost no swelling and she did not need the crutches. Still, she planned to stay off of it as much as possible, meaning she would spend the day studying because she wanted to be in tip-top shape when the festival started.

She was so engrossed in her studies that she did not realize it was almost two p.m. until Lillian arrived bearing finger sandwiches and a large shopping bag. "Did I wake you?" Lillian asked, obviously noticing Annie was still in her pajamas.

"No, no, I started reading *Accounting 101, The Fundamentals*, and lost track of the time."

"I can see how something like that could steal your entire day. You've taken the bandage off your ankle. It must be better."

"Yes, I am definitely on the mend."

"I hope you like chicken salad," Lillian said. "I had to make a tray for the garden club. As usual, I made too many."

Annie suddenly realized she was starving. She reached for one of the sandwiches and bit into it. "Mmm, this is great."

"I can't stay long," Lillian said, setting the tray on the ottoman and taking a seat on the sofa. "Guess where I've been?" she whispered. "The second-hand store," she said. "I was cleaning out my closet, and I took a load over. Look at the nice things I found in your size." She offered Annie the bag.

Annie looked inside and saw that it was crammed full of clothes—a pair of skinny jeans that looked almost new, dressy taupe-colored slacks, and a couple of sweaters. "Oh, Lillian, everything is so *nice*."

"Look at the very bottom of the bag," Lillian said excitedly.

"Oh, nice loafers," Annie said and pulled them out. "It doesn't look as though they've ever been worn."

"You wear a size seven, right? Try them on."

Annie put the loafer on her good foot. "Perfect," she said. "Thank you so much for picking these up. I love everything. How much do I owe you?"

"Don't be silly. I could buy a potted plant for what that cost me."

"I don't want you buying my clothes, Lillian."

"Okay, then buy me a potted plant. But I wanted to tell you, they have several lovely dresses that you can wear to Darla's wedding. They are very reasonable. I thought you should go look for yourself. I don't mind taking you when you're ready." She looked around. "Is it my imagination or is it a bit cool in here?"

"I did not want to turn on the heat until I checked with you to see if it needed to be serviced or checked first."

"It should be fine," Lillian said. "I bought a new heat pump when my friend moved in. The thermostat is in the hall as you've probably noticed. It has two settings, on and off. Easy as pie to operate," she added. "I'll get mad if I think you're trying to save me money by not heating the place."

"Okay," Annie said. "By the way, these are absolutely delish sandwiches."

"Glad you like them." Lillian was quiet for a moment as she studied Annie. "Well? Aren't you going to tell me what's going on with you and Sam?"

Annie blushed. "He's been very kind to me since I sprained my ankle," she said.

"And?"

"And that's all I have to report at this time, Barbara Walters."

Lillian smiled. "You know, there are a lot of women in this town who would love to sink their claws into that man. Hell, no telling what he is worth," she added. She paused and rolled her eyes heavenward. "But why am I telling you? You've got more money than all of us put together."

Annie grabbed another finger sandwich. "Correction. My father has a lot of money. He has probably disinherited me after what I did." Annie shrugged. "I don't care. Money has never held much importance with me."

"That's because you've never had to rake and scrape for it, hon."

"That's true. But I sort of like knowing I can take care of myself. It's a little scary, of course. I certainly hope I can go back to work soon."

"Annie, nobody in this town is going to let you go hungry or homeless. That's just the way we are."

"So I've noticed. It's so refreshing to live in a small town," Annie said. "And one day, when my new friends need a good accountant, I hope they'll come to me, because I'm going to give them a special deal."

"I know you will. And you'll have plenty of business, believe me. Earl

Burnsed has been my accountant since I moved here. He was old when I first hired him. I have no idea why he keeps working. Folks say he's so old, he farts graveyard dust."

Annie laughed so hard that she almost choked on her sandwich. Lillian hurried into the kitchen and grabbed a canned soda from the refrigerator. She popped the top. "Here, drink this. I don't want to have to call an ambulance." She waited until Annie had pulled herself together.

"Now, the other reason I stopped by," Lillian went on. "I thought it would be fun to throw Darla a little bachelorette party. Invite those of us who are real close to her, no more than six or eight gals. What do you think?"

Annie nodded enthusiastically. "What a great idea. But let me have it here, Lillian. After all, Darla has done so much for me."

Lillian looked around. "I suppose this place is big enough for that many people. Now, I plan to supply the food and drinks, so you needn't worry about any of that."

"When are you thinking of having it?"

"We've no time to waste. Once the Okra Festival begins, the two of you will be too busy. Is tomorrow night, after the restaurant closes, too soon?"

Annie thought about it. That would give her time to straighten the place. "That's fine," she said.

They spent twenty minutes discussing the party. "How am I going to get Darla over here?" Annie asked.

Lillian pondered the problem. "Well, she knows you're on crutches. You'll just call her and tell her—" She grinned. "Tell her you've fallen and you can't get up." They both laughed. "One more thing," Lillian said, "and you can't tell anybody. Not even the others." She leaned close and whispered. "I've hired a male stripper."

Annie's eyes almost popped out of her head, but she was grinning. "No way!"

Lillian blushed. "Yes. He's just a kid, but he looks good in blue jeans, so I have to assume he'll look just as good in a thong."

Annie shook her head, but she was more than a little amused. "Oh, Lillian, you are so bad."

The women jumped when someone knocked on the door. "Remember, not a word to anybody," Lillian said, getting up. "If Darla catches wind of it, it'll ruin the whole surprise."

"Cross my heart," Annie said.

Lillian opened the door. "Oh, hello, Sam. I see you brought lunch."

Sam stepped inside, looking a little self-conscious with Lillian there. "Hi," he said, then noticed the plate of sandwiches. "I see I'm a little late," he said, obviously disappointed.

"Oh no!" Lillian protested, "I just this minute brought these over. Annie hasn't had time to eat." She winked at Annie as she picked up the plate. "I'll just wrap these and put them in the refrigerator, and you can have them for dinner. How's that?"

Annie, who'd been stuffing finger sandwiches in her mouth since Lillian arrived, merely nodded.

"I hope you're hungry," Sam said.

"The poor girl is starving," Lillian called from the kitchen.

"I didn't know what you'd like," Sam said, "so I bought you a foot-long hot dog, large fries, and a milkshake."

Lillian rejoined them. "That sounds yummy," she said, patting Annie on the back and giving her a devilish smile.

"Why don't you stay and split it with me?" Annie suggested.

"Oh, I have to be on my way, dear. Besides, you need to eat. You're a bit on the skinny side, if you ask me." She turned to Sam. "Don't you think Annie's a bit on the skinny side?"

Sam wasn't sure how to respond. He thought Annie was perfectly proportioned; he especially liked her curves. And he should know because he had seen quite a bit of her. He smiled at Lillian. "She fills out her uniform nicely," he said. "Some of our male customers can't take their eyes off of her. Hey, don't rush off because of me," he said. "I didn't mean to interrupt."

"You're not interrupting," Lillian said. "I'm in the middle of a big project."

"Let me guess," Sam said. "You are completely redecorating your house, and Kazue is measuring for new drapes."

"Not quite *that* big," she said. "I'm cleaning out my closets this afternoon. Have to run a bunch of clothes over to the second-hand store before it closes."

Sam just looked at her; obviously he had no idea what she was talking about. "It's officially called Second Time Around, and people donate their very gently used clothes which other people buy. The profits go to local charities."

"I like the sound of it," Sam said. "Do you think I could donate a gently used waitress?" He motioned toward Annie.

"You might have to wait until her ankle heels," Lillian replied. She winked at Annie. "Enjoy your lunch," she said.

When Lillian was gone, Sam shook his head. "I feel like I missed something? What are you and Lillian cooking up?"

Annie gave him her best innocent look. "I don't know what you mean. We were just discussing what we plan to wear to the big wedding. Why don't we have lunch at the dining table," she suggested.

"Do you need help getting there?" Sam asked, then, noticed she wasn't wearing the bandage. "The ankle must be better."

"I'm still babying it a bit, but, yes, the swelling is down, and it's a lot better."

"That's good news," he said. Sam followed her the short distance to the dining room table. He pulled out a chair for her to sit and began unloading the sack. He didn't notice the dubious look on Annie's face as he shoved the gigantic hot dog and fries in front of her. "I probably should have called first," he said, "but I was afraid you wouldn't have lunch with me after the way I acted yesterday." He paused. "If that weren't bad enough, I later showed up and all but manhandled you."

She met his gaze. "You're always welcome here, Sam. You've been very kind the past couple of days. If it weren't for you rescuing me after my bicycle accident—"

"I would've stopped and helped anyone in that predicament, Annie. But I would not be looking for excuses to show up on their doorsteps. And while I'm spilling my guts, let me say that my customers aren't the only ones staring at you in that uniform. I thought my head would blow off the first day you showed up in it. I tried not to stare, but I couldn't help myself."

"I know, Sam," she said. "Why do you think I broke so many dishes?"

"Because you're clumsy?" he asked, amused.

"No. Because I knew you were staring, and I was self-conscious."

"You would have been even more so had you been able to read my thoughts," he said. He leaned forward and took her hand, and he was struck by the way that it fit so nicely in his palm. "I don't know any other way to say it other than to just blurt it out and hope I don't scare you off, but, I'm crazy about you, Annie Hartford, and there's not a damn thing I can do about it."

Chapter Nine

Annie sat very still, her gaze fixed on Sam. "I don't know what to say."

"You're probably thinking it's too soon, but—"

"It's not that, Sam." She was quiet for a moment. "It's just—" She paused. "My life has been on hold for so many years. I'm finally doing things for myself now. I'm following *my* dreams."

"I have no problem with that, Annie," Sam said, "because I *want* you to realize all your dreams."

"It's not that simple," she said. "I'm trying to make up for lost time. I want to take as many classes as I can. Between work and school I'm going to be strapped for time. I'm afraid you'll end up feeling resentful."

"Then you don't know me very well."

Annie did not reply.

"Your lunch is getting cold," Sam said.

Annie looked down at all the food and thought she might be ill. "I think I'll eat this later," she said.

"I've upset you."

"I just need time to think, that's all. And I still have more studying since I'm trying to get through several chapters in both classes. I'll feel better once I get caught up." She couldn't tell him all she needed to do to get ready for Darla's party since Lillian had practically sworn her to silence.

"You know, come to think of it, I'm not very hungry either," he said.

"Please don't let me stop you from eating," she said.

He smiled. "To be honest, I had something to eat at the restaurant right before I bought all this food."

"So, why—"

"I wanted to see you."

"So you pretended you hadn't eaten, huh? How did you expect to hold all this food down?"

"I hadn't thought that far in advance. I was just trying to get through your front door."

"Pretty sneaky of you, Sam," she said, figuring one day she would tell him about the finger sandwiches.

Sam nodded. "Oh, before I forget—" He reached into his back pocket and brought out a small sack. "I stopped by the drugstore and got you this. It's an ankle sock. See, it's made out of an Ace bandage, only it fits over your heel and ankle. It gives you the same amount of support; it's just less bulky."

Annie was touched. "Thank you, Sam. How kind of you to think of that," she said.

"I figured it would better my chances of being invited in. If that didn't work I was going to give you a used car."

Annie laughed. "You certainly are determined."

He leaned close and kissed her lightly on the lips. "So what do you think?"

"About the car?"

"About us, pretty lady. Do I stand a chance?"

Annie could see that he was sincere. She was tempted to confess she felt the same, but she didn't want to rush into anything. "Yes," she said softly. "You definitely stand a chance."

"Then, how about a picnic tomorrow at my place?" he suggested. "We can even go fishing if you like."

"Picnic?" The thought of sharing an afternoon with Sam almost made her giddy. Then she remembered the party. "What time were you thinking of having it?"

"I have clients. The last one doesn't leave until two o'clock. I'll get Martha to pack a basket for us if that's not too late for you."

"I'd love to," Annie said. "I just can't stay long because I've made plans for later." She was thinking of all she had to do for Darla's party.

Sam wanted to know what plans she'd made, but he knew it was none of his business. "Hey, if you have to study I could help you," he said, giving her a suggestive wink.

She laughed. "Forget it. Besides, if you knew that much about accounting, you wouldn't be complaining all the time about having to do it."

"I shouldn't have to do it," he said. "But the CPA I was using is so old that—"

"I've already heard," Annie said, laughing at the thought. "Perhaps it's time Pinckney had a young, attractive female CPA."

"Yeah, but where are we ever going to find someone like that?"

Annie smacked his arm playfully. "Watch it, Ballard. There may come a time when you need me to do your books. I'd hate to have to charge you more than my other friends."

"Perhaps by then we'll be more than friends." It sounded good, he told himself, but he knew he'd already crossed the friendship line and wanted more. He was falling for Annie Hartford fast and hard.

"You're being presumptuous, Mr. Ballard," Annie said. "I have not checked out all the other handsome eligible bachelors in town."

"They're all spoken for," he said quickly. "All of them are happily married. I'm all that's left."

"Oh?" she said. "How sad that nobody wanted you." She clucked her tongue.

There was a wicked gleam in his blue eyes. "Oh, they wanted me," he said. "But I run pretty fast."

"So do I," Annie said and they both laughed.

He picked up her hand and kissed her open palm. He checked his wrist-watch. "I have to go. I'm meeting with a client to discuss a real estate deal; then, some guy is bringing his daughter by to test drive that little Nissan Cube on the lot. And the ice machine is down at the restaurant. I've been meaning to replace it for a couple of years." He sighed heavily. "I'm hoping I can get a new one before the festival."

"Sam, you're too busy to have a girlfriend," Annie said laughingly.

"I'm never too busy for you." He kissed her, started for the door, then backtracked and kissed her again.

This time the kiss was slow and thorough, his tongue tracing her full bottom lip and sending Annie's stomach into a wild swirl. She kissed him back, sliding her fingers through that sexy head of hair that had beckoned her touch from the beginning.

When Sam raised his head, he was smiling. "I could get used to kissing you," he said before heading out.

Annie spent the remainder of the day studying and washing the clothes Lillian had purchased for her. Although she was determined to get through chapter three of the accounting textbook, her concentration was shot; she could not get her mind off of Sam's kisses. She thought about closing her books and cleaning, then, decided it was in her best interest to stay off her ankle for at least one more day. She planned to be ready and able when the tourists hit town. She could clean the next day after the picnic; in the meantime she would pull herself together and concentrate on schoolwork.

Darla called as Annie was getting ready for bed. "Just checking to see how you're doing, kiddo," her friend said.

Annie was about to tell her how much better her ankle was, then remembered she was supposed to call Darla the next day and pretend she was having problems. "I think I may have overdone it today," she said.

"I thought you were trying to stay off of it."

"I had to do some things around here."

"Annie, why didn't you call me? I would have come over and helped you before work this morning."

"I'm going to take it easy tomorrow," she promised.

"Well, let's hope so. The carnival people arrived this afternoon; I'm not sure how long it will take them to set up, but every kid in town will be there when the tickets go on sale. Also, there is a lot of construction work going on around the courthouse to accommodate the crafters. They rent a cubicle to show off their wares. Every motel and bed and breakfast within a twenty-five mile radius will be packed. Same goes for all the camp grounds."

"How are wedding plans coming along?"

"There's not much to do. Sam called me last night and offered to give a small reception at his place; he even found a last minute caterer. I thought that was very nice of him. And the gown is being altered a bit. And guess what?" Darla said, changing the subject. "Bo has already found a job working for a builder."

"That's good news," Annie said.

"He's always been ambitious, and you can't find a harder worker."

"It looks like everything is falling into place," Annie said.

"So you're going to stay off that ankle?" Darla asked. "Don't make me come over there and smack you."

"Yes, ma'am," Annie said. She paused. "Darla?"

"Yeah?"

"You're going to make a beautiful bride."

Sam picked up Annie shortly after two p.m. and drove her out to his place. "So what did you do all day yesterday?" he asked, helping her out of his Jeep.

"Studied. Did laundry."

"Well, now that you kept your nose to the grindstone yesterday, you can play today."

"I intend to." Annie's ankle was no longer sore, and she drew great pleasure walking about without crutches or a cumbersome Ace bandage, although she wore the sock Sam had purchased for her. The night had brought with it an early cold snap, and Annie was glad she'd worn a sweater. She thought Sam looked sexy in an off-white sweater and jeans.

She stood on a bolder and watched the sunlight shimmer on the narrow river that ran behind Sam's house. He slid his arms around her waist and nipped the back of her neck playfully. Annie shivered.

"Watch it, Ballard," she said. "That kind of stuff drives me wild."

"Really?" he said. "What else drives you wild?"

"Wouldn't you like to know?"

"Yes, as a matter of fact, I would. What does it take to find out?"

She faced him. "No way," she said. "A girl has to have a few secrets."

"I like mysterious women."

Annie gazed into his eyes. They seemed even more brilliant in the afternoon sunshine. He smelled of soap and aftershave. He smiled. "What's the smile for?" she asked.

"You want me to kiss you, don't you?"

"What makes you say that?"

"You have that look," he said. "You want me."

She laughed. "Is that so?"

"It's written all over your pretty face," he said. "Admit it, Hartford. You want my body. You've wanted it since you first laid eyes on me. Well, guess what?"

Annie arched one brow in question.

He grinned. "I'm yours, baby."

Her stomach fluttered with a typical case of butterflies. She smiled to hide her uneasiness. "I don't want to rush you, Sam."

Amusement lurked in his eyes. "Rush me, Annie. Please."

"I'll only end up hurting you. I'm far too sophisticated for you. Remember, I'm a big city girl, and you're just a country bumpkin."

"Oh, Annie, you are really asking for it. I will show you no mercy when the time comes."

See Bride Run!

"When the time comes? You're mighty sure of yourself, aren't you?"

"Oh, it's going to happen," he said, his gaze caressing her face before traveling the length of her body. "The only question in my mind is when."

Annie's body responded. There was no way to ignore the spark of excitement she felt at the prospect of making love with Sam. He wrapped his arms around her and kissed her, parting her lips with his tongue, hungry to taste all of her. He pulled her closer so that her body was pressed against his. Annie wrapped her arms around his neck and gave in to the pleasure of his mouth on hers.

When Sam raised his head, they were both breathless. He led her to a group of Adirondack chairs. "Give your ankle a rest, Babe. I'm going inside to grab our picnic lunch. I'll be right back."

Annie watched him walk away, his stance tall and straight. He was certain they were going to be lovers, and Annie had to admit the thought was more than appealing. What woman wouldn't welcome him to her bed?

But then what? Where would they go from there?

Annie was still thinking about it when Sam returned with a large picnic basket and blanket. "Let's walk closer to the river," he said. "There's sort of a beach down there."

Some minutes later they were sitting on the blanket. Sam had brought an extra in case Annie got cold. He pulled numerous plastic containers from the picnic basket—first a plate of various cheeses, added to it large ripe strawberries, and crusty French bread. It was followed by fried chicken, potato salad, and baked beans. Sam pulled out two bottles of root beer and opened them.

"Goodness," Annie said. "I was expecting a ham and cheese sandwich. I'll have to thank Martha for going to so much trouble."

"I helped," Sam said. "I sliced all the cheese."

"Oh, my," she said. "A man who cooks."

"Hey, I almost cut my finger on the cheese slicer," he said.

"You are a very brave man, Sam. Very brave indeed," she added.

"I'm glad you noticed," he said, piling food on a plate and passing it to her, "because there is nothing I wouldn't do to protect you." He sighed. "Damn, I'm getting so goofy over you, there's not much I wouldn't do to impress you."

Annie looked at the amount of food he had put on her plate. There was no way she could eat it all. She decided to play a game. "Would you take your clothes off and dive in that cold river?"

He arched one brow. "You can't stop thinking about getting me out of my clothes, can you?" He saw the pink on her cheeks and laughed. "Yes, I would swim that raging river in my birthday suit, just for you, Annie Hartford. And when they pull my frozen body from it, everyone will say I died for a good cause. Anything else?" he asked.

She laughed. "Would you purposely hit your thumb with a hammer as hard as you could?"

"I would consider it an honor, Darlin'."

She loved being referred to as Babe and Darlin'. "Step in front of an eighteen-wheeler traveling seventy miles per hour?"

"For you? In a heartbeat."

"Purposely give yourself a paper cut?" she asked.

He frowned. "Hold it right there, Annie. You've gone way too far." He cocked his head to the side. "What would you do for me?"

She pondered it. "I would eat canned spinach for you, and I can't even smell it without getting nauseous." She shuddered at the thought. "The whole can if I had to."

"Would you eat a whole can of sardines?"

This time Annie paused. She thought of the hairy, minnow-sized fish covered with oil. She almost shuddered. "If you really cared you wouldn't ask that of me."

He grinned. "And you wouldn't ask me to hit my thumb as hard as I could with a hammer."

"True," she said. "Let's agree that there is *almost* anything we would do for each other."

Once they finished lunch, Annie closed the containers and wrapped their used plates and flatware in a large dish towel. Sam lay down on the blanket, pulling Annie against his chest, and covered her with the extra blanket. They stared at the cloudless blue sky.

"What was it like growing up in a small town?" Annie asked.

"It was no different than it is today," he said. "People, for the most part, are kind, law-abiding citizens. Of course, we have our share of gossips, often it seems like everybody knows each other's business. If I got into trouble at school or did something I wasn't supposed to, my parents knew it before I got home. When I turned fourteen or fifteen I couldn't wait to grow up and get out of this town. I actually ended up in Atlanta after law school."

"Really?"

He smiled and nodded. "Went to work for a big firm. I hated every minute of it. Decided I was a small town kinda guy. I opened my practice in the building I still use. Bought the Dixieland Café so they wouldn't tear it down. Sold a few used cars here and there. Sold off a lot of livestock. It paid the bills until I got my law practice going."

Annie snuggled against Sam as he went on with his stories of life in Pinckney, Georgia. She snuggled against him, craving the warmth of his body, and the sound of his voice lulled her into a sense of well-being that she hadn't felt in many months, if ever. She closed her eyes.

Sometime later Sam nudged her. "Annie, wake up. You're trembling."

She opened her eyes, blinking as she tried to remember where she was. She was cold. She sat up and pushed her hair from her face. "I must've dozed off."

"We both fell asleep."

"What time is it?"

"Six o'clock."

"What!" She almost shrieked the word and pushed herself into a standing position. "I have to go home," she said.

He looked surprised. "Now?"

"Right this minute!"

"What's the hurry?"

"I have to clean my apartment. I haven't had time to dust."

"Is that bad?"

"I'm allergic to dust."

"You are?"

"Oh, yes, I have terrible allergies."

"Do you at least have time for a cup of coffee?" he asked.

"Look, Sam, I had a wonderful afternoon, but I told you in advance that I had plans later so I need to go." She picked up the blanket she'd used and folded it quickly. "We can do this again when I'm not rushed."

Sam stood, grabbed both blankets and the basket, and the two of them headed toward the house. "Do I have time to drop off the basket?"

"Sure. I'll wait for you in the Jeep."

Annie was already settled in the passenger's seat with her seat belt on when Sam climbed in. He looked at her. "Did I do or say something to offend you?"

"Of course not. I just have things to do." It would have been easier telling him the truth; that she was hosting Darla's bachelorette party, but she had promised to keep quiet.

"Anything I can help you with?"

"No."

They made the drive in silence. Annie figured she'd have little more than an hour to dust and vacuum the place, tidy up, and change clothes. She unbuckled her seat belt and had her hand on the door handle as Sam pulled into the driveway. She wasted no time climbing out. "Thanks, Sam, I had a great time."

He reached for his own door. "Wait a minute, I'll walk you up."

"No!" She tried to calm herself. "Don't bother," she said. "I can manage perfectly."

He shrugged, but his jaw was tense. "Fine."

Annie hurried up the stairs without a backward glance. She would explain it to Sam later. She unlocked the door and stepped inside. She headed for the kitchen, opened the refrigerator door, and chuckled when she found several large bottles of wine. Lillian had also dropped off several platters of hors d'oeuvres as well as nice serving dishes.

Quickly, Annie went to work, first cleaning the half bath in the hall, then dusting the place. She wiped down the kitchen counter, ran a wet mop over the floor, and vacuumed the large rug in the living room and the matching runners in the hall. She showered and changed into the nice slacks and sweater Lillian had purchased and tried to do something with her hair.

She was touching up her makeup when the guests arrived. "We all rode together and hid the car," Kazue said.

Another knock and Lillian walked in. "Is everybody here?" she asked Annie.

"Not quite," she said, winking at Lillian to let her know the stripper hadn't yet arrived. "Should I go ahead and call Darla?"

"Let's wait for the entertainment to arrive. I just drove by the restaurant, and there was not a customer in sight. I figure Darla is getting ready to close."

Sam had driven all over town, just trying to gather his thoughts. He was one confused man. One minute Annie acted as if she was having the time of her life. The next thing he knew, she couldn't wait to be rid of him. If he lived to be one hundred years old, he would never understand women. Perhaps he was rushing her; after all, they'd known each other less than a week, and much of that time had been spent locking horns. But he, a man who'd never believed in love at first sight, had known from the minute he'd looked into those emerald eyes that he wanted her. He supposed that's why he'd fought the attraction so hard. And he still wanted her. He didn't care that her life was a mess right now, he would gladly help her any way he could.

The thought that Annie might not feel the same about him was crushing. She'd told him he had a chance with her, and she'd responded when he'd kissed her. But if she wanted more time, he had no choice but to oblige her. He would take her to school and pick her up. He'd wine and dine her and send fresh flowers, and he would become more tolerant of her as a waitress. What did it matter if he lost a few plates now and then? He'd just buy more.

Having come to a decision about his relationship with Annie, Sam wanted to run it by her and hopefully try to find out what had happened to sour the afternoon. But as he started to turn in to the driveway leading to her apartment, he saw a young man park in front of Lillian's house and make his way up the driveway carrying one red rose.

Sam recognized him immediately, even though he was dressed differently than before. He wore a tux that was so tight, it was indecent. The shirt was open to his navel, and he was he carrying a boom box.

Sam felt his gut clench as he watched the man climb the stairs to Annie's apartment. No wonder she'd been in such a hurry to leave. She had out-and-out lied to him by saying she needed to clean her apartment. What a crock. A man didn't go to a woman's apartment wearing a tux like that unless he had something on his mind. Sam gritted his teeth as he considered what Annie might wear to complement the man's outfit.

His cell phone rang. It was Darla.

"I'm ready to blow this joint," she said. "I haven't had a customer in an hour. Flo and Patricia are already gone."

"Okay," he said. "I'll be there in five minutes."

When Annie answered the door, her jaw dropped open at the sight of the man on the other side. "Nelson, is that you?"

He grinned. "Hi, Annie."

"Do you two know each other?" Lillian asked.

"Annie and I have a couple of classes together."

"That's nice," Lillian said. She turned to Annie. "Nelson's father passed two years ago. Nelson had to drop out of school and go to work making minimum wage. Then, someone told him he could make better money, um, dancing."

Nelson nodded. "My mother almost fainted when she found out, but I was able to get back in school. I'm socking away money as fast as I can because I plan to transfer to Duke once I earn my associate's degree here."

Lillian gave Nelson a stern look. "Now, our bride-to-be is probably going to tell you to take everything off, but I'm warning you right now, I'll call your mama if you do."

"Don't worry," he said, grinning. "I do have some modesty left in me."

Lillian looked at Annie. "You can call Darla now."

"Do you have everything you need?" Annie asked Nelson.

"I need to plug in my boom box," he said. "How strong is your coffee table?"

Annie's look went blank. "I beg your pardon?"

"Oops, I forgot you needed it for your act," Lillian said. "It's plenty strong enough. I need to move the hors d'oeuvres. I'll just put everything on the dining table."

Annie hurried toward the bedroom and placed her call to Darla who was getting in her car. "I need your help," Annie said. "I tripped and fell on my bad ankle. I think I may have broken it this time. I need you to drive me to the emergency room."

Darla was clearly upset. "Annie Hartford, I told you and told you to stay off that ankle. I don't know how you think you're going to work the Okra Festival with a broken ankle. And how I'm supposed to get you down that flight of stairs by myself? Should I call Bo?"

"No, don't bother him. I'll toss my crutches to the bottom of the stairs and scoot down on my behind. Please hurry. And don't say anything to Sam."

"I'll be there in a few minutes," Darla said and hung up.

Annie made her way back to the living room, where she discovered everyone except Nelson held a glass of white wine. "Okay, Darla is on her way," she said.

"Good." Lillian handed Annie a glass of white wine. "Let's party."

Five minutes later, Darla burst through the front door and froze in shock when everyone shouted surprise.

"Welcome to your bachelorette party!" Kazue said, taking Darla's purse and handing her a glass of wine. Nelson, who'd placed the rose between his front teeth and turned on a slow song, pulled Darla into his arms for an X-rated slow dance. Darla tossed back the glass of wine and handed it to Annie.

The women stood together as Nelson and Darla danced; now and then, Nelson rubbed his crotch against her. "Oh, my Lord," Lillian said to Annie. "I hope she doesn't get pregnant."

Once the song ended, Kazue led Darla to the overstuffed chair and had her sit. Darla gave Annie a stern look. "You're going to pay for this, Annie Hartford," she said, unable to hide her amusement. "I almost got a speeding ticket getting here."

Darla had barely gotten the words out of her mouth before an old Rolling Stones song blasted "Honky-Tonk Woman." Nelson danced around the apartment, stopping to rub up against the guests while Lillian filled their glasses with more wine. Annie chuckled when he came up behind her and began pressing hot kisses to the back of her neck.

Finally, he kicked off his shoes and stepped up on the coffee table. Facing Darla, he immediately went into a bump-and-grind routine that soon had the women squealing. He reached for his bow tie, pulled it free, and tossed it to Darla.

"Take it off," Darla yelled, sending the women into a fit of giggles.

Nelson's jacket and vest came off in one tug, and he was soon bare from the waist up. Cheryl took pictures with her phone.

Another Rolling Stones song began, "I Can't Get No Satisfaction," and Nelson spent the next few minutes flexing his muscles and making suggestive moves that whipped the women into frenzy. Lillian came through with more wine, and Nelson tossed his cummerbund at her. Then, with one quick jerk, his pants came off, leaving him in a thong bikini. The

See Bride Run!

women went wild. Ira fanned herself with a magazine. Nelson motioned for Annie to join him, and, despite the blush that burned her cheeks, she joined him. The women cheered her on, and Cheryl snapped pictures.

Outside, Sam could hear screaming over the loud music and decided it was time to investigate. He shot up the stairs and through the front door like a bullet, then, stood there dumbly as he watched a barefoot Annie dance far too close to an almost naked man. Everybody was so wrapped up in the show they didn't notice him. This was not the Annie he'd come to care about, he told himself as he watched the two dance in a way that would have gotten them kicked out of most places. He shook his head sadly.

Just as he started for the door Annie saw him. She looked surprised and a lot embarrassed. "Sam, what on earth are you doing here?" she asked. She climbed off the coffee table and Kazue took her place. Annie hurried over to Sam, noting the dark scowl on his face. "Why are you here?" she asked.

Sam was glad the other women were so involved with the show that they paid him no mind. "This is what you call cleaning your apartment?" he said. "This is a helluva party you're giving, Annie. Once word gets out, you'll be the most popular girl in town."

Annie felt her temper flare. "That's not a very nice thing to say to me," she said testily. "Had you bothered to call first—"

"Oh, I get it. I'm not allowed to drop by, because Lord only knows what you'll be doing. Well, you just go ahead and party. I certainly don't want to interfere with your fun."

Annie could see that he was hurt as well as angry, but that did not give him the right to barge in uninvited and falsely accuse her. "You don't know what you're talking about, Sam Ballard. Please leave before you ruin everybody's fun."

"Gladly." He turned and stalked down the stairs. He drove straight to his office, where he tried to cool off and catch up on paperwork. But he could not get the image of Annie and the college kid doing some kind of weird mating dance on her coffee table. She obviously enjoyed it because she'd been wearing a huge grin. Further, he didn't know what to make of the other women who had been applauding loudly. Is that how the Pinckney Social Club held their private meetings, he wondered.

Sam was furious. He'd spent years being the butt of bad jokes after his ex-fiancée left town. What had started out as a fun relationship had begun to sour after her best friend accepted a job in Boston. The relationship crumbled when Sam adamantly refused to leave Pinckney, and, as his fiancée referred to, "That tacky construction trailer you call your law office." That did not sit well with Sam. He liked his office just fine.

They were between arguments when Sam presented her with a lavishly wrapped gift on Christmas Eve. She opened it to find a plane ticket for one to Boston.

Once she left town, Sam asked Lillian to give his office a face lift. She and Kazue had done a perfect job, giving it a slightly masculine feel with earthy colors and rich looking furniture. They had shelves installed for his law books and added a round table with four upholstered chairs to serve as his conference area. One counter held a dorm-sized sink, microwave oven, and refrigerator with a hip looking coffee station. They had managed to do all that *and* upgrade his small bathroom so that it was more than presentable to his clients. It would never be as fancy as a law office in Boston, but Sam didn't care. The people he worked for lived in Pinckney, Georgia, and that was just fine with him.

Still, the relationship had left a bad taste in Sam's mouth, and the teasing had only made things worse. Darla had accused him more than once of having a chip on his shoulder, which was why Sam had tried to avoid Annie when she arrived in town. But he'd soon discovered, she was not only pretty, she was good and decent and genuinely cared about people. Not only that, all he had to do was look at her, and his testosterone shot straight through the ceiling. Maybe it had been his ego talking, but he thought she felt the same.

It just proved, once a fool, always a fool. He was sure it was stamped all over his forehead.

It was coming up to ten p.m. when Sam decided to call it a night. He locked his desk and file cabinet and was about to grab his briefcase when the door was flung open.

Annie stepped inside, closed the door behind her, and planted her hands on her hips. She was clearly annoyed. "Do you have something you want to say to me?" she asked.

"How about this: My office is closed, and I'm not taking on any new clients. Have a nice life." He picked up his briefcase and headed for the door. Annie crossed her arms and stepped in front of him. He laughed. "You're going to try to stop me from leaving? Seriously?" he added. "Is your party over already? Did your boyfriend have to run home in time to make his curfew?"

"You have no idea what you're talking about," Annie said.

"I have eyes, Annie. I saw how much you enjoyed having that young stud's hands all over you."

"Thank you for mentioning that, Sam, because I need to remind you that, number one, you do not just walk into my apartment without knocking."

"I heard someone scream."

"You heard screams of laughter. That brings me to the next topic. You do not stand in judgment of how I live my life. Not you or anyone else."

"I agree. May we leave now or will you tackle me before I can get to my Jeep?"

"*After* you apologize for almost ruining Darla's bachelorette party," she said.

Sam blinked several times and cocked his head to one side. "That was Darla's bachelorette party?"

"Yes, Sam, and what you saw was a group of women letting their hair down."

"Plus, one almost naked guy," he added.

"Everybody danced with that almost naked guy, and we had a ball doing it."

"Why didn't you tell me?"

"You weren't invited."

"Is that why you were in such a hurry to leave the picnic?"

"Yes. And another reason I didn't tell you or anyone else was because Lillian asked me not to. Besides, I'm not obligated to tell you every move I make."

Sam gave a huge sigh. "You're right," he said. "On all counts," he added. "I never should have shown up at your place unannounced. I'm sorry."

"Keep going," Annie said.

"I had no right to judge you or anyone else for that matter. I'm really sorry, Annie. And embarrassed," he added. "I'm thirty-five years old, but I keep acting like I'm back in high school. My only excuse—not that I really have one—is that I'm crazy mad about you," he said, "but if I were you, I would stay as far away from me as possible because I am obviously a jerk."

Annie nodded. "You're being awfully hard on yourself, but I think I'll let you keep at it. In the meantime, would you give me and my bicycle a ride back to my place?"

"You rode your bike here? At this hour?"

"Yes, Sam, I did," she said. "Why do you ask?"

He'd almost done it again, stuck his foot in his mouth. He was going to have to practice keeping his mouth shut and minding his own business. "Well, because, that means your ankle must be completely healed. That's great news!"

Ten minutes later, they were on their way to Annie's with Kazue's bike tucked into the back of Sam's Jeep. Neither of them said anything, but Annie was still touched by his apology, and his desire to make things right.

Sam parked in Lillian's driveway and climbed from the car. He pulled the bike out, opened Lillian's garage door, and rolled it inside. He closed the door and looked at Annie. "It's safe and sound," he said. "I'll wait until you get safely inside your apartment before I leave."

Annie frowned. "That's not going to work, Sam."

"You don't want me to wait?"

"I don't want you to leave."

Chapter Ten

At first, Sam was certain he had misunderstood. He searched Annie's face, her eyes, trying to decide what she was asking of him since he had managed to get a few things wrong lately. Her eyes were soft and he thought he read the same deep longing he felt.

"I thought you were mad at me," he said.

"I *was* mad at you, but I'm over it. Do you want to come upstairs or not?"

"Hell, yeah, I want to come upstairs, but I'd like to think we were on the same page, if you know what I mean."

"We're definitely on the same page, Sam."

He followed her up the flight of stairs to her apartment. He wondered if he would ever be able to see her behind in a pair of jeans without wanting to take them off of her. Annie unlocked the door. They'd barely made it inside before Sam pulled her into his arms and kissed her deeply. When he raised his head they both sucked in air.

Annie began unbuttoning his shirt. She pulled his shirttail from his slacks.

"Are you trying to seduce me?" Sam asked jokingly.

She smiled. "Yes. How do you think I'm doing so far?"

"You're doing great. Please don't let me stop you." He kissed her again, this time slowly, leisurely, as though he had all the time in the world.

Once his tongue had explored her mouth, he cupped her face between his palms and kissed her closed eyelids, her forehead, then, pressed his lips against the hollow of her throat. Without warning, he swept her high in his arms and carried her into the bedroom where he gently placed her on the bed.

Annie pulled him close for another kiss. His mouth was hot; she drank him in and felt a tug of pleasure low in her belly. The world around her seemed to disappear, as though tucking itself behind the shadows so that the only thing left was the two of them, lost in each other's embrace.

Sam told himself to take it slow, but he could not wait to have her warm and naked under him. He pulled off her jeans and sweater, and the sight of her in a black lace bra and matching panties sent his pulse racing. He reached for the clasp on her bra, and freed her breasts before stripping away her panties. "You're beautiful," he whispered, his voice thick with emotion, "but then, I knew you would be."

He kneaded her breasts gently with his hands, then, closed his mouth around one nipple, teasing it with his tongue until he felt it tighten and quiver. He moved to her other breast before exploring the rest of her body with his mouth and tongue.

Annie's body responded to Sam's kisses and each intimate touch, filling her with a sense of longing and urgency. She felt like crying out when he pulled away and dispensed with his clothes. He quickly rejoined her, and, as Annie eagerly lifted her hips to meet him, filled her deeply. She whimpered his name once before she lost herself to him. It was the sweetest sound that Sam had ever heard. He pulled her close and wrapped his arms around her, and she snugged against him like a kitten.

When Annie opened her eyes, Sam was propped on one elbow, watching her. "Did I fall asleep?" she asked.

"You dozed off for maybe twenty minutes."

"Have you been staring at me all that time?"

"Yes, and I enjoyed every moment," he said. "Plus, I had time to think."

"About what?"

"I'm going to offer Darla the job of managing the restaurant."

"I think that's wonderful," Annie said. "She is one of the hardest workers I know."

"I want to teach her to do the books, take inventory, place the orders, and pay the bills. She has a good head on her shoulders. I think she'll catch on quickly."

"I hope she is going to get a big fat raise!"

"Yes, she will definitely get a substantial salary increase."

"Only one question," Annie said. "Darla already does a lot. How is she going to fit in all that extra work?"

"I'm working on it," Sam said. "I've already hired a busboy. He starts tomorrow, in time for the Okra Festival."

"Yes!" Annie felt like doing a happy dance.

"He will actually do more than bus tables," Sam said. "When business slows after the lunch crowd, he will do the heavy duty work up front, as well cleaning the front windows which we all know is a major job. He'll also help Flo and Patricia break down the kitchen in the evening. They'll be thrilled to know they don't have to wash the big pots and pans or sweep and mop the floor."

"That's great news for everyone, but I can't help being a bit nervous about the Okra Festival. I'm not nearly as good a waitress as Darla, and it sounds like we're going to be swamped."

"There will be three extra people on board," he said. "Patricia's daughter, who has filled in before, will work in the kitchen. Wayne, the guy I've hired, will make a huge difference up front because you girls won't have to clear the dishes off your tables and wipe everything down."

"You're right," Annie said. "That *will* make a huge difference."

"I'll be working the front as well, running the register, taking to-go orders, refilling coffee and tea, and picking up broken dishes."

"You just *had* to bring that up, didn't you? But what about your other jobs? When are you going to do your lawyerin' and selling cars?"

Sam grinned. "I cleared my lawyerin' schedule a month ago and I'm not really responsible for running the car lot so that's no big deal."

"When are you going to offer Darla the manager's position?"

"Not until after the wedding which is also the last day of the festival. She has enough on her mind right now."

"I'm concerned about her," Annie said. "I've only met Bo once, but it was a harrowing experience."

"Bo is a good man, Annie. He made mistakes, some worse than others, but he paid for them. He deserves a second chance, and the people in this town are likely to give it to him."

"Well, I'm the last one to judge," she said, giving a half-grunt, half-laugh. "I stole a car."

Sam chuckled but quickly grew serious. "When do you think your father is going to start looking for you?" he asked. "If he hasn't already," he added.

"I've been thinking about it, Sam. I'm only three hours from Atlanta. I'm not hiding out or using an alias. Don't you think someone as powerful as my father would have found me by now if he was looking?"

"I don't know how he thinks, Annie."

"He is an angry, bitter man," she said. "It's true that I humiliated him, but it did not have to be that way. I tried to break off the engagement, but he would not hear of it. I decided to leave. His good friend at the bank froze my accounts. My credit cards were canceled."

"That's illegal," Sam said.

"Not when you're Winston Hartford. He lives by his own set of laws. I had cash in my purse the day I took off, but I was in such frenzy that I left it behind. I can't reach Vera, our former housekeeper, who essentially raised Bradley and me; after our dear father sent our mother packing when we were four years old." Annie could not keep the contempt from her voice. "He filled our heads with lies, but we were too young to know better. Vera could not say much because she feared getting fired, and she was determined to see that Bradley and I had the best upbringing she could give us under the circumstances."

"I'm sorry you had to go through that, Annie," Sam said, reaching for her hand.

"I've tried figuring him out," Annie said. "On the one hand, he may want to visit long enough to tell me how much he despises me for not following his orders. On the other hand, I'm really of no importance to him now. I no longer serve a purpose. In his mind, I'm worthless, and I think he has always felt that way."

"That has to hurt," Sam said.

"That is why—" Annie suddenly felt a lump in her throat, and her eyes stung. She swallowed.

Sam squeezed her hand. "What were you about to say, Annie?" he asked gently.

She blinked several times. "That is why I am so appreciative of the kindness I've been shown since I arrived in Pinckney. I don't have to try and act a certain way. I can just be myself. It is very healing, Sam."

Sam gazed back at her for a long moment. If he'd thought her beautiful before, she was even more so now that he'd glimpsed what was inside. "I don't ever want you to change, Annie," he said.

He checked his wristwatch. "I need to go," he said, "guess we'd better get some clothes back on. Then he smiled. "Do you need a ride to school tomorrow morning or is your dance partner going to pick you up on his tricycle?"

She laughed. "You are so bad."

"Damn right I am. And don't ever forget it." But he was smiling and didn't look quite as threatening as he sounded. "I'll take you and pick you up," he added. "We've got a busy week ahead of us. I don't trust you on that bicycle." He released her hand, and they both stood. "Are you going to walk me to the door," Sam asked, "or should I find my own way out?"

Annie laughed. The door was three feet from where they stood. "I'll walk you," she said. "I don't want to have to wake my butler."

Once Sam reached the door, he kissed Annie again, this time so gently and tenderly that she felt her heart swell from the sweetness that was so unlike the passionate kisses earlier. He finally raised his head. "You know, I'm hoping that Darla will take over a lot of my responsibilities so I can start taking this certain young lady on a date once in a while. Of course, she's going to have to give up all her young studs and settle for a broken down thirty-five-year-old."

Annie tossed him a saucy smile. "I'm partial to senior citizens."

"Now who's being bad?" Sam said.

Sam opened the door and heaved a sigh. "I would stay the night if I weren't worried about your reputation. Be thankful you've got a gentleman on your hands."

Annie remembered the way they'd spent part of the evening. "You, sir, are no gentleman, and I, for one, am very glad of that fact." She offered him a beguiling smile. "Good night, Sam," she said softly.

A minute later he was on the stairs, his footsteps growing softer as he descended and headed for his Jeep. Annie felt a sudden, inexplicable yearning to run after him, ask him to stay, but her feelings were all tangled and disjointed. Was she just being hopeful that her father would stay away? Was she being unfair to Sam by encouraging him? When it came right down to it, there was no way to predict her future because she had not dealt with her past. Instead she had run from it, leaving far too many loose ends.

Annie felt better when Sam picked her up the next morning and drove her to school. She had awakened feeling baffled over her dark mood the night before. She knew one reason had to do with the fact that Vera had not texted her back on Darla's cell phone or bothered to reach her through Lillian. Annie was not only concerned for the woman, she wanted to ask Vera to mail her wallet. She could only go so long without some kind of ID and her driver's license.

"You're awfully quiet this morning," Sam said.

"Oh, sorry," she said, trying to sound upbeat. "I think we're having a quiz in my accounting class today, and I'm not as prepared as I'd like to be."

"Uh-oh," Sam said. "That's my bad for keeping you from your studies."

"I was a pretty willing accomplice," she said, offering him a smile.

He parked at the front door of the school. "You'll do fine, Babe," he said. "Just go in there and show 'em what you're made of. I'll pick you up at noon."

"Make that eleven," Annie said. "I'm going to ask to be excused early because of the festival. I don't think it will be a problem." She gave him a quick kiss, climbed from the Jeep and hurried inside. She spied Nelson in the hallway looking through a folder. He smiled when he saw her. "That was some bash, huh?" he said, approaching her.

"You do a mean bump-and-grind routine, my friend," she said. "Thank you for making the party such a huge success."

"Hey, I'll dance for you anytime, pretty lady. Perhaps you'd like a private performance. Say next weekend, after I take you to dinner? Of course, I would encourage you not to mention our plans to your uncle."

Annie laughed. "I'm too old for you, Nelson. And experienced," she added with a grin. "You need to find some sweet young thing."

"I like dating older women," he replied. "I don't have to walk very far to the front door of Walmart because they usually have handicap passes hanging from their rearview mirror."

An amused Annie tried to give him her most menacing look. "I should smack you for that comment."

He pulled his wallet from his back pocket and fished out several business cards. "Don't forget to mention my name to all your friends," he said. "Even the ones in nursing homes," he added.

"Very funny," she said with a smile. "You better keep your stripper job."

He stuffed his wallet back in his pocket. "I'll race you to class."

Annie shook her head sadly. "You are such a child."

Sam was waiting for Annie when she exited the school at 11:00. She got in the Jeep and put her books on the back seat. She had since purchased a book bag strictly for her uniform, apron, and shoes. She had discovered that, by rolling her uniform with tissue paper it kept most of the wrinkles at bay.

"Guess what? I aced the quiz!" she said.

"I knew it!" Sam said. He raised his hand. "High five."

Annie reciprocated.

"We have to hurry," Sam said. "The lunch crowd has already started coming in. If the breakfast crowd is any indication, we are going to be packed for lunch and dinner. I've already told Darla I want you girls to rest as much as you can between shifts. You'll like the busboy, Wayne," he added. "He's a hard worker."

They arrived at the restaurant in record time. The parking lot was almost half full. Annie quickly climbed from the Jeep, raced through the back door, and headed straight for the ladies room. Five minutes later she stepped out wearing her uniform and took her first order of the day. In the next booth, the busboy, Wayne, who looked to be in his mid-to-late fifties, was clearing dishes and wiping everything down. He gave her a quick smile and went back to work.

Annie was making fresh coffee and Darla was taking an order at the front counter when a customer inquired about the crowd.

"It's our annual Okra Festival," Darla said, "just something we do to get folks to visit our little town. There'll be a parade to kick things off, but the crafters and food vendors are already set up on the courthouse lawn. Unfortunately, we stay so busy that we don't have time to enjoy it. Except for next Sunday," she added with a smile. "The owner is closing for the day because I'm getting married." Darla turned and smiled at Annie who had started to fret the minute Darla mentioned the wedding.

"What's wrong, hon?" she asked.

Annie forced a smile. "Just trying to keep up with this crowd," she said and hurried away. She wasn't about to tell Darla she still didn't have a dress for the wedding. She planned to go to the secondhand store the next morning since she didn't have classes. She just hoped she could find something.

The crowd thinned, and by two o'clock the place was quiet except for a few stragglers and those stopping by for pie and coffee. Wayne finally introduced himself to Annie. He was completely gray, his face weathered, but he looked to be in excellent shape.

"You work fast," she said.

"He sure does," Darla said. "We're going to nickname him Greased Lightning."

"I'm a retired Marine," he said proudly. "I was trained to work hard."

"I have a particular fondness for Marines," Darla said, using the accent that often won sizeable tips from her gentleman customers. It was thick and slow as molasses. Annie tried to keep a straight face. "You are new in town, aren't you?" Darla said. "I never forget a handsome face."

"Yes, ma'am," he replied. "I just moved here to be close to my son and his family."

"Are you married?" Darla asked.

"My wife passed on a year ago," he said, "after almost thirty years of marriage."

"Oh, I'm sorry to hear that," Annie said.

"Me, too," Darla echoed, "but I know a lot of women in this town who would be pleased as punch to meet you, including myself if I weren't already spoken for. Do you like country music?"

A scowling Sam walked over and regarded Darla. "Are you finished interrogating the poor man?" he asked.

Darla's hand flew to her chest as though shaken by his rudeness. "I'm just being friendly," she replied. "Since when did that become against the law?"

"Well, if you can take a break from socializing, I need for you to hold down the fort while I run a couple of errands."

"But of course, Sam," she said sweetly. "Are you going by the dry cleaners to pick up Mr. Okra?"

"Very funny, Darla," he said and disappeared through the kitchen door without another word.

Annie realized her mouth was open. She closed it. "What was all *that* about?"

Darla chuckled. "You know, you couldn't find a man with a better disposition, not to mention one who is honest and fair and gets along with everyone. But once a year, when the Okra Festival comes around, he is miserable to be around on account he and all the other business owners have to wear an okra suit in the parade."

"Okra suit?" Annie asked.

"Yes, and it looks just like an okra. It's quite humiliating, but the tourists love it."

"They all look stupid if you ask me," Flo shouted through the food-order window.

Annie laughed. "I am looking forward to it."

The customers started coming in at five, and before long, Annie was in a mad race to keep up, despite the extra help. Sam had returned, and, although he wasn't frowning, Annie could tell he was not in the best of moods. Plus, she'd dropped four water glasses, and Sam had to clean up the mess because Wayne was busing a large booth. She was standing by the food window, loading her tray when Sam walked by.

"Do you need anything?" he asked.

"Yes!" she said, a bit winded. "Tables seven and nine need coffee and tea refills," she said, "and—" She paused and reached into her short apron for her ticket pad and tore off three. "I need you to total these for me. The customers are waiting for their checks."

"Okay. Once I add these up I'll deliver them to your customers if you like, then start beverage refills."

"That would be great." Annie hurried away with her tray.

The restaurant started clearing out at nine. At nine-thirty, Sam put up the closed sign. Annie and Darla had very little side work to do thanks to Wayne. Flo and Patricia, along with Patricia's daughter, had been ecstatic when they'd clocked out, having benefitted from Wayne's hard work as well.

"You need to hire that man permanently," Darla said, as she slipped on her sweater and fished inside her purse for her car keys.

"You think?" Sam asked, finishing up his book work. He stood and stretched.

"Darn right," she said. "Talk about a morale boost. Flo and Patricia were in a good mood all night." She looked at Annie. "You need a lift home?"

"I'm sure Sam would appreciate you dropping me off since he has been playing taxi on my behalf."

Sam looked surprised. "It's no trouble," he said. "I'll run you home."

Darla gave Annie a knowing smile as Sam got up and unlocked the front door. He walked Darla to her car as he had hundreds of times before to make certain she was safe.

Twenty minutes later, Sam parked in front of Annie's apartment. He pulled her into his arms the minute they stepped inside. After sharing a deep kiss, Annie pushed away. "I'm all grungy," she said. "I think I'll take a quick shower. Want to join me?" She started down the hall, and Sam followed, wearing a huge grin.

Their lovemaking began beneath a spray of hot water. Sam washed Annie's back, then, decided to give other areas special attention. Annie clung to him as waves of pleasure sent shivers of delight through her. They grabbed a towel and dried quickly before going into her bedroom for the second act.

"Promise me one thing," Sam said, as Annie snuggled against him.

"Anything," she said.

"Promise you'll still respect me after you see me dressed like a vegetable tomorrow."

Annie chuckled. "I think you will make a handsome *fresh* vegetable."

When Annie woke up the following morning, Sam was gone, but he'd left a note on her pillow, a simple thank-you inside a heart. She smiled as she remembered how they'd spent a portion of the night; and a brief shiver shook her. For the first time in longer than she could remember, she felt pure and simple joy.

She glanced at the alarm clock. It was still early, but she had a lot to do before heading to work. She climbed from the bed and hurried toward the bathroom for a hot shower.

Annie arrived at Second Time Around shortly after it opened. Elaine, the owner, had her stand before a triple mirror as she held each of the three dresses she had been holding for Annie.

"What do you think?" Elaine said as they cocked their heads to one side and then the other.

"The mint green crepe," Annie said.

"Excellent choice!" Elaine said. "That's the one I was rooting for. It also has matching four-inch heels."

"Size seven, right?" Annie said.

"Yes. Lillian made certain I had your shoe size as well."

"Okay, then," Annie said. "I'll try it on."

Annie left the store twenty minutes later, relieved that she finally had a dress. When Elaine mentioned, in a confidential whisper, that Mrs. Lillian Calhoun was dropping by later to look at a bona fide Donna Karan original, Annie asked the woman to send her dress home with Lillian. Annie was not going to risk taking the outfit back in the bike's basket, especially after shelling out seventy-five dollars for it. In her previous life that would have amounted to pennies, actually, *less* than pennies, but Annie was now a small-town waitress living on a budget.

Sam arrived at Annie's shortly before eleven. She hurried down the stairs so he wouldn't have to come up. "You may as well get ready for a long day," he said once she climbed into the jeep. "The breakfast crowd kept us running for three straight hours. Thank goodness for Wayne or we never would have pulled through." He started backing from the driveway.

"The sidewalks are filled with people, and the streets around the courthouse are roped off to accommodate thousands more. This is the biggest festival we've ever had. Plus, they let the kids out of school early."

"I suppose everyone is excited about the parade."

Sam stepped on the brake and looked at her. "What's that supposed to mean?"

"Huh?" Annie looked at him. "It means people love parades," she said.

Sam frowned. "I hate parades."

Annie laughed. "No you don't."

He gave a huge sigh. "Never mind," he replied.

The lunch shift was busier than the previous day, and it was all Annie could do to keep up, even with Darla taking on extra tables and Wayne and Sam assisting. At two-thirty, Sam excused himself and headed toward the kitchen. He returned a few minutes later in his green okra outfit which resembled a jumpsuit with a zipper that ran from his neck, almost to his crotch. He was minus the head section which he held in his right hand.

Annie quickly looked away and found Darla grinning at the sight of Sam. She put two fingers in her mouth and blasted an ear-splitting wolf whistle that startled several customers and woke a baby who howled in protest.

"I *hate* when she does that," Sam hissed to Annie. "Every year, she does the same old thing." He paused. "Annie, are you even listening to me?"

Annie refused to look his way. "I'm getting iced tea for a table of eight," she said. "I don't have time to chat."

"Is everything okay?" he asked.

"Yes, fine."

"What's wrong?"

"Nothing," she insisted.

"Something's wrong," he said. "I can tell."

A giggle escaped her. "Sam, please don't bother me right now."

"Oh, I get it. It's this outfit, right? Am I right?" he said when she didn't answer. "Is that why you won't look at me?"

Laughter bubbled up from her throat. "Go away, Sam," she ordered. "I can't work with you here."

"It's not that funny."

"Yes, it is. Trust me."

"I have to go," he said, sounding hurt. "The parade starts in fifteen minutes, and I have to take my place next to the other pathetic looking okras. I'll be back as soon as I can."

"Okay."

"Annie?"

She tried to look serious. "Yes, Sam?"

"I wish I could kiss you right here," he said.

"Please don't. There's a truck driver in the second booth who just proposed marriage. If he thinks I'm hot for Okra Man, he might lose interest."

"That's not funny," Sam said and hurried away.

Most of the customers had cleared out in time for the parade, and those who remained watched from their seats next to the window. The parade began with a marching band, each member wearing the same green as the okra outfits. It stopped right in front of the restaurant playing, *When the Saints Go Marching In*. Annie, Darla, and Wayne sat on stools at the counter trying to eat lunch and watch the parade.

Flo and Patricia craned their heads from the food window, both appearing frustrated that they could not see what was going on. A moment later, they came through the swinging doors, having dispensed of their white aprons. They watched from the front door and fell into a fit of laughter when a dozen men marched by in okra outfits. Flo laughed so hard it brought tears to her eyes. She had to sit in a booth to recover.

Once the parade moved past the restaurant, Darla and Annie refilled the sugar canisters and condiments, and wiped the vinyl menus with vinegar water. With Wayne's assistance, they got the place ready for the dinner crowd in half the time it usually took. Annie made up salads in advance and stuck them into an oversized refrigerator while Darla refilled the pie case and made tea. Wayne cleaned every booth and table in the restaurant, swept the floor, and quickly ran a damp mop over it while Flo and Patricia, along with Patricia's daughter, readied the kitchen.

Once they finished their side jobs, Darla and Annie took a well-deserved break, but Wayne kept at it, polishing the stainless steel appliances until they shone like a new penny.

Sam came through the kitchen doors, minus his okra outfit, and poured a cup of coffee. "Well that was embarrassing as hell," he said. "Next year I'm going to pay someone to break both of my legs so I can't walk, and then, just maybe, I won't have to participate in that stupid parade and make a damn fool of myself."

"Now Sam, you don't mean that," Darla said. "If you quit, all the other okras will quit, and then we won't have an Okra Festival, and this poor town will shrivel up and die. Bad enough there aren't enough jobs to keep the young people here. We need those tourists because they go home and tell their friends about our town, and that's how we get vacationers all year. But if you're determined to ruin it and turn this into a ghost town, then I'll ask Bo if he'll break your legs. First, though, I need to know how much you're willing to pay."

"Very funny, Darla," Sam said. "Next year, *you* can wear the okra suit."

An amused Annie was standing a few feet away sipping a soft drink and listening to Sam go on and on, when, all of a sudden, several young men came through the front door. Annie did a double-take at the sight of Nelson, and she almost choked on her drink as she tried to swallow a mouthful.

Nelson grinned and fixed his gaze on her. "We heard this place has the prettiest waitresses in town," he said, slurring his words. "Hey, gorgeous," he added. "I hope you're on the menu."

Annie wished she could disappear in a puff of smoke.

"Well, isn't this grand," Sam muttered to Darla. "Just when I thought the day couldn't get worse, in walks a group of drunk strippers."

"Hey, Darla," Nelson said. "You're looking real pretty in that uniform. Oh, look, it is Annie's uncle," he added.

Annie shot Darla a look of pure panic. Darla grabbed several menus. "Annie, why don't you give Sam a refill of coffee so he can take it to his office and relax, and I'll wait on these gentlemen."

Annie grabbed the coffee pot and offered Sam another cup.

"I don't want any more coffee," Sam said, "but I'll tell you what I *do* want." He took the coffee pot from Annie and set it down, then, without warning, pulled her into his arms and kissed her passionately. When he raised his head, Annie saw they had an audience. She stood there, frozen in place, as Darla and Wayne stared at her, and Flo and Patricia gaped from the other side of the food window.

"Now then," Sam said. "My day just got better." He looked at Darla. "I trust you can keep those kids under control. Please don't let them dance on any of the tables or take their clothes off." He took one last look at Annie and pushed through the doors to the kitchen.

"Oh, my Lord!" Darla said. "I never thought I would see the day. Sam Ballard is in love!" She grinned at Annie.

Annie did not think it was funny. In fact, she was both embarrassed and humiliated. "Would you please excuse me," she said and pushed through the doors just as Sam had a moment before. She found him sitting in his office filling out a deposit slip. He looked up.

Annie stepped inside, closed the door, and crossed her arms. She was as furious as the look on her face. "You listen to me, Sam Ballard, and you listen *good*," she added. "If you *ever* do that again, I'm going to walk out the back door, and that will be the last you see of me."

He looked surprised. "Are you really angry?" he asked.

"I'm so mad I feel like hitting you over the head with Flo's skillet," she said. "You do *not* have the right to embarrass me in front of the other employees *or* our customers. I'm sorry that you are annoyed because you had to be in a parade. Gee, what a terrible, horrifying, miserable experience that must've been. My advice to you is get over it." She opened the door and walked out without another word.

For the next few days, everyone raced about the Dixieland Cafe, trying to keep up with the crowds. Between studying and keeping the mad pace at work, not to mention constantly sorting through her feelings for Sam whose apology she'd finally accepted, Annie felt scrambled much of the time.

She was thankful when Sunday finally arrived. She knew Sam was taking a financial hit by closing the restaurant for the day, even more so since he'd promised everyone would still be paid for the day, but Annie figured Darla deserved it after all the years she had worked for Sam.

Annie straightened her place, took a hot shower, and spent a long time on her makeup. Once her hair dried, she sprayed it and finger-combed the waves and curls so that it came out fuller. She did her nails and waited till they were dry to begin dressing. Checking her reflection in the mirror, she was pleased with the finished product. The only thing missing was perfume. She thought of her perfume tray back home that held her favorite scents and shook her head.

She opened the door to the linen closet and looked among the shelves for perfume or body spray. She smiled when she found what she was looking for, simple lavender water, the same brand Vera had spritzed on her bed pillows for years. Annie had a sudden yearning to see the woman and decided she was going to insist that Vera visit her once the Okra Festival was over. It made no sense that Vera had not tried to reach her, but Annie couldn't think about it at the moment. She was putting on lipstick when Sam arrived. He whistled when he caught sight of Annie. "Don't you know it's not nice to outshine the bride," he said.

"That's not likely to happen," Annie said, giving a chuckle. "The bride has spent hours at the hair and nail salon, and her gown is worth umpteen-thousand-dollars. Fortunately, she will only be wearing about half as many crinolines so she'll have an easier time getting around."

"Did I tell you that Bo had to climb that tree for the tiara and veil?" Sam asked. "Darla had given up on it, said they could probably find something just as nice at the mall, but Bo knew she wanted it."

Annie smiled. "I'm glad because that's actually my wedding gift to them."

"What do you mean?"

"The diamonds in that tiara are real, Sam. Twenty karats of perfectly flawless stones, straight from Tiffany's."

"And that would be worth, um?"

"Well . . ." Annie paused. "Darla and Bo could each buy a new vehicle for starters. And they could put a huge down payment on a nice house."

"Hold it," Sam said. "You're telling me you let that tiara dangle in a tree all this time, *knowing* what it was worth?"

"Yep."

"How could you sleep at night?"

Annie smiled. "Silly boy," she said. "The tiara is insured."

As planned, Sam and Annie arrived before the bride and groom. They stood apart from the crowd while the band played soft music. The band had been moved to a grassy area nearby so the wedding would take place on the raised gazebo where everyone could see. People stood or sat in lawn chairs, patiently awaiting the couple. Lillian, Kazue, and the others stood a short distance away, waving and throwing kisses.

"I only have two requests," Sam whispered to Annie.

"Anything for you handsome."

"This is not *your* wedding. Please do not steal anybody's car and take off."

She grinned. "And your second request?"

"Do not tell Darla about the tiara until Bo and I are in position to catch her before she hits the ground."

People began clapping when a white carriage and two white horses made their way down the cobblestone street that surrounded the courthouse.

The crowd went wild when Bo helped Darla from the carriage, and they saw her dress. The band began playing the "Wedding March." Sam and Annie led the way to the gazebo and waited for the bride and groom. Annie felt a huge lump in her throat at the sight of Darla in the gown. She looked at Sam and found him watching her. He winked.

When the music died down, the minister stepped forward, and a hush fell over the crowd, except for the sound of cameras clicking. Darla's wedding would no doubt end up on the front page of the Pinckney Gazette.

The minister stepped forward. "Dearly beloved . . ." he began.

Annie tried to concentrate on the minister's words, but it was all she could do to keep from staring at Sam. She wondered what he was thinking, wondered if he knew how devastatingly handsome he looked. Most of all, she wondered if he suspected she'd fallen in love with him.

". . . The ring please."

Sam handed Bo the ring. Annie felt a giant lump in her throat as Bo, all six-foot-six, tenderly promised to love and cherish Darla for as long as they both lived. Annie's hand shook, and she felt tears gathering in her eyes when she passed the ring to Darla who repeated the same vow.

The minister pronounced them husband and wife, and the two kissed as shouts and whistles rang out from the crowd below, and the band played a lively tune.

Darla hugged Annie, both of them crying. "Thank you for the dress, honey. And thank you for helping to make this the best day of my life." Bo and Sam shook hands, and Sam kissed Darla, slipping her an envelope.

"This is for your honeymoon," Sam said. "I know Bo just started a new job, but hang on to this, maybe in a few months he can get some time off."

"Oh, Sam, you're the best," Darla said, hugging him.

He grinned. "Yeah, well wait till you find out what Annie is giving you."

Darla gave Annie an odd look. "I don't expect a gift from you," she said. "You gave me this bridal gown."

Annie shrugged. "Yes, well, I'd like to add a little something, but I would rather wait until later to give it to you."

Sam's eyes were soft as his gaze landed on Annie. He offered her his arm. "May I escort you to the reception, Miss Hartford?" he asked. She smiled and took his arm.

They were the first to arrive at Sam's house. A catering service was on standby, and they went to work immediately, pouring champagne and bringing out trays of food. There was a small table holding a wedding cake, and numerous white and gold balloons hovered overhead. "It's beautiful," Annie said.

"I was up all night baking this cake and making hors d'oeuvres and blowing up balloons," Sam told her. Nearby, the lady who owned the catering service chuckled. "Don't give me away," Sam said. "I'm trying to impress this pretty lady."

Annie laughed. "I'm already impressed," she said, patting his hand.

"You probably just came 'cause you heard there was going to be food and champagne. I hope you're not disappointed that I didn't hire a male stripper."

They kept up the lively banter until the guests arrived. Someone had helped Darla remove her train, and as she squeezed through the front door in the gown, Annie thought she looked radiant. The two women hugged again as Sam told Bo the secrets of a happy marriage. "Don't wait for your wife to ask you to take out the trash," he said. "Just do it."

"What do you know about marriage, Sam Ballard?" Lillian said, coming through the door. "You've been single all your life. Don't you think it's about time you found a good woman and tied the knot?"

Sam's gaze automatically landed on Annie, who in turn blushed and caused them to laugh. She was relieved when the caterer opened the bottles of champagne and it was time to make a toast.

"Darla," Annie began, holding an envelope with information she hoped would make life a little easier for her and Bo. "There is something you should know." She saw Sam nudge Bo, and they stepped closer to the woman. "I think you mistook the stones in the tiara as rhinestones, probably because I didn't get upset when it ended up in a tree, but that's neither here nor there. The truth is, there are twenty karats of flawless diamonds in the tiara that I purchased from Tiffany's in New York."

Darla's jaw dropped. "Does that mean I can buy a new car?"

"Yes, you can definitely buy a new car. As a matter of fact, I have the Appraisal, and the Certificate of Insurance that you might want to put in a safety deposit box, along with the tiara until you decide what to do." She handed it to Darla who gasped at the amount. She turned to Bo. "We're rich," she said and showed it to him.

Bo looked at Annie. "Is this for real?"

Annie nodded. "Absolutely."

All at once, his eyes rolled around in his head, and he staggered forward. "Oh, no!" Darla said. "He's going down!"

"Help me!" Sam said. Fortunately, two men who stood nearby joined Sam in his effort. It took all three to catch Bo, only seconds before he hit the floor.

Once everyone had eaten their fill, Bo and Darla bid their farewells and hurried to her car. Annie knew they were going back to their mobile home, and she wondered if Darla would be able to get through the door in her gown or if she'd have to take it off the way she had. When she looked up at Sam, he was smiling, and she wondered if he was thinking the same thing.

The guests left, and the caterers, who'd been cleaning up all along, took only a few minutes to get their things together. Martha and her sister were headed back to the festival to see if there were any last minute deals before the vendors closed and planned to stay for the fireworks that would start at eight p.m. Annie got the feeling that Martha was trying to make herself scarce so she and Sam could be alone.

The two were sitting on the sofa when Sam pulled Annie onto his lap. He kissed her hard. "I thought they'd never leave."

She smiled. "It was a wonderful reception. The food was excellent and everybody had a great time."

"I wouldn't know, Miss Hartford. My eyes were on you. You seem to have made a lot of friends here in very little time. In fact, I think my woman is quite popular with the townspeople."

She arched one eyebrow. "Your woman?"

"That's right. You got a problem with that?"

She leaned against him. He'd loosened his tie and dispensed with his jacket. She could feel the heat of his body through his dress shirt. "Does that mean you're my man?"

"Baby, I was yours the moment I first laid eyes on you."

Annie closed her eyes, basking in the moment. She had never felt so close to him. He turned her face to his and kissed her deeply. They held hands as they made their way upstairs to his bedroom.

Their lovemaking was slow and tender. Sam explored every inch of Annie's body. When she reached out to him, he entered her, and their sighs of pleasure wafted upward. Annie climaxed, and Sam followed right behind her.

Later they held on to each other as they waited for their breathing to return to normal. Finally, Sam looked into her eyes. "I love you, Annie Hartford."

Her insides fluttered. "I love you, too, Sam Ballard."

Darla drove everybody crazy the following week, trying to decide what to do with the tiara which was presently sitting in a safety deposit box at the bank, along with the documents. Add to that the promotion and raise Sam had given her, and Darla could not seem to get her head on straight.

"I can help you sell the tiara," Annie said.

"I hate to sell your wedding gift to me."

"That's why I *gave* it to you."

Darla nodded. "Well, I definitely need a newer model car."

"You can afford something brand new," Annie said. "You could make one heck of a down payment on a nice big house."

Darla shook her head. "I have something else in mind." She paused. "Can you keep a secret?" When Annie nodded, she went on. "I want to buy Sam out," she said. "I want to buy the Dixieland Café."

"Wow," Annie said. "I hadn't thought of that. Do you think he will sell it?"

"I plan to offer a fair price." She paused. "So I guess I'm going to need your help finding a buyer for the tiara."

Annie nodded. "I'll call Sotheby's in Atlanta. I've dealt with them before."

Two days later, Annie and Darla were cleaning up after the lunch crowd when a silver Mercedes pulled to the curb out front. Annie took one look at it, and her heart sank clear to her toes.

"Would'ja get a load of those wheels," Darla said. "Wonder whose driving it?"

"I know who it is," Annie said dully as a tall blond-haired man in expensive clothes climbed out. She felt a sense of dread as he made his way to the front door of the restaurant and opened it. He stepped inside and stared at Annie for a full minute before saying anything.

"Hello, Annie. You're looking good. That uniform becomes you."

Annie did not miss the sarcasm in his voice. She raised her hand, palm facing him. "Hold it right there, Eldon," she said. "If you're here to yell at me for skipping out on our wedding, you can turn your car around and head back to Atlanta because I'm not going to listen to it."

"In other words, you don't feel you owe me an apology."

Annie ignored his remark. "How did you find me?"

"I was forced to hire a private investigator."

"*Forced?*" Annie said.

"That's right. You probably don't give a damn, but your father suffered a massive heart attack shortly after you hit the road. I figured you'd want to know. Or not," he added.

It took a moment for Annie to grasp it, but the minute her brain registered the news she went weak-kneed. "Is he . . .?" She tried to form the word but could not.

"He is still alive," Eldon said. "The cardiologist hoped to perform a non-evasive procedure, but something went wrong, and they had to open his chest. Then, to make matters worse, your father suffered a stroke on the operating table. I don't know the specifics. Nobody will talk to me *or* Vera because we're not family. So, yeah, it was necessary that I find you."

Annie realized why she had not heard from Vera since she had arrived in Pinckney. She probably figured Annie would return home, despite all she had gone through to escape.

"What's the prognosis?" Annie asked, almost afraid to hear.

"Not good. He is in CCU. He slipped into a coma several days ago."

"Why did you wait until he was comatose to inform me?" she asked, knowing she was being ungrateful, but she was unable to conceal how much she disliked Eldon.

Eldon suddenly looked angry. "I only learned of your whereabouts a couple of days ago," he snapped, "but I sort of had my hands full. Vera and I have been taking turns sitting at the hospital. I felt it would be better if I told you in person."

Annie nodded. "I appreciate it. Thanks for stopping by."

Eldon was clearly stunned by her response. "That's *it?*"

"I can offer you coffee and pie before you head back."

"I don't think you *get it,* Annie. Your old man flat-lined at one point. He is *dying.* Don't you even care?"

"Of course I care," she said, trying to maintain her emotions. The truth was, she did not want to have to stand by his bed and watch him die. It would bring back the painful memories of losing Bradley, and it would remind her that she was alone in the world where family was concerned.

"There is nothing I can do," Annie finally said, even though her heart felt weighted, her emotions scattered like dandelion fluff in a summer breeze.

"That's really cold," Eldon said. "I hope you don't end up regretting your decision, but, hey, I did what I could so *I'll* be able to sleep at night." He made a sound of disgust. "I'll see you at the funeral," he said, "if it suits you to attend."

Darla, who had remained quiet during their conversation, stepped forward, arms crossed, her gaze fixed on Eldon. It was obvious she did not like him. "You need to watch your mouth, Slick," she said. "It just so happens I run this place and Annie is one of my dearest friends so I'm going to have to ask you to leave."

"Hold on," Annie said to Darla, and then looked at Eldon. "Could you keep quiet for two minutes?" she asked, as annoyed with him as Darla. "Give me time to think?" Eldon made the mistaking of checking his wristwatch. Annie thought she saw smoking coming out of Darla's ears.

She sighed. She wished Sam wasn't in court. She would gladly go to Atlanta if he drove her, but she had no desire to spend three hours in a car with Eldon yammering on about what a rotten person she was for backing out of the wedding. Of course, once he beat that horse to death he would accuse her of being a terrible daughter for not wanting to rush to her dying father's bedside.

Still, it was not Vera's job to see to her father's care, and if or when he passed, Annie needed to be there. She motioned for Darla to join her behind the counter. "I have to go," she whispered. "Eldon is right. I'll never be able to forgive myself if I don't."

"Then you should wait until Sam gets back and let him drive you," Darla said. "I'll text him, see what I can find out."

Annie shook her head. "No. I do not want to interrupt Sam or, heaven forbid, have him called from the courtroom. This is *my* problem, and *I* need to take care of it."

"But, honey, Sam loves you. That's what people do when they love someone. Besides, how do you know this creep won't try something?"

"I'm not afraid of Eldon," Annie whispered. "He isn't going to do anything that will shame the great Wentworth family."

Annie removed her apron and put it beneath the counter, then grabbed her small purse. "I'll call as soon as I know something." She looked at Eldon. "I'm coming with you," she said, her voice resigned. He gave Darla a smug look as if to say he had won.

"You'd better wipe that look off your face," Darla said, "because my husband is enormous, and he will turn your face into dog food if you hurt Annie."

"It is okay, Darla," Annie said, patting her arm.

Darla was not deterred. "He'll poke your eyeballs out and feed 'em to you for breakfast, and then he'll tie you to the back of his pickup truck, and drag your body—"

"Darla!" Annie said.

"Was I a bit over the top?" Darla whispered.

Eldon was clearly insulted. "Do I look like a man who would assault a woman?" he asked.

"I don't know *what* you're capable of, mister," Darla said, "but I'm giving you fair warning. My husband just got out of prison a week ago, and I don't want him to go back for wringing your neck like some yard chicken, although I would insist on a front row seat if it came to that." She suddenly smiled. "Now, then, you drive safely, y'hear?"

Eldon grunted in disgust.

Annie kissed Darla on the cheek. "You're sweet, you know that? Now stop worrying." She followed Eldon out.

Chapter Eleven

"What the hell do you mean she's gone?" Sam said to Darla when he returned.

"Shhh!" Darla said when a couple of customers looked up from the counter where they were sipping coffee and chatting. "You need to lower your voice." She stepped closer. "Annie had no choice, Sam. Her father is dying."

"Why didn't she wait for me? I would have taken her."

"We had no idea when you would get out of court. Eldon sort of gave the impression that her father was not long for this world."

Sam scowled. "From what Annie has said, the man is a pathological liar. Her father could be drinking tequila shooters in his hot tub for all we know. What hospital is he in?"

Darla looked surprised. "I don't know. Annie didn't ask and Eldon didn't say."

He looked incredulous. "Her father is supposedly in CCU, and it did not occur to you or Annie to inquire which hospital?"

"The girl was shaken by the news, and I was upset for her so I did not think to ask. Plus, I was busy telling Eldon how good-for-nothing he was."

Sam was clearly frustrated. "How long ago did they leave?"

"Thirty or forty minutes ago. I forgot to look at the clock."

"Excuse me," Sam said, "but aren't you the one who very recently asked if I would sell this place to you? How do you plan to run a restaurant if you can't think on your feet? You have to be able to act quickly. What if the walk-in freezer stops working or the fryer goes kaput? What will you do? You have to make split-second decisions if you're going to be successful."

Darla did not bother to hide her annoyance. "I've been running this restaurant almost singlehandedly for years," she said, "so that you could practice law and sell cars and whatever else you do. But I'm going to overlook your comments because I know you're upset."

Sam was prevented from answering when the bell over the door jingled, announcing a customer. Bo opened it and made a production of waving Lillian through first. She reached up, pinched his cheek, and laughed.

"Hey, sweetie," Bo said to Darla. "I came as soon as I could."

Lillian's smile faded the minute she noticed the expressions on Sam's and Darla's faces. "What's wrong?" she asked, her voice low. She gave the dining room a quick glance. "Where is Annie?"

"She, um, isn't here at the moment," Darla said.

"Has something happened to her?" Lillian asked. "Is she sick? Is she hurt? Tell me," she insisted, visibly shaken.

"She's fine," Darla said. "Well, not *fine*, but she isn't sick or hurt." She looked at Sam, then back to Lillian. "It seems her father suffered a heart attack and is very close to passing. Annie is on her way to Atlanta with Eldon."

"Eldon!" Lillian said.

"My feelings exactly," Sam said. "I'm going after her."

Lillian nodded. "I'll go with you."

"Hold on!" Bo said, waving his hands in the air. "Just hold your dang horses," he added. "Darla called me the minute they walked out that door, and that's why I'm here. You two have no business getting on the road in your present state of mind."

"Amen to that," Darla said. "Everybody needs to calm down."

Bo gave her a loving smile. "Do you remember what kinda' car the scumbag was driving?"

"I wrote it down." Darla pulled out her ticket pad. "It's a silver metallic Mercedes sedan," she said. "Looked brand-spanking new."

"Good girl," Bo said. "What time did they leave?"

Darla glanced at the clock. "I'm guessing forty-five minutes, give or take a few minutes. But this is the strange part. Instead of turning left out of the parking lot toward the interstate, he turned right, which is all back roads."

"Why would he do that?" Lillian asked.

Bo shook his head. "Good question when you consider the number of pot holes along the way. Plus, it is going to slow him down considerably."

"The whole thing smells if you ask me," Sam said. "If Annie's father is really in CCU, Eldon would take the quickest route. He is up to something."

Finally, Bo said, "We can stand here all day trying to figure it out, but we don't have time." He slapped Sam on the back. "Let's go, m'friend," he said. "My Dodge Ram has a few miles on it, but it'll outrun most anything, I gar-run-tee, and it eats up potholes and spits 'em out."

"I'm going with you," Lillian said.

All three looked at her, surprised. Bo and Sam exchanged glances. "My truck is going to be kind of tight as it is," Bo said. "It would be best if you stayed here with Darla in case Annie calls."

"I insist," Lillian said. "You're not leaving without me." Her voice trembled.

Darla took her hand. "Hon, Bo is right. Why don't you let me pour you a cup of coffee, and we'll wait for Annie's call together. You're too upset."

"Hell, yes, I'm upset," Lillian said. "We're talking about my daughter."

"This makes absolutely no sense," Annie said. "I thought we were in a hurry. Why are we taking the back roads?"

"I know a short cut," Eldon said. "Besides, I have a surprise for you."

Annie frowned. "What kind of surprise? I don't like surprises. You offered to drive me to the hospital to see my father. If you have something else in mind then you need to turn this car around, take me back to Pinckney, and I'll get another ride."

"Is your new boyfriend going to drive you to Atlanta?" he asked.

"I refuse to discuss my personal life with you." Annie wasn't sure what to make of the situation, but something did not feel right. "You never said which hospital my father was in."

"You're right, I did not."

"I should call and check on his condition. I need to borrow your cell phone."

"They aren't going to give you information over the phone," Eldon said, "what with all the laws protecting the patient's privacy. Besides, you and I need to talk."

"The only thing I want to talk about is my father's condition."

Eldon looked at her. "You sure have changed your tune since we left the restaurant. Is this your attempt to pass yourself off as a doting daughter?"

Annie's irritation flared. "Excuse me? I've put my life on hold since Bradley's death, hoping I could help my father get through his grief. If that's not a doting daughter then I don't know what is." She shook her head. "Why am I telling *you* this? I don't owe you an explanation." She took a long look at Eldon. "What's going on? Why do I feel like all is not as it should be?"

"Did you really think you would get away with humiliating me and my family in front of six hundred people?" he asked, his mouth twisting wryly.

Annie felt a prickle of unease at the back of her neck. She was not surprised that Eldon was annoyed with her for running out on him and escaping holy matrimony. He had expressed his displeasure back at the restaurant, but most of it had seemed aimed at Annie for not acting responsibly where her father was concerned. Eldon had gone out of his way to point out her shortcomings as a daughter until he had guilt tripped her into going back to Atlanta with him. Now, she realized she should not have gotten in the car with him. She should have listened to Darla and waited for Sam.

"I don't think this is the time to discuss what happened between us," she said, keeping her voice steady. She would not give Eldon the satisfaction of knowing she was anxious.

"I think it's the perfect time," Eldon said. "What you did was inexcusable. Or deplorable, as my mother has said more than once."

Annie noted his tense jaw. The skin on his face looked as though it had been stretched too tight. She realized that, despite dating and being engaged to him, she did not know him as well as she should because he had been deceitful from the beginning. All she could do was try to play things down as best she could and hope that he did not lose his cool or go into some freakish rage.

"I tried to do the right thing by calling off the engagement well in advance, Eldon. The only reason I agreed to become engaged in the first place—especially after only dating for three months—was because my father pushed and pushed until it was easier to give in. But I got sick and tired of giving in, sick and tired of being bullied."

"That's a real touching story, Annie, but it doesn't make up for what you did to me. I'm not sure you can ever make it up to me, but I'm going to see that you try."

"What are you talking about?"

He looked at her. His expression was menacing. "You'll find out soon enough."

Warning bells rang loudly in Annie's head. "Stop the car!" she said, reaching for the door handle.

Eldon hit the master lock. "Don't be stupid, Annie!" he shouted.

"I'm not going with you. Stop the car. I want out."

"Yeah, well I wanted my wife-to-be to show up at the altar, but that didn't happen, did it?"

Annie saw a gas station up ahead. "Let me off at the gas station," she said. "I'll find someone else to drive me to Atlanta."

"Shut up, Annie!" he snapped. "If you have any hope of seeing your father alive you will shut your damn mouth and do as you're told."

She glared at him. "Do as I'm told? What is that supposed to mean?"

"There is a preacher up the road who has agreed to marry us."

Annie could not believe what she was hearing. "Are you insane!" she said. "I'm not marrying you!"

"You need to rethink that," Eldon said. "I have a full tank of gas. I'll go the scenic route. By the time we get to Atlanta they will have moved your father's body to the morgue."

"Did you not *hear* me, Eldon? I will never marry you. I don't love you. I never loved you. Why would you even *want* to marry me when you know I don't have feelings for you?"

"You really have to ask?"

Annie grunted. "Oh, right, the money. It's always about the money."

"Finally, you get it. Your father and I have a contract. Once you and I marry I will be five million dollars richer."

"He was going to *pay you* to marry me?" Annie closed her eyes and leaned against the headrest. She felt sick. Finally, she opened her eyes. "I don't believe you."

"I have the contract and the marriage license."

"Show it to me."

"It's in the trunk."

"Sure it is."

Eldon slammed his hand against the steering wheel. "I am getting sick and tired of your mouth," he yelled.

"And, yet, you wish to marry me," she shouted back.

"For five million dollars I can put up with almost anything."

"You planned this all along, didn't you? How do I know my father is even ill?"

"Because I said so."

"I can't believe anything you say. What happens after the wedding, Eldon, since you seem to have everything, including my life, all figured out?"

"We live happily ever after and hope our union brings us many sons."

"Do you get a bonus check each time I birth a boy?"

"You're sole heir to a fortune, Annie. I think it's safe to say I will be well compensated."

"Why did my father choose you?"

Eldon shrugged. "He enjoys my stories. Like I said the night you called off the engagement. He believes them because he wants to believe them. You enjoyed them even more before someone told you differently."

"I can't believe my father did not check you out."

Eldon gave her an odd look. "Of course he checked me out. He knows all about my past, including getting kicked out of Duke."

"He didn't have a problem with it?"

"He isn't exactly without sin, Annie. He did not get where he is today by playing nice. I think he liked me more when he found out about my expulsion and other crap that I pulled." Eldon paused. "At the same time, he likes that I have good, um, breeding. Old people seem to get off on that sort of thing. He wants to make certain his *dynasty* will live on, and that his grandsons will one day take over."

"And *you're* supposed to run Hartford Iron and Steel until the male fruit of your loins is old enough in say twenty-five years?"

"Your father has been mentoring me. Good thing I learn fast because it looks like I'll be taking over sooner than we'd planned."

Annie noted the time on the dashboard and wondered if Sam had returned from the courthouse. What would he do once he found out she had left with Eldon? Would he be angry with her? She had promised to call, but it did not look likely. She should have done as Lillian told her some days ago and bought a prepaid phone. Lillian had even offered to get it for her, but Annie had declined. The woman already catered to her every need.

Even though Sam kept his eyes peeled out for sight of Eldon's car, he could sense Lillian was upset. She had tried to hide her tears. Finally, she had given up and pulled a small pack of tissue from her purse.

"Do you want to talk about it?" Sam asked.

Lillian sniffed. "I haven't talked about it in years," she said. "Only a couple of people know, but the bottom line, I had to give up Annie and her brother, and I was devastated."

"Why were you not able to keep them?" Bo asked.

"You would have to know how cruel and vindictive my ex-husband, Annie's father, is to understand."

"I have a fairly good idea," Sam said, "just from what Annie has told me."

Lillian sniffed and wiped her eyes again. "I was barely twenty years old and working as a secretary at his plant when he asked me out. He was forty but did not look it. I grew up lower middle-class so I was impressed with his great wealth. I think he just wanted a sweet young thing on his arm, and I'll have to say I was quite attractive."

"You still are," Sam said and Bo agreed.

Lillian chuckled. "You boys are sweet to say so."

"Anyway, a few months later, I ended up pregnant. I'll give him credit for doing the honorable thing and marrying me, but, that's when the *real* Winston Hartford showed up. He was a mean old bully who used fear, bribes, and intimidation to get what he wanted. He once told me that he had the goods on almost every judge and elected official in Atlanta. I later found he was right.

"Annie and Bradley were only four years old when I asked for a divorce, and believe me, I put up with a lot. But Winston Hartford was not about to let me take his children even though he seldom gave them the time of day. Telling him I wanted out was the absolute worst thing I could have done. In what felt like the twinkle of an eye, I no longer had access to money, credit cards, my car, or even a telephone. His henchmen practically moved into the house so they could watch every move I made.

"In the meantime, Winston filed for an emergency divorce on grounds of adultery and habitual drunkenness. He had affidavits from half the people who worked for him. People who lied for him because they were afraid of losing their jobs. Long story short, he was granted full custody of both kids, and I ended up on the street. When I tried to fight back, one of his men broke into my apartment while I was out and planted a crap-load of cocaine. The next thing I know there are police searching my apartment, and I'm in jail facing a ten year sentence for dealing illegal drugs. It was hopeless. My mother and father went to the editor of the newspaper because they hoped to get my story out so people could see how crooked Winston and his cronies were." Lillian paused and shook her head. "A week later their house burned to the ground."

"What a bastard," Bo said.

"That's not even the worst of it," Lillian replied. "One day Winston and his lawyer showed up with papers for me to sign, handing over any and all rights to my children. I was told if I signed the papers, all charges against me would be dropped. If I refused, I would go to prison for a long time, and—" Lillian choked on a sob.

"You don't have to say anything more," Sam told her.

"I have to get it out," Lillian replied. "Winston said if I did not do exactly as I was told, he was going to put Annie up for adoption, meaning she would be separated from her twin."

"Da-um," Bo said.

Lillian nodded. "I knew he would do it because he only cared about having a son who could one day take over his stupid plant. He was obsessed. I could not bear the thought of Bradley and Annie being separated. Twins need to be together."

Sam and Bo exchanged looks as Lillian began to cry in earnest. Sam held her close. "It's okay," he said. "Annie is the last person in the world who would judge you."

"I thought maybe I could finally see them when they were older," Lillian said. "I figured once they moved out of their father's house and had a life of their own, I would ask them to meet with me so I could try to explain why I did what I did. But I was too afraid of having them say no. I figured their father had turned them against me, although Vera claimed she had taught them differently, bless her heart." Lillian sniffed again.

"But then Bradley died in the auto accident, and I think something inside me died as well. I did a good job of hiding it from folks. I'm ashamed that I did not try to see Annie, but I figured she was going through enough pain, what with losing her twin. The last thing she needed was for me to show up and confuse things." Lillian was quiet for a moment as though gathering her thoughts.

"When Vera told me Annie had skipped out on her wedding and was on her way to Pinckney, I had a full-blown panic attack. I considered leaving town, and that's no lie. But Vera said Annie would need help so I had to pull myself together and be there for her, even though she had no idea who I was."

"Why haven't you told her the truth?" Sam asked.

"I'm afraid. If she were to reject me for waiting so long to make an appearance in her life I would be crushed. I just can't risk it, Sam. I decided it would be best if I gave her time to get to know me before I broke the news. Besides, the poor girl had enough on her mind."

Eldon turned on his blinker and slowed the car.

Annie glanced out the window and saw a small cinderblock building in dire need of painting. "What's this?" she asked.

"It's a church," Eldon said. "Actually, it is just a shell of a building with an altar and folding chairs, but I've promised the minister a sizeable donation."

"You're paying him off in exchange for marrying us. How is it going to look when you have to handcuff me, knock me unconscious, and drag me down the aisle by my hair?"

"I warned him in advance you might be reluctant."

"You do know I'm going to charge you with kidnapping first chance I get?"

"Really?" Eldon said. "Don't forget that your redneck girlfriend saw you leave with me of your own free will."

"Do *not* call my friend a redneck."

"Sweetheart, it's written all over her."

"Do *not* call me sweetheart."

He parked in front of the building. "What's it going to be, Annie? I've made myself very clear as to what will happen if you don't go through with the wedding this time. If your father passes away before you get there you will have to live with the knowledge that it was all your fault. If you go through with the wedding, I'll hop on the interstate and get you to Atlanta in record time."

Annie sat quietly for a moment trying to formulate a plan. Damned if she wasn't always trying to find a way to get out of marrying Eldon. She wondered if there was a support group for that sort of thing. Still, she had to find a way to get out of the locked car, which meant she would have to lie and do it in such a way that Eldon did not see right through it. Annie thought about the clothes she had packed for her honeymoon and prayed that the suitcases were still in Eldon's trunk.

"Okay, dammit, you win," she said in her nastiest tone, "although I'm doing so under great duress, but you have to swear that we will head straight to Atlanta afterward."

"Of course."

"Then let's get it over with," she snapped. "Are my suitcases still in the trunk?"

"Yes. Why do you ask?"

"I want to grab an outfit and shoes from my suitcase so I can change clothes. I don't care what I look like at this sham of a wedding, but I do not want to show up at the hospital in my waitress uniform."

"That's a relief," he said, "but honest-to-God, Annie, if you try something I'm going to see that you pay."

"You're just like my father. You wear me down and bully me until all I can do is go along with whatever you want."

"Give me your shoes."

Annie looked at him. "What?"

"The grounds have not been cleared. The whole lot is filled with thorns and stinging nettles. If you try to run you won't get far because they're very painful." Eldon winked. "See, Annie, I've thought of everything."

"How am I supposed to get my clothes out of my suitcase, Einstein?"

"Don't talk to me that way, Annie. Don't ever talk to me like that again."

"Then stop acting like a jerk. If you don't trust me, hold my wrist."

Eldon shook his head. "I don't like it."

"Hello?" Annie shouted. "I don't *care* what you like and don't like. You've won, Eldon. What more do you want from me?" Annie's eyes suddenly filled with tears.

"Oh, great!" Eldon said. "Just what I need. Dry it up, Annie because I'm not going to deal with a crying female." He slammed the door, hurried around the front and opened her door. "Come on," he said. "And don't try any funny business."

He grasped her wrists, pulled her from the car, and all but dragged her toward the trunk. Once he opened it, Annie saw her suitcases. They had been pushed toward the very front of the trunk, out of her reach. She saw a metal box with a keyhole. "What's that?" she asked.

"Important papers. Which suitcase do you want?"

Annie suspected the box held their marriage license and the contract Eldon and her father had signed. "The larger one," she said.

"I'm going to release your wrist for two seconds, Annie. If you try to run I'll catch you. And I'll have to take your shoes."

"A tough guy. How romantic."

Eldon let go of her wrist and reached for the suitcase, but it was a stretch. He glanced at Annie who simply stood there sniffing and wiping her tears.

Finally he inched closer to the suitcases and grabbed the handle on the larger one and tugged. He did not see Annie grab the metal box, but he yowled when she slammed it on his head as hard as she could. He released the suitcase and turned toward her, and Annie hit him again. The third time did the trick. He staggered, and his eyes rolled around in their sockets.

Annie dropped the box, shoved him as hard as she could, and he fell forward, the upper half of him landing in the trunk. He stopped struggling. Annie lifted one leg and then the other, folding them into the trunk before giving his backside a hard push. Once he was completely inside, Annie picked up the metal box and tossed it in the trunk. She winced when it bounced and hit him smack on the side of his head. She slammed the door to the trunk and pulled the key from the lock.

Annie leaned against the closed trunk, trembling from the adrenaline that still gripped her. There were no sounds coming from inside the trunk. She called out to Eldon several times, but there was no answer.

"Hold it!" Sam said. "I see Annie!"

"That's the car all right," Bo said.

Lillian blinked back fresh tears. "Oh, Lord, let her be okay."

Annie was so cloaked in her misery that she did not hear the approaching vehicle, did not see it pull into the drive next to Eldon's car. But when she glanced up, she saw Sam. He pulled her into his arms.

"Are you okay, babe?" he asked.

She sank against him. "Yeah, I'm good," she said tearfully.

Bo and Lillian hurried toward them. "Where is the no good lying skunk?" Lillian demanded. "I just want to take one shot at him."

Annie pointed to the trunk. "In there," she said. "I think I killed him."

See Bride Run!

Sam yanked Eldon from the trunk of his Mercedes and shoved him inside the cab of Bo's pickup truck while Bo chatted briefly with Darla on his cell phone, assuring her that Annie was okay. Eldon banged his head on the gun rack which held an old shotgun and what looked to be a new rifle.

"I need to go to the hospital," Eldon said.

"Listen to me," Sam said, taking care to control his temper. "See that big guy on the phone? He's crazy. You make one wrong move, and there is no telling what he'll do to you."

Eldon looked from Sam to Bo then back at Sam. "Is he going to shoot me?"

Bo ended his call, slipped his cell into the pocket of his denim vest and climbed into the truck. "I don't need to shoot you, pal," he said. "I got my bare hands."

"Tell you what, Bo," Sam said. "If sissy britches here gives you any trouble we'll sic Annie on him again."

Bo looked at Eldon. "Any man who'd let a skinny gal like that beat him up is a big wuss." Bo grinned at Sam. "Tell Annie I'll flash my lights if I need help."

Eldon leaned back in the seat and closed his eyes.

Sam drove Eldon's car. Annie sat in the front and Lillian in the back. They were less than a half hour from the Hartford mansion when Sam asked Lillian if she had something she wanted to tell Annie.

Lillian's face turned a bright red. "I don't know where to start," she said to Sam.

"The beginning is always the best place," he replied.

Annie turned in her seat and looked at Lillian. "What is it?" she asked.

Lillian struggled to tell her story, stopping several times when she had to wipe her eyes and blow her nose. By the time she was finished, Annie's face was streaked with tears.

"I'm so sorry," Lillian said. "I feel like I let you and Bradley down."

Annie unbuckled her seatbelt and climbed into the back with Lillian. "You never have to apologize to me," she said. "Starting right here and now, we're going to make up for lost time."

Lillian hugged her. "I'm so proud of you, Annie. You are the sweetest and the prettiest daughter a mother could ask for."

"She might be sweet," Sam said from the front seat, "but she's tough. She sure gave Eldon a good butt-kick."

"He had it coming," Annie said, but her gaze was fixed on Lillian. She was touched by the love and tenderness she saw in her eyes, her mother's eyes. "I wish you'd gotten to know Bradley," she said. "He and I were so close."

"I look forward to hearing all about him," Lillian said. "I will always be grateful to Vera for doing such a fine job." She suddenly laughed. "I'll let you in on a little secret," she said. "I pulled one over on Winston."

"This, I got to hear," Sam said.

"I told him I absolutely and positively did *not* want Vera Holmes raising my children."

Annie laughed, as did Sam.

Lillian grinned. "Vera later told me he hired her that very day to act as nanny."

Annie's smile faded once they reached the Hartford estate. The guard opened the gate when he caught sight of her in Eldon's car. Vera opened the front door as Sam and Bo parked beside them in the wide circular drive. Annie climbed from the car and hurried toward Vera, giving her a warm hug. She noted how tired the woman looked, how worn, and she felt guilty for not being there to help.

"Eldon told me Father had a heart attack," Annie said, "although I'm not sure how much is truth and how much is fiction."

Vera offered Annie a sad smile. "Sweetie, your father passed away this morning."

Annie stood there a moment trying to deal with the blow. Despite her father's many sins, she felt a deep sense of loss because she suddenly recalled good times as well. People were not just all good or all bad; they were more complex. Even as she stood there, her eyes filling with tears,

Annie promised herself to try and remember the good times.

Lillian, Vera, and Sam took turns hugging her as they moved toward the house. "I'll help any way I can," Lillian said to Annie.

"Same here," Vera told her, then paused when she caught sight of Bo leading a bruised and battered Eldon from his truck.

"What happened to Eldon?" Vera asked.

"Annie beat him up," Sam said.

"Really?" Vera looked at Annie. "I hate I missed that."

Once inside the house, Vera hurried to the kitchen to see to refreshments. Sam and Bo were discussing what to do with Eldon who was annoyed that nobody seemed to appreciate the trouble he'd gone to by alerting Annie of her father's impending demise.

"Let him go for now," Annie said. "Please get my suitcases out of his trunk first. Oh yeah, a*nd* the metal box." She gave Eldon a hard look. "I plan to take that box to my father's attorney. You had better hope he doesn't find anything that could land you in prison. Additionally, I am going to the courthouse tomorrow and obtain a restraining order. If you ever, *ever* come near me again I'll have you arrested."

Sam and Bo escorted him out the front door. Annie went into the guest bathroom and washed her face. Vera knocked on the door. "Your eyes are a bit swollen, sweetie," she said. "You should probably lie down and rest awhile."

"I'll be okay," Annie said, "once I get over feeling guilty."

Vera frowned. "Why on earth would you feel guilty?"

"It's my fault that Father was under so much stress," Annie said. "I caused his heart attack by running off like I did."

"Annie, that's the craziest thing I've ever heard," Vera said. "Your father has been battling heart disease for several years. He was taking medication for it. Not that it mattered," she added. "We both know he did not take care of himself."

"Why didn't somebody tell me?" she asked.

"Your father did not want anyone to know because he feared it would be a sign of weakness, especially where his competitors were concerned. The only reason I knew was because I picked up his prescriptions now and then. I thought I was protecting you by staying silent, but I did you an injustice, and I'm sorry." She touched Annie's cheek. "He's gone now, but you have your whole life in front of you. More than anyone, you deserve to be happy."

"That makes two of us," Annie said.

"Oh, by the way, your father's attorney was at the hospital when he passed away."

"I'm not surprised," Annie said. "Mr. Yeager has always been kind."

"He asked me to get in touch with you and have you call him. I'm sure it's about your father's will."

"Oh, jeez, I'm probably headed to the poor house," Annie said, then laughed. "But I have a really good job waiting for me in Pinckney."

"Silly girl. You just might end up being one of the wealthiest young ladies in the state of Georgia." Vera winked.

"You obviously know something I don't," Annie said. "Eldon must suspect Father provided for me in his will. That would explain why he showed up wanting a quickie marriage. He told me how he sat at the hospital night after night."

"Eldon isn't in the picture anymore, Annie. Your father kicked him to the curb when the wedding did not take place. Eldon only showed up at the hospital once. I think he was hoping you'd be there or that he might hear something regarding the will, so that's just one more lie." Vera shrugged. "But none of it matters now." She kissed Annie's forehead. "I'll let you finish washing up," she said, but try to hurry. I've ordered all sorts of goodies from the kitchen and asked the cook to put on fresh coffee. You look like you could use a cup of coffee and something to eat."

Annie splashed more water on her face and dried it with a towel. She felt numb but exhausted. She knew the next few days would be busy ones, and she dreaded it, although she knew Vera and Lillian would help, as would Sam if she asked. She expected to be sad for a while, but she looked forward to the day that she could put it all behind her.

She opened the door and almost bumped into Sam. He pulled her into his arms. "I'm sorry about your father," he said.

"Thank you, Sam," she said.

"Are you okay?"

"I will be once I get everything out of the way. I just want it to be over so I can go home."

"Where is home, babe?" he asked.

"Wherever you are, Sam. Home is with you."

Epilogue

One year later...

Annie's contractions began at two a.m. on Christmas Eve. She was surprised. While she and Sam were eagerly awaiting the births of their twins, the babies weren't due for almost two weeks. Annie still had a long to-do list—she'd only wrapped half her gifts—but she, with the help of her father's attorney, had spent the past month negotiating the sale of Hartford Iron and Steel for a staggering sum. The bulk of the money had gone into The Bradley Hartford Foundation, along with monies from the Hartford Estate which had sold for twice what her father had paid thirty years earlier.

Annie had already put some of the money to work. She'd hired painters, contractors, and brick masons to restore the exterior of the old courthouse which was clearly showing its age. Annie had commissioned a local nursery to replace old shrubs, design and plant flowerbeds, and get the lawn in shape. The gazebo had been scraped and repainted, and the old park benches replaced. Annie felt proud of what she and her team had accomplished. The residents of Pinckney had been so kind to her, she wanted to give back.

Four a.m. . . .

Annie's back was beginning to hurt. She suddenly remembered she had a meeting later with an architect. She was building a Boys & Girls Club of America. She'd heard rumors of under-age drinking at the local pool hall, high school students not applying themselves, and, worse, bullying. After visiting several BGCAs in neighboring cities and listening to young people describe how the clubs had changed them for the better—actually saving lives!—Annie had contacted the national headquarters in Atlanta and asked for guidance so she could put the project on fast-track. They had been happy to oblige.

Five a.m. . . .

Annie's labor had kicked up a notch. She had been brainstorming ways to create more commerce and job growth for those living in Pinckney, while maintaining the simple small town feel she'd come to love. She no longer shopped at Saks, Gucci, Neiman Marcus, and Tiffany's. She had donated her designer wardrobe to the Second Hand Store. She had wanted to make a fresh start in life, and getting rid of a lot of *stuff* had felt good. She had even sold her custom pearl-colored Jaguar with its ultra-posh interior and purchased two Dodge Ram Pickup Trucks, black for Sam and candy apple red for her. He'd been embarrassed.

"I don't want folks thinking I married you for your money."

"Don't be silly," she said. "They know you married me because I'm gorgeous and look good in a waitress uniform. Besides, I bought you a pickup truck, not a fleet of Lamborghinis."

"You need to save your money for a rainy day," he said.

"Really? Where do I buy a billion dollar umbrella?"

His jaw had dropped almost to his chest. "Holy hell, Annie! Is that what you're worth? No, don't tell me because I don't want to know. Just don't go buying me a bunch of expensive gifts."

"Okay, from now on I'll just buy you cheap crap."

Sam had grinned. Annie had not lost that mouthy side of her personality, but to be honest it was one of the things he loved most. He'd kissed her. When he raised his face, his look was tender. "Nobody has ever given me a nicer gift, Annie. Thank you."

"You're welcome, Sam. See how easy that was."

Six thirty a.m.

Annie glanced at the alarm clock. She had ridden out the light contractions for four and a half hours, using the relaxation techniques she had learned in childbirth classes; but she sensed a change, the muscles in her stomach were growing tighter, her back ached something fierce. Still, as she glanced at the alarm clock on her night table, she noted her contractions were uneven and sporadic. She would wake Sam when they got closer together. If only she could ease her back pain.

Seven forty-five a.m.

Annie was suddenly hit with the whammy of all contractions. She grabbed her stomach, bolted upright in the bed, and cried out. "Holy Mother of God!"

Sam jumped up. "What is it? Are you in labor? Are the babies coming?"

"It huurrts!" Annie said, kicking the covers aside, hoping to ease her pain. I've been in labor for almost seven hours, but—"

"Seven hours! Why didn't you wake me?" Sam leaped from the bed, and threw on his clothes. "We need to time the contractions!"

"They're five minutes apart."

"We have to get you dressed and to the hospital pronto!" he said, helping her from the bed. As Annie slipped out of her nightgown, he rushed to the closet and yanked the first thing he came across. "How's this?" he asked.

"That's a summer dress, Sam."

He tossed it aside.

"This?" he said, holding up a pencil skirt. He looked from the skirt to Annie. "Maybe not."

She pointed to an overstuffed chair. "I've already got my things laid out just in case." She waddled toward it.

"No! Don't move!" Sam said. "You might stir things up." He hurried across the room, grabbed her dress. "Here we go."

Annie suddenly grabbed one of his arms, her nails digging into his flesh. "Arggggg. Owwwww!"

Sam winced, certain she had drawn blood. "I know it hurts, babe, but don't worry. As soon as we get to the hospital I'm going to demand they put you on really good drugs. By the time you wake up our twins will have graduated high school."

Annie struggled to get through the contraction. Her eyes crossed.

"Raise your arms so I can slip the dress over your head," he said after the contraction had passed.

Annie did as she was told. Once Sam had the dress in place, he fumbled with the zipper. "Something is wrong here."

"You put my dress on wrong side out," Annie said.

"Oh, hell," he muttered. "Well, we don't have time to worry about it."

"I can't go to the hospital with my dress inside-out."

Sam gave huge sigh and started over. "If we keep messing around, our babies are going to be born in the backseat of my pickup truck." He looked her over. "Where are your shoes?" He glanced about frantically.

Annie pointed to the closet. "I need the brown loafers. The others are too tight."

Sam grabbed the shoes and stuffed her feet into them as quickly as he could, then took her hand and led her toward the stairs. They had managed to get half way down before Annie stopped and screeched.

Sam heard Martha's bedroom door open. She came into the hall. "Is Annie in labor?" she asked.

Annie doubled over as the contraction intensified. "Oh crap, oh crap, oh, crap," she cried.

"I guess she is," Martha said. She helped Sam get Annie into her coat. "It's going to be okay, honey," Martha said. "Just practice what you and Sam learned in those classes. Won't be long before you're holding your babies."

"Don't forget my suitcase," Annie said as Sam tried to shuffle her through the front door. He grabbed the suitcase beside the door and led her toward his truck.

"I'll start making phone calls," Martha called out.

Sam was able to time Annie's contractions, even as he made the drive to Pinckney General Hospital. He parked in front of the emergency room, and an orderly hustled Annie into a wheelchair.

"I'm going to park my truck," Sam said and sped toward the parking garage. He joined Annie a few minutes later in the reception area. They were quickly processed because the forms and insurance had been taken care of in advance. One of the staff fitted Annie with a hospital bracelet.

Lillian and Vera rushed through the door. "How are you feeling?" Lillian asked.

Annie suddenly doubled over in the wheelchair and gave a yelp, obviously in the throes of another contraction. A breathless Darla came through the main doors, spotted Annie and hurried toward her. "Oh, hon, I'm sorry you're in so much pain." She paused. "Would you like a valium?" she whispered.

Finally, the orderly pushed Annie through a set of double doors leading to maternity and Annie's room. Lillian and Vera followed. Both were thrilled they were going to witness the births. A sweet-faced nurse named Daisy appeared, and they waited outside while the woman and Sam helped Annie out of her clothes and into a hospital gown.

"Uh-oh," Annie said as soon as she was situated on the hospital bed. "I think my water just broke."

Daisy slipped a large dry pad beneath her and took a peek at Annie's progress. "Holy cow!" she said. "I'd better page your doctor." She looked at Sam. "You'll have to wash up and put on scrubs," she said. "I'll show you where to go."

"I'll be right back, sweetheart," he told Annie and followed the nurse out.

Lillian and Vera exchanged worried looks. "Is there a problem?" Lillian asked Daisy when she returned.

See Bride Run!

"Mrs. Ballard is doing fine," Daisy said. "She is dilated almost nine centimeters. Dr. Newton is on his way." She motioned them into the room.

Daisy and another nurse gently prepped Annie, putting her feet in stirrups and draping sterile sheets in place. Lillian stood on one side of the hospital bed and Vera on the other. "Have you picked out names yet?" Lillian asked, having posed the same question a dozen times, only this time it was obvious she was trying to take Annie's mind off her pain.

"We're . . . um, undecided," Annie said, sweat beading her brow and upper lip. Vera quickly wet a paper towel with cold water and wiped Annie's face. "I guess we'll call them Baby Number One and Baby Number Two," Vera said.

Sam returned wearing scrubs. Lillian and Vera stepped aside so he could take his place next to Annie. He held her hand. "How are you doing, sweetheart?" he asked. He'd barely gotten the words out before a contraction hit. "Remember your breathing," he said and coached her through several contractions.

Annie was in the midst of another contraction when she suddenly felt the need to push and announced to everyone in the room. "I need to push! I need to push!" she said, just as soon as her doctor sailed into the room. He grabbed a stool and placed it at the foot of the hospital bed between Annie's legs. "Looks like you're ready to rock-n-roll, Mrs. Ballard," he said.

"She's in a lot of pain," Sam said. "Can you give her anything?"

"It's too late for that," the doctor said, "but I'll ask my nurse to make her a gin and tonic. Okay, Mrs. Ballard, I've got a baby crowning. On the next contraction you can start pushing."

Annie did as she was told. After several pushes, a couple of grunts, and one huge groan, a baby slipped into Dr. Newton's hands. "A fine boy!" he said, presenting the baby to Sam who looked to be in shock.

Lillian and Vera stepped closer. "He's beautiful," Lillian said.

Sam smiled. "Ladies, meet Bradley Samuel Ballard."

Both women immediately became tearful.

Sam passed the baby to Annie, and she studied his red face. "Oh, look, he has your nose and blue eyes, Sam."

"He definitely has Bradley's mouth and jaw," Vera said.

Dr. Newton put a clamp on the baby's umbilical cord and asked Sam if he wanted to cut the cord. A nervous Sam followed the doctor's instructions and did so. Lillian and Vera clapped softly.

"May I have your son for a moment, Mrs. Ballard?" one of the nurses asked. "I need to suction him, put eye drops in those pretty blues, and clean him up a bit. Won't take long."

Annie struggled through several more contractions. "When can I start pushing?" she asked the doctor.

"Your little girl is taking her time," he said. "That's a woman for you. They like being fashionably late. Okay, Mrs. Ballard, let 'er rip."

Annie pushed as hard as she could, and her baby daughter slid into Dr. Newton's waiting hands. He passed her to Sam, and all three women stared at the newborn adoringly. "She's got your green eyes, Annie!" Sam said and held her up. "Ladies, meet Lillian Bethany Ballard."

Lillian gave a small squeal of delight, but Vera looked stunned. "You named her after my mother?" she asked.

Annie nodded. "I've always loved the name Bethany. We plan to call her Lily."

Sam passed the baby to Annie, cut the umbilical cord, and kissed Annie's lips softly. They simply stared at the infant in awe.

Dr. Newton was still busy with Annie, even after one of the nurses took Lily. Sam knew the doctor had more to do, but he grinned and questioned him. "I'm almost afraid to ask what you're doing," he said. "You don't see another baby, do you?"

The doctor smiled. "No, but I think I see a Jack Russell Terrier."

Everyone laughed.

Lillian tried to hide the tears streaming down her cheeks. "I can't believe I'm a grandmother," she said. She looked at Vera. "And so are you."

Vera put her arms around Lillian, and they hugged. Sam and Annie watched the nurses clean the babies. A few minutes later, they were returned to their proud parents.

Annie held her son. Tears rolled down her cheeks. "Hello, Bradley," she said, a bit choked. "You're too little to understand right now, but one of these days I'm going to tell you all about the uncle you were named after. He was my very best friend. Just like you and Lily will be best friends."

Lillian kissed Annie on the forehead. "I'd better go out and give Darla the news," she said, "or she's going to storm through that door and demand to know what's taking so long."

"I'll go with you," Vera said. "Let's give the new parents a little privacy."

Sam looked into his daughter's face and saw Annie's reflection. "She's beautiful, sweetheart. Just like her mother. And I could not ask for a finer looking son. My parents are going to be so proud."

"You need to call them," Annie said, "as well as your sister," she added. She'd felt bad that her pregnancy had interfered with their annual Christmas celebration, but they'd feared their presence would create a hardship during Annie's late stage pregnancy. Instead, they were planning to visit after New Year's.

Annie smiled, but despite all the excitement she felt drained. She tried to keep her eyes open. Finally, two nurses returned. "Mrs. Ballard, we're going to take the babies for now. The next time you see them they'll be bathed and dressed in fresh gowns. In the meantime, you should rest."

Sam stayed with Annie, holding her hand long after she drifted off. "Thank you, Annie," he whispered. He knew Annie could not hear him, but it didn't matter. He continued the sit there, watching her sleep, and he fell in love with her all over again.

About The Author

Charlotte Hughes published her first category romance in 1987, a Bantam Books' *Loveswept*, titled *Too Many Husbands,* which immediately shot to #1 on the Waldenbooks Bestseller list. She went on to write almost thirty books before the line closed in 1998.

Although Charlotte is widely known for her laugh-out-loud romantic comedies, she went on to pen three Maggie-Award winning thrillers for Avon Books in the late nineties, before resuming her first love, funny stories about people falling in love. She thrilled readers with her hilarious books, *A New Attitude* and *Hot Shot,* the latter of which won the Waldenbooks Greatest Sales Growth Achievement in 2003.

Her books received so many accolades that she was invited to co-author the very popular Full House series with mega-star author Janet Evanovich.

With that series behind her, Charlotte began her own, starring psychologist Kate Holly; *What Looks Like Crazy, Nutcase,* and *High Anxiety,* creating a list of somewhat kooky but always loveable and funny ensemble characters.

Charlotte hopes you loved *See Bride Run!* as much as she loved writing it. Let her know what you think of it; she loves to hear from her readers.

You can also visit her website at readcharlottehughes.com and follow her on Twitter @charlottehughes.

If you enjoyed reading *See Bride Run!* keep up with Charlotte Hughes news by joining her readers group (http://readcharlottehughes.com/Newsletter.html). You probably will also enjoy other independently published books by her including *Tall Dark and Bad*, and *Welcome to Temptation*, available at Amazon. Look for other titles by Charlotte in the near future, especially *Miss Goody Two Shoes* and *Just Married, Again*.

Printed in Great Britain
by Amazon